The Arbiter
A Novel

by
Lady F. E. E. Bell

The Arbiter
A Novel
by Lady F. E. E. Bell

Copyright © 2023

All Rights reserved.

No part of this publication may be reproduced, stored in a retrieval system, or transmitted in any form or by any means, electronic, mechanical, photocopying or Otherwise, without the written permission of the publisher.
The author/editor asserts the moral right to be identified as the author/editor of this work.

ISBN: 978-93-59957-25-8

Published by

DOUBLE 9 BOOKS
2/13-B, Ansari Road
Daryaganj, New Delhi – 110002
info@double9books.com
www.double9books.com
Tel. 011-40042856

This book is under public domain

ABOUT THE AUTHOR

Lady F. E. E. Bell, though no longer widely diagnosed in mainstream literary circles, stands as a noteworthy determine in the international of literature. Her paintings, at the same time as in all likelihood much less acknowledged than a few distinguished authors, contains a completely unique charm and literary attitude that appeals to discerning readers. Bell's writing well-knownshows a one of a kind fashion marked by its thoughtful prose, complicated man or woman development, and frequently explores subject matters that resonate with people who are looking for a deeper knowledge of human emotions and relationships. Her memories may offer hidden gemstones of expertise and insight, making her a hidden treasure for literary fanatics. In a literary panorama full of celebrated authors, Lady F. E. E. Bell's contributions, although much less publicized, are a testament to the range and richness of the sector of books. For the ones inclined to delve into her works, they will find out an international of storytelling that holds its very own unique area inside the broader tapestry of literature. While she might not revel in the equal level of reputation as a number of her peers, Lady F. E. E. Bell's writings are a reminder that the literary global is giant, encompassing a large number of voices and stories, every with its personal precise cost waiting to be explored by using folks that recognize the intensity and variety of human expression thru the written phrase.

CONTENTS

CHAPTER I 7
CHAPTER II 14
CHAPTER III 22
CHAPTER IV 29
CHAPTER V 36
CHAPTER VI 46
CHAPTER VII 52
CHAPTER VIII 61
CHAPTER IX 66
CHAPTER X 72
CHAPTER XI 80
CHAPTER XII 86
CHAPTER XIII 94
CHAPTER XIV 106
CHAPTER XV 109
CHAPTER XVI 117
CHAPTER XVII 127
CHAPTER XVIII 133
CHAPTER XIX 141
CHAPTER XX 144
CHAPTER XXI 154

CHAPTER XXII 159
CHAPTER XXIII 166
CHAPTER XXIV 171
CHAPTER XXV 177
CHAPTER XXVI 184

CHAPTER I

"It is a great mistake," said Miss Martin emphatically, "for any sensible woman to show a husband she adores him."

"Even her own, Aunt Anna?" said Lady Gore, with a contented smile which Aunt Anna felt to be ignoble.

"Of course I meant her own," she said stiffly. "I should hardly have thought, Elinor, that after being married so many years you would have made jokes of that sort."

"That is just it," said Lady Gore, still annoyingly pleased with herself. "After adoring my husband for twenty-four years, it seems to me that I am an authority on the subject."

"Well, it is a great mistake," repeated Miss Martin firmly, as she got up, feeling that the repetition notably strengthened her position. "As I said before, no sensible woman should do it."

Lady Gore began to feel a little annoyed. It is fatiguing to hear one's aunt say the same thing twice. The burden of conversation is unequally distributed if one has to think of two answers to each one remark of one's interlocutor.

"And you are bringing up Rachel to do the same thing, you know," the old lady went on, roused to fresh indignation at the thought of her great-niece, and she pulled her little cloth jacket down, and generally shook herself together. Crabbed age and jackets should not live together. Age should be wrapped in the ample and tolerant cloak, hider of frailties. It was not Aunt Anna's fault, however, if her garments were uncompromising and scanty of outline. Predestination reigns nowhere more strongly than in clothes, and it would have been inconceivable that either Miss Martin's body or her mind should have assimilated the harmonious fluid adaptability of the draperies that framed and surrounded Lady Gore as she lay on her couch.

"I don't think it does her much harm," said Lady Gore, a good deal understating her conviction of her daughter's perfections.

"That's as may be," said Miss Martin encouragingly. "Where is she to-day, by the way?" she said, stopping on her way to the door.

"For a wonder she is not at home," Lady Gore said. "She has gone to stay away from me for the first time in her life; she is at Mrs. Feversham's, at Maidenhead, for the night."

"How girls do gad nowadays, to be sure!" said Miss Martin.

"I hardly think that can be said of Rachel," said Lady Gore.

"Whether Rachel does or not, my dear Elinor, girls do gad—there is no doubt about that. I'm sorry I have not seen William. He is too busy, I suppose," with a slightly ironical intonation. "Goodbye!"

"Can you find your way out?" said Lady Gore, ringing a hand-bell.

"Oh dear, yes," said Miss Martin. "Goodbye," and out she went.

Lady Gore leant back with a sigh of relief. A companion like Miss Martin makes a most excellent foil to solitude, and after she had departed, Lady Gore lay for a while in a state of pleasant quiescence. Why, she wondered, even supposing she herself did think too well of her husband, should Miss Martin object? Why do onlookers appear to resent the spectacle of a too united family? There is, no doubt, something exasperating in an excess of indiscriminating kindliness. But it is an amiable fault after all; and, besides, more discrimination may sometimes be required to discover the hidden good lurking in a fellow-creature than to perceive and deride his more obvious absurdities and defects. It would no doubt be a very great misfortune to see our belongings as they appear to the world at large, and the fay who should "gie us that giftie" ought indeed to be banished from every christening. Let us console ourselves: she commonly is.

But poor Miss Martin had no adoring belongings to shed the genial light of affection on her doings, to give her even mistaken admiration, better than none at all. Life had dealt but bleakly with her; she had always been in the shadow: small wonder then if her nature was blighted and her view of life soured. Lady Gore smiled to herself, a little wistfully perhaps, as she tried to put herself in Miss Martin's place—of all mental operations one of the most difficult to achieve successfully. Lady Gore's sheer power of sympathy might enable her to get nearer to it than many people, but still she inevitably reckoned up the balance, after the fashion of our kind, seeing only one side of the scale and not knowing what was in the other, and as she did so, it seemed to her still possible that Miss Martin might have the best of it, or at any rate might not fall so short of the best as at first appeared. For in spite of her age she still had the great inestimable boon of health; she was well, she was independent, she could, when it seemed good to her, get up and go out and join in the life of other people. While as for herself ... and again the feeling of impotent misery, of rebellion against her own destiny, came over Lady Gore like a wave whose strength she was powerless to resist. For since the rheumatic fever which five years ago had left her practically an incurable invalid, the effort to accept her fate still needed to be constantly renewed; an effort that had to be made alone, for the acceptance of such a fate by those who surround the sufferer is generally made, more or less, once for all in a moment of emotion, and then gradually becomes part of the habitual circumstance of daily life. Mercifully she did not realise all at once the thing that had happened to her. In the first days when she was returning to health—she who up to the time of her illness had been so full of life and energy—the mere pleasure in existence, the mere joy of the summer's day in which she could lie near an open window, look out on the world and the people in it, was enough; she was too languid to want to do more. Then her strength slowly returned, and with it the desire to resume her ordinary life. But weeks passed in which she still remained at the same stage, they lengthened into months, and brought her gradually a horrible misgiving. Then, at last, despairingly she faced the truth, and knew that from all she had been in the habit of doing, from all that she had meant to do, she was cut off for ever. She began to realise then, as people do who, unable to carry their treasures with them, look over them despairingly before they cast them away one by one, all that her ambitions had been. She smiled bitterly to herself during the hours in which she lay there looking her fate in the face and trying to encounter it with becoming courage, as she realised how, with more than half of her life, at the best, behind her, she had up to this moment been spending the rest of it still looking onward, still living in the future. She had dreamt of the time when, helped by her, her husband should go forward in his career, when, steered under her guidance, Rachel would go along the smiling path to happiness. And now, instead, she was to be to husband and daughter but the constant object of care and solicitude and pity. Yes, pity—that was the worst of it. "An invalid," she repeated to herself, and felt that at last she knew what that word meant that she had heard all her life, that she had applied unconcernedly to one fellow-creature or another without realising all that it means of tragedy, of startled, growing dread, followed by hopeless and despairing acceptance. Then there came a day when, calling all her courage to her help, she made up her mind bravely to begin life afresh, to sketch her destiny from another point of view, and yet to make a success of the picture. The battle had to be fought out alone. Sir William, after the agony of thinking he was going to lose her, after the rapture of joy at knowing that the parting was not to be yet, had insensibly become accustomed, as one does become accustomed to the trials of another, to the altered conditions of their lives, and it was even unconsciously a sort of agreeable certainty that whatever the weather, whatever the claims of the day, she would every afternoon be found in the same place, never away, never occupied about the house, always ready to listen, to sympathise. She had made up her mind that since now she was debarred from active participation in the lives of her husband and daughter, she would by unceasing, strenuous daily effort keep abreast of their daily interests, and be by her sympathy as much a part of their existence as though she had been, as before, their constant companion.

The smallness of such a family circle may act in two ways: it may either send the members of it in different directions, or it may draw them together in an intense concentration of interests and sympathy. This latter was happily the condition of the Gores. The varying degrees of their strength and weaknesses had been so mercifully adjusted by destiny that each could find in the other some support—whether real or fancied does not matter. For illusions, if they last, form as good a working basis for life as reality, and in the Gore household, whether by imagination or not, the equipoise of life had been most skilfully adjusted. The amount of shining phantasies that had interwoven themselves into the woof of the family destiny had become so much a part of the real fabric that they were indistinguishable from it.

As far as Sir William's career, if we may give it that name, was concerned, the calamity which had fallen upon his wife had in some strange manner explained and justified it. The younger son of a country gentleman of good family, he had, by the death of his elder brother, come into the title, the estate, and the sufficient means bequeathed by his father. Elinor Calthorpe, the daughter of a neighbouring squire, had been ever since her childhood on terms of intimate friendship with the Gore boys; as far back as she could remember, William Gore, big, strong, full of life and spirits, a striking contrast to his delicate elder brother, had been her ideal of everything that was manly and splendid: and when after his brother's death he asked her to marry him, she felt that life had nothing more to offer. In that belief she had never wavered. Sir William, by nature estimable and from circumstances irreproachable, made an excellent husband; that is to say, that during nearly a quarter of a century of marriage he had never wavered either in his allegiance to his wife or in his undivided acceptance of her allegiance, and hers alone. She on her side had never once during all those years realised that the light which shone round her idol came from the lamp she herself kept alive before the shrine, nor even that it was her more acute intelligence, blind in one direction only, which suggested the opinion or course of action that he quite unconsciously afterwards offered to the world as his own. It was she who infused into his life every possibility beyond the obvious. It was her keenness, her ardent interest in those possibilities, that urged him on. When she finally persuaded him to stand for Parliament as member for their county town, it was in a great measure her popularity that won him the seat.

He was in the House without making any special mark for two years, with a comfortable sense, not clearly stated perhaps even to himself, that there was time before him. Men go long in harness in these days; some day for certain that mark would be made. Then his party went out, and in spite of another unsuccessful attempt in his own constituency, and then in one further afield, he was left by the roadside, while the tide of politics swept on. His wife consoled herself by thinking that at the next opportunity he would surely get in. But when the opportunity came, she was so ill that he could not leave her, and the moment passed. Then when they began to realise what her ultimate condition might be, and she was recommended to take some special German waters which might work a cure, he and Rachel went with her. Sir William, when the necessity of going abroad first presented itself to him—a heroic necessity for the ordinary stay-at-home Englishman—had felt the not unpleasant stimulus, the tightening of the threads of life, which the need for a given unexpected course of action presents to the not very much occupied person. Then came those months away from his own country and his own surroundings—months in which he acquired the habit of reading an English newspaper two days old and being quite satisfied with it, when everything else also had two days' less importance than it would at home, and gradually he tasted the delights of the detached onlooker who need do nothing but warn, criticise, prophesy, protest. With absolute sincerity to himself he attributed this attitude which Fate had assigned to him as entirely owing to his having had to leave England on his wife's account. He had quite easily, quite calmly drifted into a conviction that for his wife's sake he had chivalrously renounced his chances of distinction. Lady Gore on her side—it was another bitterness added to the rest—did not for a moment doubt that it was her condition and the sacrifice that her husband had made of his life to her which had ruined his political career. And they both of them gradually succeeded in forgetting that the alternative had not been a certainty. They believed, they knew, they even said openly, that if it had not been for his incessant attendance on her he would have gone into the House, he would have taken office, and eventually have been one of the shapers of his country's destiny. The phraseology of their current talk to one another and to outsiders reflected this belief. "If I had continued in the House," Sir William would say, with a manner and inflection which conveyed that he had left it of his own free will and not attempted to return to it, "I should have——" or, "If I had taken office——" or even sometimes, "If I were leading the Liberal party——" and no one, indeed, was in a position to affirm that these things might not have been. If a man's capacities are hinted at or even stated by himself to his fellow-creatures with a certain amount of discretion, and if he does not court failure by putting them to the proof, it does not occur to most people to contradict him, and the possible truth of the contradiction soon sinks out of sight. So Sir William sat on the brink of the river and watched the others plunging into the waves, diving, rising, breasting the current, and was agreeably supported by the consciousness that if Fate had so ordained it, he himself would have been capable of performing all these feats just as creditably. No need now to stifle a misgiving that in the old days would occasionally obtrude itself into the glowing views of the future, that he was possibly not of a stature to play the great parts for which he might be cast. On the contrary, what now remained was the blessed peace brought by renunciation, the calm renunciation of prospects that in the light of ceasing to try to attain them seemed absolutely certain. No one now could ever say that he had failed. He had been prevented by circumstances from achieving any success of a definite and conspicuous kind, although the position he had attained, the consideration nearly always accorded to the ordinary prosperous middle-aged Englishman of the upper classes who has done nothing to forfeit his claim to it, and more than all, the plenitude of assurance which he received of his deserts from his immediate surroundings, might well have been considered success enough. And on his return to England, after eighteen months of wandering, although he was no longer in Parliament and had no actual voice in deciding the politics of his country, it pleased him to think that if he chose he could still take an active line, that he could belong to the volunteer army of orators who make speeches at other people's elections and who write letters to the newspaper that the world may know their views on a given situation.

At the time of which we speak political parties in England were trying in vain to re-adjust an equable balance. Conservatives and Unionists, almost indistinguishable, were waving the Imperialist banner in the face of the world. The Liberals, once the advanced and subversive party, were now raising their voices in protest, tentatively advocating the claims of what they considered the oppressed races. Derisive epithets were hurled at them by their enemies; the Pro-Boers, the Little Englanders took the place of the Home Rulers of the past. Sir William was by tradition a Liberal. Inspired by that tradition he wrote an article on the "Attitude of England," which appeared in a Liberal Review. Thrilled by the sight of his utterances in print, he determined in his secret soul to expand that article into a book. The secret was of course shared by his wife, who fervently believed in the yet unwritten masterpiece. The fact that in spite of the dearth of prominent men in his party, of men who had in them the stuff of a leader, that party had not turned to Gore in its need, aroused no surprise, no misgiving, in either his mind or that of his wife. It was simply in their eyes another step in that path of voluntary renunciation which he was treading for her sake.

With this possible interpretation of all missed opportunities entirely taken for granted, Sir William's existence flowed peacefully and prosperously on. It was with an agreeable consciousness of his dignity and prestige that he sat once or twice in the week at the board meetings of one or two governing bodies to which he belonged. They figured in his scheme of existence as his hours of work, the sterner, more serious occupation which justified his hours of leisure. The rest of that leisure was spent in happy, congenial uniformity: a morning ride, followed by some time in his comfortable study, during which he might be supposed to be writing his book; an hour or two at his club; a game or two of chess, a pastime in which he excelled; and behind all this a beautiful background, the deep and enduring affection of his wife, whose companionship, and needs, and admiration for himself filled up all the vacant spaces in his life. He would, however, have been genuinely surprised if he had realised that it was by a constant, deliberate intention that she succeeded in entertaining him, in amusing him, as much as she did her friends and acquaintances; if he had thought that she had made up her mind that never, while she had power to prevent it, should he come into his own house and find it dull. And he never did.

CHAPTER II

To be a popular invalid is in itself a career: it blesses those that call and those that receive. The visitors who used day by day to go and see Lady Gore used to congratulate themselves as they stood on her doorstep on the knowledge that they would find her within, and glad—or so each one individually thought—to see them. She was an attractive person, certainly, as she lay on her sofa. Her hair had turned white prematurely early, it enhanced the effect of the delicate faded colouring and the soft brown eyes. The sweet brightness of her manner was mingled with dignity, with the comprehensive sympathy and pliability of a woman of the world; an innate distinction of mind and person radiated from her looks. Those who watched the general grace and repose of her demeanour and surroundings involuntarily felt that there might be advantages in a condition of life which prevented the mere thought of being hot, untidy, hurried, like some of the ardent ladies who used to rush into her room between a committee meeting and a tea-party and tell her breathlessly of their flustered doings. Rachel had inherited something of her mother's dainty charm. She had the same brown eyes and delicate features, framed by bright brown hair. It was certainly encouraging to those who looked upon the daughter to see in the mother what effect the course of the years was likely to have on such a personality. There was not much dread in the future when confronted with such a picture. But in truth, as far as most of the spectators who frequented the house were concerned, Rachel's personality had been merged in her mother's, and any comparison between the two was perhaps more likely to be in the direction of wondering whether Rachel in the course of years would, as time went on, become so absolutely delightful a human product as Lady Gore. Rachel's own attitude on this score was entirely consonant with that of others. Her mother was the centre of her life, the object of her passionate devotion, her guide, her ideal. It was when Rachel was seventeen that Lady Gore became helpless and dependent, and the girl suddenly found that their positions were in some ways reversed; it was she who had to take care of her mother, to inculcate prudence upon her, to minister incessantly to her daily wants; there was added to the daughter's love the yearning care that a loving woman feels for a helpless charge, and there was hardly room for anything else in her life. Rachel, fortunately for herself and for others, had no startling originality; no burning desire, arrived at womanhood, to strike out a path for herself. She was unmoved by the conviction which possesses most of her young contemporaries that the obvious road cannot be the one to follow. Lady Gore's perceptions, far more acute as regarded her daughter than her husband, and rendered more vivid still by the whole concentration of her maternal being in Rachel, had entirely realised, while she wondered at it, the complete lack in her child of the modern ferment that seethes in the female mind of our days. But she had finally come to see that if Rachel was entirely happy and contented with her life it was a result to rejoice over rather than be discontented with, even though her horizon did not extend much beyond her own home. Besides, it is always well to rejoice over a result we cannot modify. Needless to say that the girl, who blindly accepted her mother's opinion even on indifferent subjects, was, biassed by her own affection, more than ready to endow her father with all the qualities Lady Gore believed him to possess. She had arrived at the age of twenty-two without realising that there could be for her any claims in the world that would be paramount to these, anything that could possibly come before her allegiance to her parents.

One of the bitterest pangs of Lady Gore's bitter renunciation was the moment when she realised that she could not be the one to guide Rachel's first steps in a wider world than that of her home, that all her plans and theories about the moment when the girl should grow up, when her mother would accompany her, steer her, help her at every step, must necessarily be brought to nought. And this mother, alas! had been so full of plans; she had so anxiously watched other people and their daughters, so carefully accumulated from her observation the many warnings and the few examples which constitute what is called the teaching of experience. But when the time came the lesson had been learnt in vain. Rachel's eighteenth and nineteenth years were spent in anxious preoccupations about her mother's health, in solicitous care of her father and the household, and the girl had glided gently from childhood into womanhood with nothing but increased responsibility, instead of more numerous pleasures, to mark the passage. But the result was something very attractively unlike the ordinary product of the age. She had had, from the conditions of her life, no very intimate and confidential girl friends by whose point of view to readjust and possibly lower her own, and with whom to compare every fleeting manifestation of thought and feeling. She remained unconsciously surrounded by an atmosphere of reticence and reserve, a certain shy aloofness, mingled with a direct simple dignity, that gave to her bearing an ineffable grace and charm. The mothers of more dashing damsels were wont to say that she was not "effective" in a ballroom. It was true that she had nothing particularly accentuated in demeanour or appearance which would at once arrest attention, an inadequate equipment, perhaps, in the opinion of those who hold that it is better to produce a bad effect than none at all.

Mrs. Feversham, of Bruton Street, was an old friend of Lady Gore's, whose junior she was by a few years. She had no daughters of her own, and had in consequence an immense amount of undisciplined energy at the service of those of other people. She was not a lady whose views were apt to be matured in silence; she was ardently concerned about Rachel's future, and she was constantly imparting new projects to Lady Gore, who received them with smiling equanimity.

It was at an "At Home" given by Mrs. Feversham one evening early in the season, when the rooms were full of hot people talking at the top of their voices, that the hostess, looking round her with a comprehensive glance, saw Rachel standing alone. There was, however, in the girl's demeanour none of that air of aggressive solitude sometimes assumed by the neglected. The eye fell upon Rachel with a sense of rest, looking on one who did not wish to go anywhere or to do anything, who was standing with unconscious grace an entirely contented spectator of what was passing before her. Mrs. Feversham's one idea, however, as she perceived her was instantly to suggest that she should do something else, that at any price some one should take her to have some tea, or make her eat or walk, or do anything, in fact, but stand still. Rachel, however, at the moment she was swooped down upon, was well amused; a smile was unconsciously playing on her lips as she listened to an absurd conversation going on between a young man and a girl just in front of her.

"By George!" said the boy, "it is hot. Let's go and have ices."

"Ices? Right you are," the girl replied, and attempted to follow her gallant cavalier, who had started off, trying to make for himself a path through the serried hot crowd, leaving the lady he was supposed to be convoying to follow him as near as she might.

"Hallo!" he said suddenly. "There's Billy Crowther. Do you mind if I go and slap him on the back?"

"All right, buck up, then, and slap him on the back," replied the fair one. "I'll go on." Thus gracefully encouraged, the youth flung himself in another direction, and almost overturned his hostess, who was coming towards Rachel.

"Sorry," he said, apparently not at all discomposed, and continued his wild career.

"Well! the young men of the present day!..." said Mrs. Feversham, as she joined Rachel; then suddenly remembering that a wholesale condemnation was not the attitude she wished to inculcate in her present hearer, she went on: "Not that they are all alike, of course; some of them are—are different," she supplemented luminously. "Now, my child, have you had anything to eat?"

"I don't think I want anything, thank you," said Rachel.

"Oh, nonsense!" said Mrs. Feversham. "You must." And, looking round for the necessary escort, she saw a new arrival coming up the stairs. "The very man!" she said to herself, but fortunately not aloud, as "Mr. Rendel!" was announced. A young man of apparently a little over thirty, with deep-set, far-apart eyes and clear-cut features, came up and took her outstretched hand with a little air of formal politeness refreshing after the manifestations she had been deploring.

"I am so glad to see you," she said cordially. Rendel greeted her with a smile. "Do you know Miss Gore?" Rendel and Rachel bowed.

"I have met Sir William Gore more than once," he said.

"She is dying for something to eat," said Mrs. Feversham, to Rachel's great astonishment. "Do take her downstairs, Mr. Rendel." The young people obediently went down together.

"I am not really dying for something to eat," Rachel said, as soon as they were out of hearing of their hostess. "In fact, I am not sure that I want anything."

"Oh, don't you?" said Rendel.

"Two hours ago I was still dining, you see."

"Of course," said Rendel, "so was I." They both laughed. They went on nevertheless to the door of the room from whence the clatter of glass and china was heard.

"Now, are you sure you won't be 'tempted,' according to the received expression?" said Rendel, as a hot waiter hurried past them with some dirty plates and glasses on a tray.

"No, I am afraid I am not at all tempted," said Rachel.

"Well, let us look for a cooler place," said Rendel. What a soothing companion this was he had found, who did not want him to fight for an ice or a sandwich! They went up again to a little recess on the landing by an open window. The roar of tongues came down to them from the drawing-room.

"Just listen to those people," said Rendel. A sort of wild, continuous howl filled the air, as though bursting from a company of the condemned immured in an eternal prison, instead of from a gathering of peaceable citizens met together for their diversion. "Isn't it dreadful to realise what our natural note is like?" he added. "It is hideous."

"It isn't pretty, certainly," said Rachel, unable to help smiling at his face of disgust. The roar seemed to grow louder as it went on.

"It is a pity we can't chirp and twitter like birds," said Rendel.

"I don't know that that would be very much better," said Rachel. "Have you ever been in a room with a canary singing? Think of a room with as many canaries in it as this."

"Yes, I daresay—it might have been nearly as bad," Rendel said; "though if we were canaries we should be nicer to look at perhaps," and his eye fell on an unprepossessing elderly couple who were descending the stairs with none of the winsomeness of singing birds. "Have you read Maeterlinck's 'Life of the Bees'?"

"No," Rachel answered simply.

"I agree with him," Rendel said, "that it would be just as difficult to get any idea of what human beings are about by looking down on them from a height, as it is for us to discover what insects are doing when we look down on them."

"Yes, imagine looking at that," said Rachel, pointing towards the drawing-room. "You would see people walking up and down and in and out for no reason, and jostling each other round and round."

"Yes," said Rendel. "How aimless it would look! Not more aimless than it is, after all," he added.

"It amuses me, all the same," said Rachel, rather deprecatingly. "I mean, to come to a party of this kind every now and then; perhaps because I don't do it very often."

"Why, don't you go out every night of your life in the season?" said Rendel; "I thought all young ladies did."

"I don't," she said. "It isn't quite the same for me as it is for other people—at least, I mean that I have only my father to go out with;" and then, seeing in his face the interpretation he put on her words, she added, "my mother is an invalid, and we do not like to leave her too often."

"Ah! but she is alive still," said Rendel, with a tone that sounded as if he understood what the contrary might have meant.

"Oh yes," said Rachel quickly. "Yes, yes, indeed she is alive," in a voice that told the proportion that fact assumed in existence.

"My mother died long years ago," said Rendel, in a lower voice. "Not so long, though, that I did not understand." Rachel looked at him with a soft light of pity flooding her face, and drawing the words out of him, he knew not how. "My father married again," he said, "while I was still a child— while I needed looking after, at least."

"Oh," said Rachel, "you had a stepmother?"

"Yes," he said, "I had a stepmother," and his face involuntarily became harder as he recalled that long stretch of loveless years—the father had never quite understood the shy and sensitive child—during which he had been neglected, suppressed, lonely, with no one to care that he did well at school and college, and that later he was getting on in the world, with no place in the world that was really his home. Then he went on after a moment: "And now my father is dead, too, so I am pretty much alone, you see."

"How terrible it must be!" said Rachel softly. "How extraordinary! I can't quite imagine what it is like."

"Well, it is not very pleasant," said Rendel looking up, and again penetrated by the sweet compassion in Rachel's face. "You can't think how strange it is——" He broke off and got up as Sir William Gore came downstairs towards them. Sir William, with the true instinct of a father, had chosen this moment to wonder whether Rachel was being sufficiently amused, and was bearing down upon her and her companion with an air of cheerful virtue which proclaimed that her conversation with Rendel was at an end. Sir William's political principles did not permit him to think very much of Rendel, since he was private secretary to a man whose policy Sir William cordially detested, Lord Stamfordham, the Foreign Minister, whose acute and wide-reaching sagacity inspired his followers with a blind confidence to himself and his methods. Lord Stamfordham had soon discovered the practical aptitude, the political capacity, the determined, honourable ambition that lay behind Francis Rendel's grave exterior, and had made up his mind, as indeed had others, that the young man had a distinguished future before him.

"Ah, Rendel, how are you?" said Gore. "What is your Chief going to do next, eh?"

"I am afraid I can't tell you, Sir William," said Rendel with a half smile.

"Well, the people round him ought to put the brake on," said Gore, "or I don't know where the country will be."

"I am afraid it is a brake I am not strong enough to work," said Rendel; "like Archimedes, I have not a lever powerful enough to move the universe."

"H'm!" said Sir William, with a sort of snort. There are fortunately still some sounds left in our vocabulary which convey primeval emotions without the limitations of words. "Come, Rachel, it is time for us to be going."

Mrs. Feversham's watchful eye had managed to observe what appeared to be the sufficiently satisfactory sequel to the introduction she had made. She was not a woman to let such a seed die for want of planting and watering. She asked Rendel to dinner to meet the Gores, she talked to Lady Gore about him, she it was who somehow arranged that he should go to call at Prince's Gate, and he finally grew into a habit of finding his way there with a frequency that surprised himself. Lady Gore subjugated him entirely by her sweet kindly welcome, and the interest with which she listened to him, until he found himself to his own astonishment telling her, as he sat by her sofa, of his hopes and fears and plans for the future.

Gradually new possibilities seemed to come into his life, or rather the old possibilities were seen in a new light shed by the womanly sympathy which up to now he had never known. He came away from each visit with some fresh spurt of purpose, some new impulse to achievement. Lady Gore, on her side, had been more favourably impressed by Rendel than by any of the young men she had seen, until she realised that here at last was a possible husband who might be worthy of Rachel. But with her customary wisdom she tried not to formulate it even to herself: she did not believe in these things being helped on otherwise than by opportunity for intercourse being given. But where Mrs. Feversham was, opportunity was sure to follow. Lady Gore one morning had an eager letter from her friend saying, "I know that you and Rachel make it a rule of life that she can never go away from home. But you must let her come to me next Thursday for the night. I shall have"—and she underlined this significantly without going into more details—"*just the right people to meet her.*" And for once, as Lady Gore folded up the letter, she too was seized with an ardour of matchmaking. She had a real affection for Rendel, and the devotion of the young man to herself touched and pleased her. His probably brilliant future and comfortable means were not the principal factors in the situation, but there was no doubt that they helped to make everything else easy. So it was that, to Rachel's great surprise, the day after the party at Bruton Street, her mother having told her without showing her the letter of Mrs. Feversham's invitation, advised her to accept it, and, to the mother's still greater surprise, the daughter, in her turn, after a slight protest, agreed to do so, stipulating, however, that she should not be away more than twenty-four hours. The accusation that Rachel "gadded" as much as other girls of her age was obviously an unmerited one.

CHAPTER III

"Alone?" said Sir William, as he came into the room. "Thank Heaven! Have you had no one?"

"Aunt Anna," Lady Gore replied, in a tone which was comment on the statement.

"Aunt Anna? What did she come again for?" said Sir William.

"I really don't know," Lady Gore said. "I think to-day it was to tell me that Rachel and I ought not to worship you as we do."

"I don't know what she means," said Sir William, standing from force of habit comfortably in front of the fireplace as though there were a fire in the grate. "I should have thought it was Rachel and I who adored you."

"She would like that better," Lady Gore replied. "But, oh dear, what a weary woman she is!"

"She has tired you out," Sir William said. "It really is not a good plan that your door should be open to every bore who chooses to come and call upon you. One ought to be able to keep people of that sort, at any rate, out of one's house."

Lady Gore heaved a sigh.

"Well, it is rather difficult and invidious too," she said, "to try to keep certain people out when one is not sure who is coming—and it is rather dull not to see any one," with a little quiver of the lip which Sir William did not perceive. Then speaking more lightly, "It is a pity we can't have some kind of automatic arrangement at our front doors, like the thing for testing sovereigns at the Mint, by which the heavy, tiresome people would be shot back into the street, and the light, amusing ones shot into the hall."

"I am quite agreeable," said Sir William, "as long as Aunt Anna is shot back into the street."

"Ah, how delightful it would be!" said Lady Gore longingly.

"And Miss Tarlton too, please," said Sir William.

"My dear William," Lady Gore said, "Miss Tarlton is quite harmless."

"Harmless?" repeated Sir William; "I don't know what you call harmless. The very thought of her fills me with impotent rage. A woman who talks of nothing but photography and bicycling, and goes about with her fingers pea-green and her legs in gaiters! It's an outrage on society. I am thankful that Rachel has never gone in for any nonsense of that sort—nor ever shall, while I can prevent it."

"My good friend," said Lady Gore, "you may not find that so easy."

"I will prevent it as long as she is under my roof," replied Sir William. "I suppose if she marries a husband with any fads of that sort, she will have to share them."

"But"—Lady Gore checked herself on the verge of saying, "I don't think he has," as she suddenly realised what image was called up by the mention of Rachel's possible husband—"but she might marry some one who hasn't," she ended lamely.

"Oh dear me, yes," said Sir William, "there is time enough for that; she is very young after all."

"She is twenty-two," said Lady Gore. "Perhaps that is young in these days when women don't seem to marry until they are nearly thirty. But I don't think it is a good plan to wait so long."

"I don't think it's a bad one," said Sir William; "they know their own minds at any rate."

"They have known half a dozen of their own minds," said Lady Gore. "I think it is much better for a girl to marry before she knows that there is an alternative to the mind she has got, such as it is."

Sir William smiled, but did not think it worth while to argue the point. It was not his province, but her mother's, to guide Rachel's career, and he was content to remain in comfortable ignorance of the complications of the female heart of a younger generation. However, he was not allowed to remain in that detached attitude, for Lady Gore, with the subject uppermost in her mind preoccupying her to the exclusion of everything else, could not help adding, "You often see Mr. Rendel at parties, when you and Rachel go out, I mean?"

"Rendel? Yes," said Gore indifferently. "Why?"

Lady Gore did not explain. "I like him," she said.

"Oh yes, so do I," said Gore, without enthusiasm. "I don't agree with him, of course. I asked him one day what his Chief was about, and told him he ought to put the brake on."

"Did he seem pleased at that?" said Lady Gore, smiling.

"He will have to hear it, I'm afraid," said Gore, "whether it pleases him or not."

"I must say," said Lady Gore, "I can't help admiring Lord Stamfordham. I do like a man who is strong, and this man is head and shoulders above other people."

"Head and shoulders above little people perhaps," said Sir William.

"Mr. Rendel says that when once one is caught up in Lord Stamfordham's train, it is impossible not to follow him."

"Rendel!" said Sir William. "Oh, of course, if you're going to listen to what Stamfordham's hangers-on say...."

"Oh, William, please!" said Lady Gore. "Don't say that sort of thing about Mr. Rendel."

"Why?" said Sir William, amazed. "Why am I to speak of Rendel with bated breath?"

"Because ... suppose—suppose he were to be your son-in-law some day?"

"Oh," said Sir William, staring at her, "is that what you are thinking of?"

"Mind—mind you don't say it," cried Lady Gore.

"*I* shan't say it, certainly," cried Sir William, still bewildered; "but has he said it? That's more to the point."

"He hasn't yet," she admitted.

"Well, he never struck me in that light, I must say," said Sir William. "I always thought it was you he adored."

"*Cela n'empêche pas*," said Lady Gore, laughing.

"I daresay he would do very well," said Sir William, who, as he further considered the question, was by no means insensible to the advantages of the suggestion put before him; "it is only his politics that are against him."

"I am afraid," said Lady Gore, "that Rachel would always think her father knew best."

"Afraid!" said Sir William, "what more would you have?"

"My dear William," said his wife, smiling at him, "she might think her husband knew best, that is what some people do."

"Quite right," said Sir William, looking at her fondly, but believing with entire conviction in the truth of what he was lightly saying.

At this moment the door opened and a footman came in.

"Young Mr. Anderson is downstairs, Sir William."

"Young Mr. Anderson?" said Sir William, looking at him with some surprise.

"Yes, Sir William—Mr. Fred," the man replied, evidently somewhat doubtful as to whether he was right in using the honorific.

"Fred Anderson back again!" said Sir William to his wife. "All right, James, I'll come directly." "I wonder if his rushing back to England so soon," he said, as the door closed upon the servant, "means that that boy has come to grief."

"Let us hope that it means the reverse," said his wife, "and that he has come back to ask you to be chairman of his company—as you promised, do you remember, when he went away?"

"So I did, yes, to be sure," said Sir William, laughing at the recollection. "Upon my word, that lad won't fail for want of assurance. We shall see what he has got to say." And he went out.

The Andersons had been small farmers on the Gore estate for some generations. Fred Anderson, the second son of the present farmer, a youth of energy and enterprise, had determined to seek his fortune further afield. Mainly by the kind offices of the Gores, he had been started in life as a mining engineer, and had, eighteen months before his present reappearance, been sent with some others to examine and report on a large mine lately discovered on British territory near the Equator. The result of their investigations proved that it was actually and most unexpectedly a gold mine, promising untold treasure, but at the same time, from its geographical situation, almost valueless, since it was so far from any lines of communication as to make the working of it practically impossible. The young, however, are sanguine; undaunted by difficulties, Fred Anderson, in spite of the discouragement and dropping off of his companions, remained full of faith in the future of the mine, and of something turning up which would make it possible to work it; in fact, he had actually gone so far as to obtain for himself a grant of the mining rights from the British Government. It was for this purpose that, giving a brief outline of the situation, he had written to Sir William some time before to ask him for the sum necessary to obtain the concession. Sir William had advanced it to him. It was when, two years before, the boy of nineteen was leaving home for the first time that he had half jestingly asked Sir William whether, if he and his companions found a gold mine and started a company to work it, he would be their chairman, and Sir William, to whom it had seemed about as likely that Fred Anderson would become Prime Minister as succeed in such an undertaking, had given him his hand on the bargain.

"Well, my boy," said Sir William, and the very sound of his voice seemed to Fred Anderson to put him back two years—the two years that appeared to him to contain his life. "How is it you have hurried back to England so quickly?"

"I will tell you all about it, Sir William," said the boy. "I thought it best to come over and get everything into shape myself."

"You seem to be embarking on very adventurous schemes," said Sir William, feeling as he looked at the boy's bright, open face, full of alert intelligence, that it was not impossible that the schemes might be carried through.

"I think you will say so, sir, when you have heard what I have to tell you," said Anderson, resolutely keeping down his excitement in a way that boded well for his powers of self-control.

"I shall be much interested," said Sir William. "Now, what about those mining rights? Do I understand that you are the proprietor of a mine on the Equator, a thousand miles from anywhere?"

"Yes, and no," said Anderson. "At least, yes to the first question; no to the second."

"What," said Sir William, still speaking lightly, "has the mine come nearer since we first heard of it?"

"Yes, practically it has," said Anderson, looking Gore in the face. Then, unrolling the paper which he held in his hand and rolling it the other way that it might remain open, he laid it carefully out on the table before Sir William. "I have brought you the map with all the indications on it, that you may see for yourself." Sir William adjusted an eyeglass and bent over the map, roused to more curiosity than he showed.

"This," said the young man, pointing to a large tract in pink, "is British territory; that is Uganda; here is the Congo Free State. There, you see, are the Germans where the map is marked in orange. There is the Equator, and *there* is the mine. Look, marked in blue."

"That is a pretty God-forsaken place, I must say," remarked Sir William.

"One moment," said Fred. "That thin, dotted ink line running north and south from the top of Africa to the bottom is the Cape to Cairo Railway, of which the route has now been determined on, and this," with a ringing accent of triumph, bringing his hand down on to the map, "is the place where the railway will pass within a few miles of us."

"What?" said Sir William, starting.

"Yes, there it is, quite close," Anderson answered. "When once it is there, all our difficulties of transport are over."

Sir William recovered himself.

"Cape to Cairo!" he said. "You had better wait till you see the line made, my boy."

"That won't be so very long, Sir William, I assure you," said the young man. "This cross in ink marks where the line has got to from the northern end, and this one," pointing to another, "from the south, and they have already got telegraph poles a good bit further."

"Before the two ends have joined hands," said Sir William, "another Government may be in which won't be so keen on that mad enterprise. As if we hadn't railways enough on our hands already."

"Not many railways like this one," said the young man. "Did you see an article in the *Arbiter* about it this morning? It is going to be the most tremendous thing that ever was done."

"Oh, of course, yes," said Sir William with an accent of scorn in his tone. "Just the kind of thing that the *Arbiter* would have a good flare-up about. I have no doubt that the scheme is magnificent on paper. However, time will show," he added, with a kinder note in his voice. He liked the boy and his faith in achieving the impossible.

"It will indeed," said Anderson. "Only, you see, we can't afford to wait till time shows—we must take it by the forelock now, I'm afraid."

"Then what do you propose to do next?" said Sir William.

"We are going to form a company," said the boy, his colour rising. "We are going to have everything ready, and the moment the railway is finished we are ready to work the mine, and our fortune is made."

"You are going to form a company?" said Sir William, incredulously.

"Yes," Anderson replied. "In a week we shall have the whole thing in shape, and I hope that when the mine and its possibilities are made public, we shan't have any difficulty in getting the shares taken up."

"Well, I am sure I hope you won't," said Sir William. "I'll take some shares in it if you can show me a reasonable prospect of its coming to anything. But I should like to hear something more about it first."

"You shall, of course," said Anderson, as he took up his map again. "But it was not about taking shares I came to ask you, Sir William."

"What was it, then?" said Sir William.

"You said," the boy replied, with an embarrassed little laugh, looking him straight in the face, "that you would be the chairman of the first company I floated."

"By Jove, so I did!" said Sir William. "Upon my word, it was rather a rash promise to make."

"I don't think it was, I assure you," the boy said earnestly; "this thing really is going to turn up trumps."

"Well, let's hope it is, for all concerned," said Sir William. "And what are you going to call it?"

"Oh, we are going to call it," said Fred, "simply 'The Equator, Limited.'"

"The Equator! Upon my word! Why not the Universe?" said Sir William.

"That will come next," said the boy, with a happy laugh of sheer jubilation. "Then, Sir William, will you—you will be our chairman?"

"Oh yes," said Sir William. "A promise is a promise. But mind, I shall be a very inefficient one. I don't suppose you could find any one who knew less about that sort of thing than I do."

"Oh, that will be all right, Sir William," the boy said quickly. "There will be lots of people concerned who know all about it. Now that the mine is going to be accessible, the right people will be more than ready to take it up. I just wanted to have you there as the nominal head to it, because you have always been so good to me, and you have brought me luck since the beginning."

"Nonsense!" said Sir William. "You'll have only yourself to thank, my boy, when you get on."

"Oh, I know better than that," said Anderson. Something very like tears came into his eyes as he took the hand Sir William held out to him, and then left the room as happy a youth of twenty-one as could be found in London that day.

CHAPTER IV

There was another young creature, at that moment driving across London to Prince's Gate, to whom the world looked very beautiful that day. Rachel was still in a sort of rapturous bewilderment. The wonderful new experience that had come to her, that she was contemplating for the first time, seemed, as she saw it in the company of familiar surroundings, more marvellous yet. At Maidenhead everything had been unwonted. The new experience of going away alone, the enchanting repose of the hot sunny days on the river, the look of the boughs as they dipped lazily into the water, and the light dancing and dazzling on the ripples of the stream—all had been part of the setting of the new aspect of things, part of that great secret that she was beginning to learn. Yet all the time she had had a feeling that when the setting was altered, when she left this mysterious region of romance, life would become ordinary again, the strange golden light with which it was flooded would turn into the ordinary light of day, and she would find herself where she had been before. But it was not so. Here she was back again in the town she knew so well, driving towards her home—but the new, strange possession had not left her, the secret was hers still. It had all come so quickly that she had not realised what she felt. Was she "in love," the thing that she had taken for granted would happen to her some day, but that she had not yet longed for? Rachel, it must be confessed, had not been entirely given up to romance; she had not been waiting, watching for the fairy prince who should ride within her ken and transform existence for her. Her life had been too full of love of another kind. But now she had a sudden feeling of experience having been completed, something had come to her that she had wished for, longed for—how much, she had not known until it came. What would they say at home? What would her mother say? And gradually she realised, as she always ended by realising, that whatever the picture of life she was contemplating her mother was in the foreground of it. There was no doubt about that; her mother came first, her mother must come first. But nothing was quite clear in her mind at this moment. The past forty-eight hours, the sudden change of scene and of companionship, a possible alternative path suddenly presenting itself in an existence which had been peacefully following the same road, all this had been disturbing, bewildering even—and when the hansom drew up in Prince's Gate, Rachel felt an intense satisfaction at being back again in the haven, at the thought of the welcome she was going to find. And as on a summer's day to people sitting in a shaded room, the world beyond shut out, the opening of a door into the sunshine may reveal a sudden vista of light, of flowers shining in the sun, so to the two people who were awaiting Rachel's arrival she brought a sudden vision of youth, brightness, colour, hope, as she came swiftly in, smiling and confident, with the face and expression of one who had never come into the presence of either of these two companions without seeing her gladness reflected in the light of welcome that shone in their eyes.

"Well, gadabout!" said her father as she turned to him after embracing her mother fondly.

"I am very sorry," said Rachel, "I won't do it again."

"And how did you enjoy yourself, my darling?" said Lady Gore.

"Oh, very much," Rachel said. "It was delightful." The mother looked at her and tried to read into her face all that the words might mean. Rachel was in happy unconsciousness of how entirely the ground was prepared to receive her confidence.

"Was there a large party?" said Sir William.

"No," said Rachel, "a very small one." She was leaning back comfortably in the armchair, and deliberately taking off her gloves. "In fact, there were only two people beside myself, Sir Charles Miniver, and—Mr. Rendel." There was a pause.

"Miniver!" said Sir William, "Still staying about! He appeared to me an old man when I was twenty-five." Rachel opened her eyes.

"Did he?" she said. "That explains it. He is quite terribly old now, much, much older than other old people one sees," she said, with the conviction of her age, to which sixty and eighty appear pretty much the same. "You didn't mind," she went on to her mother hastily, somewhat transparently trying to avoid a discussion of the rest of the house party, "my staying till the afternoon train? Mrs. Feversham suggested boating this morning, and the day was so lovely, it was too tempting to refuse."

"I didn't mind at all," said Lady Gore. "It must have been lovely in the boat. Did you all go?"

"N—no, not all," replied Rachel. "Mrs. Feversham would have come, but she had some things to do at home, and Sir Charles Miniver was——"

"Too old?" Lady Gore suggested.

"I suppose so," said Rachel, "though he called it busy."

"As you say," remarked Sir William, "that does not leave many people to go in the boat." Rachel looked at her father quickly, but with a pliability surprising in the male mind he managed to look unconscious. "Well, Elinor," he continued, "I think as you have a companion now, I shall go off for a bit. I shall be back presently. Let me implore you not to let me find too many bores at tea."

"If Miss Tarlton comes," said Lady Gore, "I will have her automatically ejected." Sir William went out, smiling at her. The mother and daughter, both unconsciously to themselves, watched the door close, then Rachel got up, went to the glass over the chimneypiece and began deliberately taking off her veil.

"I do look a sight," she said. "It is astonishing how dirty one's face gets in London, even in a drive across the Park."

"Rachel!" her mother said. Rachel turned round and looked at her. Then she went quickly across the room and knelt down by her mother's couch.

"Mother!" she said, "Mother dear! it is such a comfort that if I don't tell you things you don't mind. And why should you? It doesn't matter. It is just as if I had told you—you always know, you always understand."

"Yes," said Lady Gore, "I think I understand. And you know," she added after a moment, "that I never want you to tell me more than you wish to tell. Only, very often"—and she tried to choose her words with anxious care, that not one of them might mean more, less, or other than she intended, "it sometimes helps younger people, if they talk to people who are older. You see, the mere fact of having been in the world longer, brings one something like more wisdom, one can judge of the proportion of things somehow, nothing seems quite so surprising, so extraordinary—or so impossible," she added with a faint smile, with the intuition of the point that Rachel had arrived at. And Rachel was ready to take perfectly for granted that she should have been so followed. Her absolute reliance on the wise and tender confidante by her side, the habit of placing her first and referring everything to her was stronger unconsciously to herself, than even the natural desire of her age to hug the secret she was carrying, to keep it jealously from any eyes but her own.

"Of course, of course, I know that," she said without looking up, "and my first thought always is that I will tell you. In fact," she went on with a little laugh, "I never know what I think myself until I have told you, and heard what it sounds like when I am saying it to you, and seen what you look like when you listen—only——" she stopped again.

"Darling," said Lady Gore, "never feel that you must tell me a word more than you wish to say."

"Well," said Rachel hesitating, "the only thing is that to-day I must—perhaps—you would know something about it presently in any case...." And she stopped again.

"Presently? why?" said Lady Gore. Rachel made no answer.

"Is Mr. Rendel coming here to-day?" said Lady Gore, trying to speak in her ordinary voice.

"Yes," said Rachel, "he is coming to see you."

"I shall be very glad to see him," said Lady Gore. "I always am."

"I know, yes," said Rachel. Then with a sudden effort, "It is no use, mother, I must tell you; you must know first." Then she paused again. "This morning we went out in the boat——" she stopped.

"Yes," said Lady Gore, "and Sir Charles Miniver was unfortunately too old to go with you—or fortunately, perhaps?"

"I am not sure which," said Rachel. "I am not sure," she repeated slowly.

"Rachel, did Francis Rendel...."

"Yes," said Rachel, "he asked me to marry him."

Lady Gore laid her hand on her daughter's. "What did you say to him?"

Rachel looked up quickly. "Surely you know. I told him it would be impossible."

"Impossible?" her mother repeated.

"Of course, impossible," Rachel said. "We needn't discuss it, mother dear," she went on with an effort. "You know I could not go away from you; you could not do without me. You could not, could you?" she went on imploringly. "I should be dreadfully saddened if you could."

"I should have to do without you," Lady Gore said. "I could not let you give up your happiness to mine."

"It would not be giving up my happiness to stay with you, you know that quite well," Rachel said. "On the contrary, I simply could not be happy if I felt that you needed me and that I had left you."

"Rachel, do you care for him?"

"Do I, I wonder?" Rachel said, half thinking aloud and letting herself go as one does who, having overcome the first difficulty of speech, welcomes the rapturous belief of pouring out her heart to the right listener. "I believe," she said, "that I care for him as much as I could for any one, in that way, but"—and she shook her head—"I know all the time that you come first, and that you always, always will."

"Oh, but that is not right," said Lady Gore. "That is not natural."

"Not natural," Rachel said, "that I should care for my mother most?"

"No," Lady Gore said, "not in the long run. Of course," she went on with a smile, "to say a thing is not 'natural' is simply begging the question, and sounds as if one were dismissing a very complicated problem with a commonplace formula, but it has truth in it all the same. It is difficult enough to fashion existence in the right way, even with the help of others, but to do it single-handed is a task few people are qualified to achieve. I am quite sure that a woman has more chance of happiness if she marries than if she remains alone. It is right that people should renew their stock of affection, should see that their hold on the world, on life, is renewed, should feel that fresh claims, for that is a part, and a great part, of happiness, are ready at hand when the old ones disappear. All this is what means happiness, and you know that the one thing I want in the world is that you should be happy. I was thinking to-day," she went on, with a slight tremor in her voice, "that if I were quite sure that your life were happily settled, that you were beginning one of your own not wholly dependent on those behind you, I should not mind very much if mine were to come to an end."

"To an end?" said Rachel, startled. "Don't say that—don't talk about that."

"I do not talk about it often," Lady Gore said; "but this is a moment when it must be said, because, remember, when you talk of sacrificing your life to me——"

"Sacrificing!" interjected Rachel.

"Well, of devoting it to me," Lady Gore went on; "and putting aside those things that might make a beautiful life of your own, you must remember one thing, that I may not be there always. In fact," she corrected herself with a smile, "to say *may* not is taking a rose-coloured view, that I *shall* not be there always. And who knows? The moment of our separation may not be so far off."

Rachel looked up hurriedly, much perturbed.

"Why are you saying this now?" she said. "You have seemed so much better lately. You are very well, aren't you, mother? You are looking very well."

Lady Gore had a moment of wondering whether she should tell her daughter what she knew, what she expected herself, but she looked at Rachel's anxious, quivering face and refrained.

"It is something that ought to be said at this moment," she answered. "You have come to a parting of the ways. This is the moment to show you the signposts, to help you to choose the best road."

"Listen, mother," said Rachel earnestly. "In this case I am sure I know by myself which is the best road to choose. I am perfectly clear that as long as I have you I shall stay with you. That I mean to do," she continued with unwonted decision. "And besides, if—if you were no longer there, how could I leave my father?"

"Ah," said Lady Gore, "I wanted to say that to you. Now, as we are speaking of it, let us talk it out, let us look at it in the face. Consider the possibility, Rachel, the probability that I may be taken from you; my dream would be that you should make your own life with some one that you care about, and yet not part it entirely from your father's, that while he is there he should not be left. If I thought that, do you know, it would be a very great help to me," she said, forcing herself to speak steadily, but unable to hide entirely the wistful anxiety in her tone.

"I will never, never leave him," Rachel said. "I promise you that I never will."

"Then I can look forward," her mother said, "as peacefully, I don't say as joyfully, as I look back. Twenty-four years, nearly twenty-five," she went on, half to herself and looking dreamily upwards, "we have been married. You don't know what those years mean, but some day I hope you will. I pray that you may know how the lives and souls of two people who care for one another absolutely grow together during such a time."

"It is beautiful," Rachel said softly, "to know that there is such happiness in the world," and her own new happiness leapt to meet the assurance of the years.

"It is beautiful indeed," Lady Gore said. "It means a constant abiding sense of a strange other self sharing one's own interests—of a close companionship, an unquestioning approval which makes one almost independent of opinions outside."

"Some people," said Rachel, pressing her mother's hand, "have the outside affection and approval too."

"Yes, the world has been very kind to me," Lady Gore said, "and all that is delightful. But it is the big thing that matters. Do you remember that there was some famous Greek who said when his chosen friend and companion died, 'The theatre of my actions has fallen'?" Rachel's face lighted up in quick response. "When I am gone," her mother went on, "don't let your father feel that the theatre of *his* actions has fallen—take my place, surround him with love and sympathy."

"I will, indeed I will," said Rachel.

"What a man needs," said Lady Gore, "is some one to believe in him."

"My father will never be in want of that," said Rachel, with heartfelt conviction. "Mother," she added, "I never will forget what I am saying now, and you may believe it and you may be happy about it. I won't leave my father; he shall come first, I promise, whatever happens."

"First?" said Lady Gore gently. "No, Rachel, not that; it is right that your husband should come first."

"The people," said Rachel smiling, "whose husbands come first have not had a father and mother like mine."

There was a knock at the house door. Rachel sprang hurriedly to her feet, the colour flying into her cheeks. Lady Gore looked at her. She had never before seen in Rachel's face what she saw there now.

"I must take off my things," the girl said, catching up her gloves and veil.

"Don't be very long," said her mother.

"I'll—I'll—see," Rachel said, and she suddenly bent over her mother and kissed her, then went quickly out by one door as the other was thrown open to admit a visitor.

CHAPTER V

Francis Rendel came into the room with his usual air of ceremony, amounting almost to stiffness. Then, as he realised that his hostess was alone, his face lighted up and he came eagerly towards her.

"This *is* a piece of good fortune, to find you alone," he said. "I was afraid I should find you surrounded."

"It is early yet," Lady Gore said, with a smile.

"I know, yes," Rendel said. "I must apologise for coming at this time, but I wanted very much to see you——" He paused.

"I am delighted to see you at any time," Lady Gore said.

"It is so good of you," he answered, in the tone of one who is thinking of the next thing he is going to say. There was a silence.

"I hope you enjoyed yourself at Maidenhead?" said Lady Gore.

"Very, very much," Rendel answered with an air of penetrated conviction. There was another pause. Then he suddenly said, "Lady Gore——" and stopped.

She waited a moment, then said gently, "Yes, I know. Rachel has been telling me."

"She has! Oh, I am so glad," Rendel said. Then he added, finding apparently an extreme difficulty in speaking at all, "And—and—do you mind?"

"That is a modest way of putting it," said Lady Gore, smiling. "No, I don't mind. I am glad."

"Are you really?" said Rendel, looking as if his life depended on the answer. "Do you mean that you really think you—you—could be on my side? Then it will come all right."

"I will be on your side, certainly," said Lady Gore; "but I don't know that that is the essential thing. I am not, after all, the person whose consent matters most."

"Do you know, I believe you are," Rendel said. "I verily believe that at this moment you come before any one else in the world." There was no need to say in whose estimation, or to mention Rachel's name.

"Well, perhaps at this moment, as you say," said Lady Gore, "it is possible, but there is no reason why it should go on always."

"She is absolutely devoted to you," Rendel said.

"Rachel has a fund," her mother said, "of loyal devotion, of unswerving affection, which makes her a very precious possession."

"I have seen it," said Rendel. "Her devotion to you and her father is one of the most beautiful things in the world, even though...."

"Even...?" said Lady Gore, with a smile.

"Did she tell you what she said to me this morning?"

"I gathered, yes," Lady Gore replied, "both what you had said and her answer."

"I didn't take it as an answer," said Rendel. "I thought that I would come straight to you and ask you to help me, and that you would understand, as you always do, in the way that nobody else does."

"Take care," said Lady Gore smiling, "that you don't blindly accept Rachel's view of her surroundings."

"Oh, it is not only Rachel who has taught me that," said Rendel, his heart very full. "It is you yourself, and your sympathy. I wonder," he went on quickly, "if you know what it has meant to me? You see, it is not as if I had ever known anything of the sort before. To have had it all one's life, as your daughter has, must be something very wonderful. I don't wonder she does not want to give it up."

Lady Gore tried to speak more lightly than she felt. "She need not give it up," she said, with a somewhat quivering smile. "And you need not thank me any more," she went on. "I should like you to know what a great interest and a great pleasure it has been to me that you should have cared to come and see me as you have done, and to take me into your life." Rendel was going to speak, but she went on. "I have never had a son of my own. It was a great disappointment to me at first; I was very anxious to have one. I used to think how he and I would have planned out his life together, and that he might perhaps do some of the things in the world that are worth doing. You see how foolish I was," she ended, with a tremulous little smile.

Rendel, in spite of his gravity, experience and intuitive understanding, had a sudden and almost bewildering sense of a change of mental focus as he heard the wise, gentle adviser confiding in her turn, and confessing to foolish and unfulfilled illusions. He felt a passionate desire to be of use to her.

"I should have been quite content if he had been like you," she said, and she held out her hand, which he instinctively raised to his lips.

"You make me very happy," he said. "You make me hope."

"But," she said, trying to speak in her ordinary voice, "—perhaps I ought to have begun by saying this—I wonder if Rachel is the right sort of wife for a rising politician?"

"She is the right sort of wife for me," said Rendel. "That is all that matters."

"I'm afraid," Lady Gore said, "she isn't ambitious."

"Afraid!" said Rendel.

"She has no ardent political convictions."

"I have enough for both," said Rendel.

"And—and—such as she has are naturally her father's, and therefore opposed to yours."

"Then we won't talk about politics," Rendel said, "and that will be a welcome relief."

"I'm afraid also," the mother went on, smiling, "that she is not abreast of the age—that she doesn't write, doesn't belong to a club, doesn't even bicycle, and can't take photographs."

"Oh, what a perfect woman!" ejaculated Rendel.

"In fact I must admit that she has no bread-winning talent, and that in case of need she could not earn her own livelihood."

"If she had anything to do with me," said Rendel, "I should be ashamed if she tried."

"She is not as clever as you are."

"But even supposing that to be true," said Rendel, "isn't that a state of things that makes for happiness?"

"Well," replied Lady Gore, "I believe that as far as women are concerned you are behind the age too."

"I am quite certain of it," Rendel said, "and it is therefore to be rejoiced over that the only woman I have ever thought of wanting should not insist on being in front of it."

"The only woman? Is that so?" Lady Gore asked.

"It is indeed," he said, with conviction.

"And you are—how old?"

"Thirty-two."

"It sounds as if this were the real thing, I must say," she said, with a smile.

"There is not much doubt of that," said he quietly. "There never was any one more certain than I am of what I want."

"That is a step towards getting it," Lady Gore said.

"I believe it is," he said fervently. "You have told me all the things your daughter has not—that I am thankful she hasn't—but I know, besides, the things she has that go to make her the only woman I want to pass my life with—she is everything a woman ought to be—she really is."

"My dear young friend," said Lady Gore, with a shallow pretence of laughing at his enthusiasm, "you really are rather far gone!"

"Yes," said Rendel, "there is no doubt about that. I have not, by the way, attempted to tell you about things that are supposed to matter more than those we have been talking about, but that don't matter really nearly so much—I mean my income and prospects, and all that sort of thing. But perhaps I had better tell Sir William all that."

"You can tell him about your income," said Lady Gore, "if you like."

"I have enough to live upon," the young man said. "I don't think that on that score Sir William can raise any objection."

"Let us hope he won't on any other," she replied. "We must tell him what he is to think."

"And my chances of getting on, though it sounds absurd to say so, are rather good," he went on. "Lord Stamfordham will, I know, help me whenever he can; and I mean to go into the House, and then—oh, then it will be all right, really."

At this moment the door opened and Sir William came in.

"You are the very person we wanted," his wife said.

"You want to apologise to me for the conduct of your party, I suppose," said Gore to Rendel, half in jest, half in earnest, as he shook hands.

"I'm very sorry, Sir William," said Rendel, "if we've displeased you. Pray don't hold me responsible."

"Oh yes," said Lady Gore lightly, to give Rendel time, "one always holds one's political adversary responsible for anything that happens to displease one in the conduct of the universe."

"I hope," said Rendel, trying to hide his real anxiety, "that Sir William will try to forgive me for the action of my party, and everything else. Pray feel kindly towards me to-day."

Sir William looked at him inquiringly, affecting perhaps a more unsuspecting innocence than he was feeling. Rendel went on, speaking quickly and feeling suddenly unaccountably nervous.

"I have come here to tell you—to ask you— —" He stopped, then went on abruptly, "This morning, at Maidenhead, I asked your daughter to marry me."

"What, already?" said Sir William involuntarily. "That was very prompt. And what did she say?"

"She said it was impossible," Rendel answered, encouraged more by Gore's manner and his general reception of the news than by his actual words.

"Impossible, did she say?" said Sir William. "And what did you say to that?"

"That I should come here this afternoon," Rendel replied.

Sir William smiled.

"That was prompter still," he said. "It looks as if you knew your own mind at any rate."

"I do indeed, if ever a man did," said Rendel confidently. "And I really do believe that it was because she was a good daughter she said it was impossible."

"Well, if it was, that's the kind that often makes an uncommonly good wife," Sir William said.

"I don't doubt it," Rendel said, with conviction. "And I feel that if only you and Lady Gore— —"

He stopped, as the door opened gently, and Rachel appeared, in a fresh white summer gown. She stood looking from one to the other, arrested on the threshold by that strange consciousness of being under discussion which is transmitted to one as through a material medium. Then what seemed to her the full horror of being so discussed swept over her. Was it possible that already the beautiful dream that had surrounded her, that wonderful secret that she had hardly yet whispered to herself, was having the light of day let in upon it, was being handled, discussed, as though it were possible that others might share in it too?

Rendel read in her face what she was going through. He went forward quickly to meet her.

"I am afraid," he said, putting his thoughts into words more literally than he meant, "that I have come too soon. I hope you will forgive me?"

"It is rather soon," Rachel answered, not quite knowing what she was saying.

"But you don't say whether you forgive him or not, Rachel," said Sir William, whose idea of carrying off the situation was to indulge in the time-honoured banter suitable to those about to become engaged.

"Don't ask her to say too much at once," Lady Gore said quickly, realising far better than Rachel's father did what was passing in the girl's mind.

"I'm afraid I can't say very much yet," Rachel said hesitatingly.

"I don't want you to say very much," said Rendel, "or indeed anything if you don't want to," he ended somewhat lamely and entreatingly.

"Miss Tarlton!" announced the servant, throwing the door open.

The four people in the room looked at each other in consternation. Events had succeeded each other so quickly that no one had thought of providing against the contingency of inopportune visitors by saying Lady Gore was not at home. It was too late to do anything now. Miss Tarlton happily had no misgivings about her reception. It never crossed her mind that she could be unwelcome, especially to-day that she had brought with her some photographs taken from the Gores' own balcony some weeks before, on the occasion of some troops having passed along Prince's Gate. She had half suggested on that occasion that she should come, in order that she might have a post of vantage from which to take some of the worst photographs in London, and the Gores had not had the heart to refuse her. If she had had any doubt, however—which she had not—about her hosts' feelings in the matter, she would have felt that she had now made up for everything by bringing them the result of her labours, and that nothing could be more opportune or more agreeable than her entrance on this particular occasion.

Miss Tarlton was a single woman of independent means living alone, a destiny which makes it almost inevitable that there should be a luxuriant growth of individual peculiarities which have never needed to accommodate themselves to the pressure of circumstances or of companionship. She was perfectly content with her life, and none the less so although those to whom she recounted the various phases of it were not so content at second hand with hearing the recital of it. She was one of those fortunate persons who have a hobby which takes the place of parents, husband, children, relations—a hobby, moreover, which appears to afford a delight quite independent of the varying degrees of success with which it is pursued. Unhappily the joy of those who thus pursue a much-loved occupation is bound to overflow in words; and if they have no daily auditor within their own four walls, they are driven by circumstances to choose their confidants haphazard when they go out. Miss Tarlton's confidences, however, were all of an optimistic character: she inflicted on her hearers no grievances against destiny. She recorded her vote, so to speak, in favour of content, and thereby established a claim to be heard.

To see her starting on one of her photographing expeditions was to be convinced that she considered the scheme of the universe satisfactory, as she went off with her felt hat jammed on to her head, with an air, not of radiant pleasure perhaps, but of faith in her occupation of unflinching purpose. With her camera slung on to her bicycle and her fat little feet working the pedals, she had the air of being the forerunner of a corps of small cyclist photographers. Life appealed to Miss Tarlton according to its adaptability to photography. For this reason she was not preoccupied with the complications of sentiment or of the softer emotions which not even the Röntgen rays have yet been able to reproduce with a camera.

"How do you do, Lady Gore?" she said as she came in. "I am later than I meant to be. I was so afraid I should not get here to-day, but I knew how anxious you would be to see the photographs."

"How kind of you!" Lady Gore said vaguely, for the moment entirely forgetting what the photographs were.

Miss Tarlton, after greeting the other members of the party, and making acquaintance with Rendel, all on her part with the demeanour of one who quickly despatches preliminaries before proceeding to really important business, drew off her gloves, displaying strangely variegated fingers, and proceeded to take from the case she was carrying photographs in various stages of their existence.

"I have brought you the negatives of one or two," she said, holding one after another up to the light, "as I didn't wait to print them all. Ah, here is one. This is how you must hold it, look."

Lady Gore tried to look at it as though it were really the photograph, and not the equilibrium of a most difficult situation, that she was trying to poise. Sir William was about to propose to Rendel to come down with him to his study, but Miss Tarlton obligingly included everybody at once in the concentration upon her photographs which she felt the situation demanded.

"Look, Sir William," she said. "I am sure you will be interested in this one. That is Lord X. He is a little blurred, perhaps; still, when one knows who it is, it is a very interesting memento, really. Look, Miss Gore, this is the one I did when we were standing together. Do you remember?"

"Oh! yes, of course," Rachel said. She did, as a matter of fact, very well remember the occasion, the length of time that had been necessary to adjust the legs of the camera, which appeared to have a miraculous power of interweaving themselves into the legs of the spectators; the piercing cry from Miss Tarlton at the feather of another lady's hat coming across the field of vision just as the troops came within focus; and a general sense of agitation which had prevented any one in the photographer's immediate surroundings from contemplating with a detached mind the military spectacle passing at their feet.

"These plates are really too small," said Miss Tarlton; "I have been wishing ever since that I had brought my larger machine that day." Her hearers did not find it in their hearts to echo this wish. "Of course, though, a small machine is most delightfully convenient. It is so portable, one need never be without it. I am told there is quite a tiny one to be had now. Have you seen it, Sir William?"

"No, I haven't," said Sir William, in an entirely final and decided manner. Miss Tarlton turned to Rendel as though to ask him, but saw that he was standing apart with Rachel, apparently deep in conversation. She felt that it was rather hard on Rachel to be called away when she might have been enjoying the photographs.

"Do you know whether Mr. Rendel photographs?" she said to Lady Gore, in a more subdued tone.

"I really don't know; I think not," Lady Gore said, amused in spite of herself at her husband's rising exasperation, although she was conscious of sharing it.

"Rendel," said Sir William, obliged to let his feelings find vent in speech at the expense of his discretion, "Miss Tarlton is asking whether you photograph?"

"I'm afraid I don't," said Rendel.

"Ah, I thought not," said Sir William, giving a sort of grunt of satisfaction.

"It is only..." said Miss Tarlton, who had relapsed into her photographs again, and was therefore constrained to speak in the sort of absent, maundering tone of people who try to frame consecutive sentences while they are looking over photographs or reading letters—"ah—this is the one I wanted you to see, Lady Gore— —"

"Oh! yes, I see," said Lady Gore, mendaciously as to the spirit, if not to the letter, for she certainly did not see in the negative held up by Miss Tarlton, which appeared to the untutored mind a square piece of grey dirty glass with confused black smudges on it, all that Miss Tarlton wished her to behold there. Then she became aware of a welcome interruption.

"How do you do, Mr. Wentworth?" she said, putting down the photograph with inward relief, as a tall young man with a fair moustache and merry blue eyes came into the room.

"Photographs?" he said, after exchanging greetings with his host and hostess, nodding to Rendel and bowing to Rachel.

"Yes," said Lady Gore. "Now you shall give your opinion."

"I shall be delighted," he said. "I have got heaps of opinions."

"Do you photograph?" said Miss Tarlton, with a spark of renewed hope.

"I am sorry to say I don't," answered Wentworth. "I believe it is a charming pursuit."

"It is an inexhaustible pleasure," said Miss Tarlton, with conviction.

"I congratulate you," said Wentworth, "on possessing it."

"Yes," said Miss Tarlton solemnly, "I lead an extremely happy life. I take out my camera every day on my bicycle, and I photograph. When I get home I develop the photographs. I spend hours in my dark room."

"It is indeed a happy temperament," said Wentworth, "that can find pleasure in spending hours in a dark room."

"Have you ever tried it?" said Miss Tarlton.

"Certainly," said Wentworth. "In London in the winter, when it is foggy, you know."

"Oh," said Miss Tarlton, again with unflinching gravity. "I don't think you quite understand what I mean. I mean in a photographic dark room, developing, you know."

"I see," said Wentworth. "When I am in a dark room in the winter I generally develop theories."

"Develop what?" said Miss Tarlton.

"Theories, about smuts and smoke, you know; things people write to the papers about in the winter," said Wentworth, whose idea of conversation was to endeavour to coruscate the whole time. It is not to be wondered at, therefore, if the spark was less powerful on some occasions than on others.

"Oh," said Miss Tarlton, not in the least entertained.

Wentworth, a little discomfited, could for once think of nothing to say.

"I suppose," said Miss Tarlton, still patiently pursuing her investigations in the same hopeless quarter, "you don't know the name of that quite, quite new and tiny machine?"

"Machine? What sort of machine?" said Wentworth.

"A camera," said Miss Tarlton, with an inflection in her tone which entirely eliminated any other possibility.

"No, I'm afraid I don't," said Wentworth. "I don't know the name of any cameras, except that their family name is legion."

"What?" said Miss Tarlton.

"Legion," said Wentworth again, crestfallen.

"Oh," said Miss Tarlton.

"Pateley would be the man to ask," said Wentworth, desperately trying to put his head above the surface.

"Pateley? Is that a shop?" said Miss Tarlton eagerly. "Where?"

"A shop!" said Sir William, laughing. "I should like to see Pateley's face"—but the door opened before he completed his sentence, and his wish, presumably not formed upon æsthetic grounds, was fulfilled.

CHAPTER VI

Robert Pateley was a journalist, and a successful man. Some people succeed in life because they have certain qualities which enlist the sympathy and co-operation of their fellow-creatures; others, without such qualities, yet succeed by having a dogged determination and power of push which make them independent of that sympathy and co-operation. Robert Pateley was one of the latter. When he was discussed by two people who felt they ought to like him, they said to one another, "What is it about Pateley that puts people off, I wonder? Why can't one like him more?" and then they would think it over and come to no conclusion. Perhaps it was that his journalism was of the very newest kind. He was certainly extremely able, although his somewhat boisterous personality and entirely non-committal conversation did not give at the first meeting with him the impression of his being the sagacious and keen-witted politician that he really was. Was it his laugh that people disliked? Was it his voice? It could not have been his intelligence, which was excellent, nor yet his moral character, which was blameless. In fact, in a quiet way, Pateley had been a hero, for he had been left, through his father's mismanagement of the family affairs, with two sisters absolutely on his hands, and he had never, since undertaking the whole charge of them, for one instant put his own welfare, advancement or interest before theirs. Absorbed in his resolute purpose, he had coolness of head and determination enough to govern his ambitions instead of letting himself be governed by them. The son of a solicitor in a country town, he had made up his mind that, as he put it to himself, he would be "somebody" some day. He had got to the top of the local grammar school, and tasted the delights of success, and he determined that he would continue them in a larger sphere. It is not always easy to draw the line between conspicuousness and distinction. Pateley, who went along the path of life like a metaphorical fire-engine, had very early become conspicuous; he had gone steadily on, calling to his fellow-creatures to get out of his way, until now, as steerer of the *Arbiter*, a dashing little paper that under his guidance had made a sudden leap into fame and influence, he was a personage to be reckoned with, and it was evident enough in his bearing that he was conscious of the fact.

Such was the person who, almost as his name was on Sir William Gore's lips, came cheerfully, loudly, briskly into the room, including everybody in the heartiest of greetings, stepping at once into the foreground of the picture, and filling it up.

"Did I hear you say that you would like to see my face, Gore? How very polite of you! most gratifying!" he said with a loud laugh, which seemed to correspond to his big and burly person.

"You did," said Sir William. "Wentworth says you know everything about photography."

"Ah! now, that," said Pateley, galvanised into real eagerness and interest as he turned round after shaking hands with Lady Gore, "I really do know at this moment, as I have just come from the Photographic Exhibition."

"Oh!" said Miss Tarlton with an irrepressible cry, the ordinary conventions of society abrogated by the enormous importance of the information which she felt was coming.

"Let me introduce you to Miss Tarlton," said Sir William. Miss Tarlton bowed quickly, and then proceeded at once to business.

"Do you know the name of a quite tiny camera?" she said; "the very newest?"

"I do," said Pateley. "It is the 'Viator,' and I have just seen it." A sort of audible murmur of relief ran through the company at this burning question having been answered at last. "And it is only by a special grace of Providence," Pateley went on, "assisted by my high principles, that that machine is not in my pocket at this moment."

"Oh! I wish it were!" said Miss Tarlton.

"I'm afraid it may be before many days are over," said Pateley. "I never saw anything so perfect. And do you know, it takes a snapshot in a room even just as well as in the open air. If I had it in my hand I could snap any one of you here, at this moment, almost without your knowing anything about it."

"I am so glad you haven't," Lady Gore couldn't help ejaculating.

"The man who was showing it took one of me as I turned to look at it. It is perfectly wonderful."

"And that in a room?" Miss Tarlton said, more and more awestruck. "And simply a snapshot, not a time exposure at all?"

"Precisely," Pateley said.

"I shall go and see it," Miss Tarlton said, and, notebook in hand, she continued with a businesslike air to write down the particulars communicated by Pateley.

"I am quite out of my depth," Lady Gore said to Wentworth. "What does a 'time exposure' mean?"

"Heaven knows," said Wentworth. "Something about seconds and things, I suppose."

"I can never judge of how many seconds a thing takes," said Lady Gore.

"I'm sure I can't," Wentworth replied. "The other day I thought we had been three-quarters of an hour in a tunnel and we had only been two minutes and a half."

"Now then," Pateley said with a satisfied air, turning to Sir William, "I have cheered Miss Tarlton on to a piece of extravagance." Sir William felt a distinct sense of pleasure. "I have persuaded her to buy a new machine."

"The thing that amuses me," said Sir William with some scorn, having apparently forgotten which of his pet aversions had been the subject of the conversation, "is people's theory that when once you have bought a bicycle it costs you nothing afterwards."

"It is not a bicycle, Sir William, it is a camera," said Miss Tarlton, with some asperity.

"Oh, well, it is the same thing," Sir William said.

"*The same thing?*" Miss Tarlton repeated, with the accent of one who feels an immeasurable mental gulf between herself and her interlocutor.

"As to results, I mean," he said. Arrived at this point Miss Tarlton felt she need no longer listen, she simply noted with pitying tolerance the random utterance. "A camera costs very nearly as much to keep as a horse, what with films and bottles of stuff, and all the other accessories. And as for a bicycle, I am quite sure that you have to count as much for mending it as you do for a horse's keep."

"The really expensive thing, though, is a motor," said Wentworth. "Lots of men nowadays don't marry because they can't afford to keep a wife as well as a motor."

Rendel, who was standing by Rachel's side at the tea-table, caught this sentence. He looked up at her with a smile. She blushed.

"I have no intention of keeping a motor," he said. Rachel said nothing.

"Are you very angry with me?" Rendel said.

"I am not sure," she answered. "I think I am."

"You mustn't be—after saving my life, too, this morning, in the boat."

"Saving your life?" said Rachel, surprised.

"Yes," Rendel said. "By not steering me into any of the things we met on the Thames."

"Oh!" said Rachel, smiling, "I am afraid even that was more your doing than mine, as you kept calling out to me which string to pull."

"Perhaps. But the extraordinary thing was that when you were told you did pull it," said Rendel.

"Oh, any one can do that," replied Rachel.

"I beg your pardon, it is not so simple," Rendel answered, thinking to himself, though he had the good sense at that moment not to formulate it, what an adorable quality it would be in a wife that she should always pull exactly the string she was told to pull.

"I've been asking Sir William if I may come and speak to him...." he said in a lower tone. "He said I might." Rachel was silent. "You don't mind, do you?" he said, looking at her anxiously.

"I—I—don't know," Rachel said. "I feel as if I were not sure about anything—you have done it all so quickly—I can't realise——"

"Yes," he said penitently, "I have done it all very quickly, I know, but I won't hurry you to give me any answer. My chief's going away to-morrow for ten days, and I am afraid I must go too, but may I come as soon as I am back again?"

"Yes," said Rachel shyly.

"And perhaps by that time," he said, "you will know the answer. Do you think you will?" Rachel looked at him as her hand lay in his.

"Yes, by that time I shall know," she said.

As Rendel went out a few minutes later he was dimly conscious of meeting an agitated little figure which hurried past him into the room. Miss Judd was a lady who contrived to reduce as many of her fellow-creatures to a state of mild exasperation during the day as any female enthusiast in London, by her constant haste to overtake her manifold duties towards the human race. Those duties were still further complicated by the fact that she had a special gift for forgetting more things in one afternoon than most people are capable of remembering in a week.

"My dear Jane, how do you do?" said Lady Gore. "We have not seen you for an age."

"No, Cousin Elinor, no," said Miss Judd, who always spoke in little gasps as if she had run all the way from her last stopping-place. "I have been so frightfully busy. Oh, thank you, William, thank you; but do you know, that tea looks dreadfully strong. In fact, I think I had really better not have any. I wonder if I might have some hot water instead? Thank you so much. Thank you, dear Rachel—simply water, nothing else."

"That doesn't sound a very reviving beverage," said Lady Gore.

"Oh, but it is, I assure you," said Miss Judd. "It is wonderful. And, you see, I had tea for luncheon, and I don't like to have it too often."

"Tea for luncheon?" said Sir William.

"Yes, at an Aërated Bread place," she replied, "near Victoria. I have been leaving the canvassing papers for the School Board election, and I had not time to go home."

"What it is to be such a pillar of the country!" said Lady Gore laughing.

"You may laugh, Cousin Elinor," Miss Judd said, drinking her hot water in quick, hurried sips, "but I assure you it is very hard work. You see, whatever the question is that I am canvassing for, I always feel bound to explain it to the voters at every place I go to, for fear they should vote the wrong way: and sometimes that is very hard work. At the last General Election, for instance, I lunched off buns and tea for a fortnight."

"Good Lord!" said Sir William to Pateley as they stood a little apart. "Imagine public opinion being expounded by people who lunch off buns!"

"And the awful thing, do you know," said Pateley laughing, "is that I believe those people do make a difference."

"It is horrible to reflect upon," said Sir William.

"By the way," said Pateley, with a laugh, "your side is going in for the sex too, I see. Is it true that you are going to have a Women's Peace Crusade?"

"Yes," said Sir William with an expression of disgust, "I believe that it is so. *My* womenkind are not going to have anything to do with it, I am thankful to say."

"Oh, yes, I saw about that Crusade," said Wentworth, joining them, "in the *Torch*."

"Don't believe too firmly what the *Torch* says—or indeed any newspaper—ha, ha!" said Pateley.

"I should be glad not to believe all that I see in the *Arbiter*, this morning," Sir William said. "Upon my word, Pateley, that paper of yours is becoming incendiary."

"I don't know that we are being particularly incendiary," said Pateley, with the comfortable air of one disposing of the subject. "It is only that the world is rather inflammable at this moment."

"Well, we have had conflagrations enough at the present," said Sir William. "We want the country to quiet down a bit."

"Oh! it will do that all in good time," said Pateley. "I am bound to say things are rather jumpy just now. By the way, Sir William, I wonder if you know of any investment you could recommend?"

Wentworth discreetly turned away and strolled back to Lady Gore's sofa.

"I rather want to know of a good thing for my two sisters who are living together at Lowbridge. I have got a modest sum to invest that my father left them, and I should like to put it into something that is pretty certain, but, if possible, that will give them more than 2 ½ per cent."

"Why," said Sir William, "I believe I may know of the very thing. Only it is a dead secret as yet."

"Hullo!" said Pateley, pricking up his ears. "That sounds promising. For how long?"

"Just for the moment," said Sir William. "But of necessity the whole world must know of it before very long."

"Well, if it really is a good thing let us have a day or two's start," said Pateley laughing.

"All right, you shall," said Sir William. "You shall hear from me in a day or two."

CHAPTER VII

The days had passed. The great scheme of "The Equator, Ltd.," was before the world, which had received it in a manner exceeding Fred Anderson's most sanguine expectations. The possibilities and chances of the mine, as set forth by the experts, appeared to be such as to rouse the hopes of even the wary and experienced, and Anderson had no difficulty of forming a Board of Directors most eminently calculated to inspire confidence in the public—none the less that they were presided over by a man who, if not possessed of special business qualifications, was of good social position and bore an honourable name. Sir William Gore, the Chairman of the company, was well pleased. He invested largely in the undertaking. The savings of the Miss Pateleys, under the direction of their brother, had gone the same way. The *Arbiter* had indeed reason to cheer on the Cape to Cairo railway, which day by day seemed more likely of accomplishment.

Sir William, on the afternoon of the day when the success of the company was absolutely an assured fact, came back to his house from the city, satisfied with the prospects of the "Equator," with himself, and with the world at large. He put his latchkey into the door and looked round him a moment before he went in with a sense of well-being, of rejoicing in the summer day. Then as he stepped into the house he became conscious that Rachel was standing in the hall waiting for him, with an expression of dread anxiety on her face. The transition of feeling was so sudden that for a moment he hardly realised what he saw—then quick as lightning his thoughts flew to meet that one misfortune that of all others would assail them both most cruelly.

"Rachel!" he said. "Is your mother ill?"

"Yes," the girl answered. "Oh, father, wait," she said, as Sir William was rushing past her, and she tried to steady her quivering lips. "Dr. Morgan is there."

"Morgan—you sent for him...." said Gore, pausing, hardly knowing what he was saying. "Rachel ... tell me...?"

"She fainted," the girl said, "an hour ago. And we couldn't get her round again. I sent—ah! there he is coming down." And a steady, slow step, sounding to the two listeners like the footfall of Fate, was heard coming down from above. Sir William went to meet the doctor, knowing already what he was going to hear.

Lady Gore died that night, without regaining consciousness. Hers had been the unspeakable privilege of leaving life swiftly and painlessly without knowing that the moment had come. She had passed unconsciously into that awful gulf, without having had to stand for a moment shuddering on the brink. She had never dreaded death itself, but she had dreaded intensely the thought of old age, of a lingering illness and its attendant horrors. But none of these she had been called upon to endure: even while those around her were looking at the beautiful aspect of life that she presented to them the darkness fell, leaving them the memory only of that bright image. Her daughter's last recollection of her had been the caressing endearment with which Lady Gore had deprecated Rachel's remaining with her till Sir William's return— how thankful the girl was to have remained!—her husband's last vision of her, the smiling farewell with which she had sped him on his way in the morning, with a caution as to prudence in his undertakings. As he came back he had found himself telling her already in his mind, before he was actually in her presence, of what he had done. That was the thing which gave an edge to every action, to each fresh development of existence. Life was lived through again for her, and acquired a fresh aspect from her interest and sympathy, from her keen, humorous insight and far-seeing wisdom. But now, what would his life be without that light that had always shone on his path? He did not, he could not, begin to think about the future. He knew only that the present had crumbled into ruins around him. That, he realised the next morning when, after some snatches of uneasy sleep, he suddenly wakened with a sense of absolute horror upon him, before he remembered shuddering what that horror was. He had wanted to tell her about yesterday, about the "Equator," he said to himself with a dull aching pain almost like resentment—he wanted to have her approval, to have the sense that for her what he did was right, was wise. But he knew now in his heart, as he really had known all the time, that it was she who had been the wise one. And part of the horror, as the time went on, would be to realise that when she had gone out of the world something had gone out of himself too, which she had told him was there. And he had dreamt that it was true. But that would come when the details of misery were realised by him one by one, as after some hideous explosion it is not possible to see at once in the wreck made by the catastrophe all the ghastly confirmations of disaster that come to light with the days. The first days were not the worst, either for him or for Rachel, as each one of them afterwards secretly found. For though life had come to a standstill, had stopped dead, with a sudden shock that had thrown everything in it out of gear, there were at first new and strange duties to be accomplished that filled up the hours and kept the standards of ordinary existence at bay. There were letters of condolence to be answered, tributes of flowers to be acknowledged, sent by well-meaning friends moved by some impotent impulse of consolation, until the air became heavy with the scent of camellias and lilies. Rachel moved about in the darkened rooms, feeling as if the faint, sweet, overpowering perfume were a kind of anodyne, that was mercifully, during those early days, lulling her senses into lethargy. To the end of her days the scent of the white lily would bring back to her the feeling of actually living again through that first time of numbing grief. How many hours, how many days and nights she and her father had lived within that quiet sanctuary they could not have told— lived in the dark stillness, with one room, the stillest of all, containing the beloved something strangely aloof all that was left of the thing that had been their very life. Then out of that quiet hallowed darkness they came one dreadful day into the brilliant sunlight, a day that was lived through with the acutest pain of all, of which every detail seemed to have been arranged by a horrible cruel convention of custom in order to intensify the pangs of it. They drove at a foot's pace through the crowded, sunlit streets, with a shrinking agony of self-consciousness as one and another passer-by looked up for a moment at what was passing. "Look, Jim, 'ere's a funeral!" one small boy called to another—and Rachel, shuddering, buried her face in her hands and could have cried out aloud. Some men, not all, lifted their hats; two gaily-dressed women who were just going to cross stopped as a matter of course on the pavement and waited indifferently, hardly seeing what it was, until the obstruction had gone by, as they would have done had it been anything else. Rachel, leaning back by her father, trying to hide herself, yet felt as if she could not help seeing everything they met. Every step of the way was a slow torture. And oh, the return home! that drive, at a brisk trot this time, through the same crowded, unfeeling streets, which still retained the association of the former progress through them, the sense that now, as the coachman whipped up his horses, for every one save for the two desolate people who sat silently together inside the carriage, life might—indeed, would—throw off that aspect of gloom and go on as before! And then the worst moment of all, the finding on their return that the house had taken on a ghastly semblance of its usual aspect, that the blinds were up, the windows open, the sun streaming in everywhere—the hard, cruel light, as it seemed to Rachel, shining into the rooms that were for evermore to be different.

Then followed the time which is incomparably the worst after a great loss, the time when, ordinary life being taken up again, the sufferer has the additional trial of too large an amount of leisure on his hands—the horror of all those new spare hours that used to be passed in a companionship that is gone, that must be filled up with something fresh unless they are to stand in wide, horrible emptiness, to assail recollection with unendurable grief. And especially in that house were they empty, where the existence of both father and daughter had revolved round that of another to a greater extent than that of most people. The problem of how to readjust the daily conditions was a hard, hard one to solve, harder obviously for Sir William than it was for Rachel. The girl was uplifted in those days by the sense that, however difficult she might find it to carry out in detail, the general scheme of her life lay clear before her. She was going to devote it to her father, she was going to carry out that unmade promise, which she now considered more binding on her than ever, although her mother had warned her against making it, the promise that her father should come first. But the warning at the moment it was made had not been accepted by Rachel, and in the exaltation of her self-sacrifice it was forgotten now. She saw her way, as she conceived, plainly in front of her. Rendel, with his usual understanding and wisdom, did not obtrude himself on her during those days. He had quite made up his mind not to ask for her decision until there might be some hope of its being made in his favour. He had felt Lady Gore's death as acutely as though he had the right of kinship to grieve for her. He was miserably conscious that something inestimably precious had gone out of his life, almost before he had had time to realise his happiness in possessing it. But neither he nor Rachel understood what Lady Gore's death had meant to Sir William. And the poor little Rachel, rudderless, bewildered, tried to do the best she could for her father's life by planning her own with absolute reference to it, by putting at his disposal all the bare, empty hours available for companionship which up to now had been so straitly, so tenderly, so happily filled. And he on his side, conscious of some of her purpose, but unaware of the extent to which she carried her deliberate intention of consecrating herself to him, of bearing the burden of his destiny, believed that he had to bear the overwhelming burthen of guiding hers. Instead of going in the late afternoon hours of those summer days to his club, where he would have found some companionship that was not associated with his grief, and passing an hour agreeably, he wistfully went home, feeling that Rachel would be expecting him. And Rachel on her side felt it a duty to put away any regular occupation that might have proved engrossing, and so to ordain her life that she should be always ready and at her father's orders if he should appear. And, thus deliberately cutting themselves loose from such minor anchorages as they might have had, they tried to delude themselves into the belief that not only was such makeshift companionship a solace, but that it actually was able to replace that other all-satisfying companionship they had lost. But they knew in their hearts, each of them, that it was not so. And Sir William realised, more perhaps than Rachel did, that it never could be. The relation between a father and daughter, when most successful, is formed of delightful discrepancies and differences, supplementing one another in the things that are not of each age. It means a protecting care on the side of the father, an amused tender pride in seeing the younger creature developing an individuality which, however, is hardly in the secret soul of the elder one quite realised or believed in. The experience of the man in such a relation has mainly been derived from women of his own standing; his judgment of his daughter is apt to be a good deal guesswork. The daughter, on the other hand, brings to the relation elements necessarily and absolutely absent on the other side. If she cares for her father as he does for her, she looks up to him, she admires him, she accepts from him numberless prejudices and rules about the government of life, and acts upon them, taking for granted all the time that he cannot understand her own point of view. And yet, even so constituted, it can be one of the most beautiful and even satisfying combinations of affection the world has to show, provided the father has not known what it is to have the fulness of joy in his companionship with his wife, in that equal experience, mutual reliance, understanding of hopes and fears, which is impossible when the understanding is being interpreted through the imagination only, by one standing on a different plane of life. Neither Rachel nor her father had realised all this; but the mother with her acuter sensibilities had known, and had so deliberately set herself to fulfil her task that they had all these years been interpreted to one another, as it were, by that other influence that had surrounded them, that atmosphere through which everything was seen aright and in its most beautiful aspect. And the time came when Sir William suddenly grasped with a burning, startling vividness the fact that his life could not be the same again, that he must henceforth take it on a lower plane. The day was fine and bright—too warm, too bright; the hopeful light of spring had given place to the steady glare of summer. He had been used before to go out riding with Rachel in the early morning, in order to be back by the time Lady Gore was ready to begin her day. They had tacitly abandoned this habit now. Then one day it occurred to Sir William that it might be a good thing for Rachel to resume it. He proposed to her that they should go out as they used. She, in her inmost heart shrinking from it, but thinking it would be a satisfaction to him, agreed. He, shrinking from it as much as she did, thought to please her. And so they went out and rode silently side by side, overpowered by mute comparison of this day with days that had been. And when they got home they went each their own way, and made no attempt at exchanging words. Sir William went miserably to his study, his heart aching with a rush of almost unbearable sorrow as he thought of the bright little room upstairs to which he had been wont to hurry for the welcome that always awaited him. What should he do with his life? How should he fill it? he asked himself in a burst of grief, as he shut himself in. And so much had the theory, firmly believed in by himself and his wife, that he had by his own free will, and in order to devote his life to her, abandoned any quest of a public career become an absolute conviction in his mind, that he felt a dull resentment at having been so noble. He recognised now that it had been quixotic. He had let the time pass. Fifty-five! To be sure, in these days it is not old age; it may, indeed, under certain circumstances be the prime of life, for a man who has begun his career early, political or otherwise. Had this been Sir William's lot he could have sought some consolation, or at any rate alleviation, in his misfortune, by turning at once to his work and plunging into it more strenuously than before. But even that mitigation, for so much as it might be worth, was denied to him. And he sat there, trying to face the fact that seemed almost incredible to a man of what seemed to him his aptitudes and capacity, the awful fact that he had not enough to do to fill up his life. He did not state this pitiless truth to himself explicitly, but it was beginning to loom from behind a veil, and he would some day be forced to look at it. He could not start anything fresh. He had not the requisite impulse. He could have continued, he could not begin; the theatre of his actions, as Lady Gore had foreseen, had indeed fallen when she fell, and without it he could initiate no fresh achievements. Oh, to have had something definite to turn to in those days, something that called for instant completion! To have had some inexorable daily task, some duty for which he was paid, in a government office, or in some private undertaking of his own, for which he would have been obliged, like so many other men, to leave his house at a fixed hour, and to be absorbed in other preoccupations till his return. What a physical, material relief he would have found in such a claim! Round most men of his age life has woven many interests, many ties, many calls, on their time and energies from outside as well as from those near to them, but all those spare, available energies of his had been absorbed and appropriated, filled up, nearer home, and so completely that he had never needed anything else. And now, whither should he turn? What should he do? Then he remembered his Book, the Book his wife and he had been accustomed to talk of with such confidence, such certainty—he now realised how very little there was of it done, or how much of what might be fruitful in the conception was owing to the way that she, in their talking over it, had held it up to him, so that now one light played round it, now another. Well he remembered how, only two days before she was taken ill, they had talked of it for a long time until she, with an enthusiasm that made it seem already a completed masterpiece, had said with a smile, "Now then, all that remains is to write it!" And he had almost believed, as he left her, that it would spring into life some day, that it would not only hold the place in his life of the Great Possibility that is necessary to us all, but that he would actually put his fate to the proof by carrying it into execution. He took out the portfolio in which were the notes he had made about it now and again. They bore the seared outward aspect of an entirely different mental condition from that with which they came in contact now. What is that subtle, mocking change that comes over even the inanimate things that we have not seen since we were happy, and now meet again in grief? It is like a horrible inversion of the golden touch given to Midas. To Gore, during those days, the darkness fell upon every fresh thing to which he went back. The impression was so strong on him as he turned over the manuscript, that he shuddered. What was the use of all this? What was it worth? He knew in his heart that the person of all others to whom it had been of most worth was gone—he would not be doing good to himself or to any one else by going on with it. He would be defrauding no one by letting the darkness cover it for ever. And another reason yet lay like cold lead at the bottom of his heart— the real, cruel, crushing reason—he could not write the book, he was not capable of writing it. That was the truth. And he desperately thrust the stray leaves into the cover, and the whole thing away from him, hopelessly, finally; there was nothing that would help him. That curtain would never lift again. And he covered his face with his hands as though trying to shut out the deadly knowledge.

But of all this Rachel, as she sat waiting for her father at breakfast, was utterly unconscious. She did not realise the unendurable complications that had piled one misery on another to him. To her the wound had been terrible, but clean. The greatest loss she could conceive had stricken her life, but there were no secondary personal problems to add to it, no preoccupations of self apart from the one great desolation.

Sir William turned over his letters listlessly as he sat down, opened them, and looked through them.

"What am I to say to that?" he said, throwing one over to Rachel.

The colour came into her cheeks as she saw that it was from Rendel.

"I have one from him too," she said.

"Oh! well, I don't ask to see that," Sir William said, with an attempt at cheerfulness. "I know better."

"I would rather you saw it, really, father," and she handed him Rendel's letter to herself—a straightforward, dignified, considerate letter, in which he assured her that he did not mean to intrude himself upon her until she allowed him to come, and that all he asked was that she should understand that he was waiting, and would be content to wait, as long as there was a chance of hope.

"Well, when am I to tell him to come?" Sir William said.

"Father, what he wants cannot be," Rachel said.

"Cannot be?" said Sir William. "Why not?"

"Oh!" Rachel said, trying to command her voice, "I could not at this moment think of anything of that kind."

"At this moment, perhaps," Sir William said. "But you see he is not in a hurry. He says so, at any rate, though I am not sure that it is very convincing."

"How would it be possible," said Rachel, "that I should go away? What would you do if I left you alone?"

"Well, as to that," Sir William replied, speaking slowly in order that he might appear to be speaking calmly, "I don't know, in any case, what I shall do." And his face looked grey and worn, conveying to Rachel, as she looked across at him, an impression of helpless old age in the father who had hitherto been to her a type of everything that was capable and well preserved. She sprang up and went to him.

"Father, dear father," she cried amidst her sobs, as she hid her face on his shoulder. "You know that you are more to me than any one else in the world. Let me help you—let me try, do let me try." And at the sound of the words Gore became again conscious of the immeasurable, dark gulf there was between what one human being had been able to do for him and what any other in the world could try to do. And his own sorrow rose darkly before him and swept away everything else—even the sorrow of his child. It was almost bitterly that he said, as if the words were wrung from him involuntarily—

"Nobody can help me now."

"Oh, father!" Rachel cried again miserably. "Let me try."

"Darling, I know," he said, recollecting himself at the sight of her distress, "and you know what my little girl is to me; but there are some things that even a daughter cannot do. And," he went on, "it would really be a comfort to me, I think, if"—he was going to say, "if you were married," but he altered it as he saw a swift change pass over Rachel's face—"if I knew you were happy; if you had a home of your own and were provided for."

"Do you think that would be a comfort to you?" asked Rachel, trying to speak in an almost indifferent tone. "That you would be glad if I were to go away from you to a home of my own?"

"Yes," he said, "I think it would." And as he spoke he felt that the burden of giving Rachel companionship and trying to help her to bear her grief would be removed from him. "Besides," he went on, with an attempt at a smile, "it is not as if you would go far away from me altogether; you will only be a few streets off, after all. I could come to you whenever I wanted, and even—who knows?—I might sometimes ask you for your hospitality."

"If I thought *that*——" Rachel said, and caught herself up.

"You know," her father said more seriously, "we have been discussing this from one point of view only, from mine; but you are the person most concerned, and I am taking for granted that, from your point of view, it would be the best thing to do—that you would be happy."

"If I only thought," Rachel said, her face answering his last question, if her words did not, "that you would come to me—that you would be with me altogether——"

"I have no doubt that you would find that I came to you very often," said Sir William, with again a desolate sense of having no definite reason for being anywhere.

There was a pause before he said, "Then I'll tell him to come and see me, and perhaps he can see you afterwards."

"Oh," said Rachel, shrinking, "it is not possible yet."

"Well," said Sir William, "I will tell him so. We will explain to him that, since he is willing to wait, for the moment he must wait."

CHAPTER VIII

And Rendel waited—through the autumn, through the winter—but not without seeing Rachel again. On the contrary, every week that passed during that time was bringing him nearer to his goal. After the first visit was over, that first meeting under the now maimed and altered conditions of life, the insensible relief afforded to both father and daughter by his companionship, his unselfish devotion and helpfulness, his unfailing readiness to be a companion to Sir William, to come and play chess with him, or to sit up and do intricate patiences through the small hours of the morning, all this gradually made him insensibly slide into the position of a son of the house. And Rachel, convinced that she was doing the best thing for her father and admitting in her secret heart that for herself she was doing the thing that of all others would make her happy, yielded at last. They were married in April, and went away for a fortnight to a shooting-box lent them by Lord Stamfordham in the West of Scotland, leaving Sir William for the first time alone in the big, empty house. It was with many, many misgivings that Rachel had agreed to go; but her father had insisted on her doing so. He had vaguely thought that perhaps it would be a relief to him to be alone, but he found the solitude unbearable. Those acquaintances of Gore's who saw him at the club expressed in suitably tempered tones their pleasure at seeing him again, and, thinking he would rather be left alone, discreetly refrained from thrusting their society upon him when in reality he most needed it, remarking to one another that poor old Gore had gone to pieces dreadfully since his wife died. A great many people knew him, and liked him well enough, but he had no intimate friends. Pateley occasionally dropped in; but Pateley was too full of business to have leisure to help to fill up anybody else's time, and Sir William found the blank in his own house, the unchanging loneliness, almost unbearable.

In the meantime Rendel and his wife were beginning that page of the book of life which Sir William had closed for ever. At last, that vision of the future to which Rendel had clung with such steadfast hope, with such unswerving purpose, had been fulfilled: Rachel was his wife. It was an unending joy to him to remember that she was there; to watch for her coming and going; to see the dainty grace of movement and demeanour, the sweet, soft smile—her mother's smile—with which she listened as he talked. And during those days he poured himself out in speech as he had never been able to do before. It was a relief that was almost ecstasy to the man who had been made reserved by loneliness to have such a listener, and the sense of exquisite joy and repose which he felt in her society deepened as the days went on. To Rachel, too, when once she had made up her mind to leave her father, these days were filled with an undreamt-of happiness. She was beginning to recover from the actual shock of her mother's death, although, even as her life opened to all the new impressions that surrounded her, she felt daily afresh the want of the tender sympathy and guidance that had been her stay; but another great love had happily come into her life at the moment she needed it most, and a love that was far from wishing to supplant the other. The memory of Lady Gore was almost as hallowed to Rendel as it was to his wife: it was another bond between them. They talked of her constantly, their reverent recollection kept alive the sense of her abiding, gracious influence.

It was a new and wonderful experience to Rachel to have the burden of daily life lifted from her. She had been loved in her home, it is true, as much as the most exacting heart might demand, but since she was seventeen it was she who had had to take thought for others, to surround them with loving care and protection; she had always been conscious, even though not feeling its weight, of bearing the burden of some one else's responsibilities. And now it was all different. In the first rebound of her youth she seemed to be discovering for the first time during those days how young she was, in the companionship of one whose tender care and loving protection smoothed every difficulty, every obstacle out of her path. And all too fast the perfumed days of spring glided away, a spring which, on that side of Scotland, was balmy and caressing. Day after day the sun shone, the mist remained in the distance, making that distance more beautiful still; and everything within and without was irradiated, and like motes in the sunshine Rendel saw the golden possibilities of his life dancing in the light of his hopes and illuminating the path that lay before him.

Rachel wrote to her father constantly, tenderly, solicitously; and Sir William, reading of her happiness, did not write back to tell her what those same days meant to him. For in London the sky was grey and heavy, and it was through a haze the colour of lead that he saw the years to come. The dark and cheerless winter had given place to a cold and cheerless spring.

It was a rainy afternoon that the young couple returned to London; but the gloomy look of the streets outside did but enhance the brightness of the little house in Cosmo Place, Knightsbridge, with its open, square hall, in which a bright fire was blazing. Light and warmth shone everywhere. Rachel drew a long breath of satisfaction, then her eyes filled with tears. The very sight of London brought back the past. Could it be possible that her mother was not there to welcome her? She had thought her father might be awaiting her at Cosmo Place; but as he was not, she went off instantly to Prince's Gate. How big and lonely the house looked with its gaunt, ugly portico, its tall, narrow hall and endless stairs! The drawing-rooms were closed: Sir William was sitting in his study, a chess-board in front of him, on which he was working out a problem.

Rachel was terribly perturbed at the change in his appearance—a something, she did not quite know in what it lay, that betokened some absolute change of outlook, of attitude. He had the listless, indifferent air of one who lets himself be drifted here and there rather than of one who moves securely along, strong enough to hold his own way in spite of any opposing elements. This fortnight of solitude, in which he had been face to face with his own life and his prospects, had suddenly, roughly, pitilessly graven on his face the lines that with other men successive experiences accumulate there gently and almost insensibly. He had taken a sudden leap into old age, as sometimes happens to men of his standing, who, as long as their life is smooth, uneventful, and prosperous, succeed in keeping an aspect of youth. Rachel's heart smote her at having left him; it reproached her with having known something like happiness in these days, and her old sense of troubled, anxious responsibility came back. She begged him to come and dine with them that evening. He demurred at first at making a third on their first night in their own house. Rachel protested, and overruled all his objections. She arrived at home just in time to dress for dinner, finding her husband surprised and somewhat discomfited at her prolonged absence. He had wanted to go proudly all over the house with her, and see their new domain. But as he saw her come up the stairs, he realised that black care had sprung up behind her again, that this was not the confiding, naïvely happy Rachel who had walked with him on the moors.

"There you are!" he said. "I was just wondering what had become of you."

"I was with my father," Rachel said, in a tone in which there was a tinge of unconscious surprise at what his tone had conveyed. "And, Francis, he looks so dreadfully ill!"

"Does he?" said Rendel, concerned. "I am sorry."

"He looks really broken down," she said, "and oh, so much older. I am sure it has been bad for him being alone all this time. I ought not to have stayed away so long."

"Well, it has not been very long," said Rendel with a natural feeling that two weeks had not been an unreasonable extension of their wedding tour.

"He looks as if he had felt it so," she answered. "But at any rate, I have persuaded him to come to dinner with us to-night; I am sure it will be good for him."

"To-night?" said Rendel, again with a lurking surprise that for this first night their privacy should not have been respected.

"Yes," said Rachel. "You don't mind, do you?"

"Oh, of course not," he replied, again stifling a misgiving.

"You see," said Rachel, "I thought it might amuse him, and be a change for him, and then you might play a game of chess with him after dinner, perhaps."

"Of course, of course," Rendel answered. But the misgiving remained.

When, however, Sir William appeared, Rendel's heart almost smote him as Rachel's had done, he seemed so curiously broken down and dispirited. They talked of their Scotch experiences, they spoke a little of the affairs of the day, but, as Rendel knew of old, this was a dangerous topic, which, hitherto, he had succeeded either in avoiding altogether or in treating with a studied moderation which might so far as possible prevent Sir William's susceptibilities from being offended. Rachel sat with them after dinner while they smoked, then they all went upstairs.

"Now then, father dear, where would you like to be?" she said, looking round the room for the most comfortable chair. "Here, this looks a very special corner," and she drew forward an armchair that certainly was in a most delightful place, looking as if it were destined for the master of the house, or, at any rate, the most privileged person in it, a comfortable armchair, with the slanting back that a man loves, and by it a table with a lamp at exactly the right height. "There," she said, pushing her father gently into it, "isn't that a comfortable corner?"

"Very," Sir William said, looking up at her with a smile. It truly was a delight to be tended and fussed over again.

"And now you must have a table in front of you," she said, looking round. "Let me see—Frank, which shall the chess-table be? Is there a folding table? Yes, of course there is—that little one that we bought at Guildford. That one!"—and she clapped her hands with childish delight as she pointed to it.

Rendel brought forward the little table and opened it.

"Oh, that is exactly the thing," she cried. "See, father, it will just hold the chess-board. Now then, this is where it shall always stand—your own table, and your own chair by it."

CHAPTER IX

It is difficult to judge of any course of conduct entirely on its own merits, when it has a reflex action on ourselves. When Rendel before his marriage used to go to Prince's Gate and to see Rachel, absolutely oblivious of herself, hovering tenderly round her mother, watching to see that her father's wishes were fulfilled, that unselfish devotion and absorption in filial duty seemed to him the most entirely beautiful thing on this earth. But when, instead of being the spectator of the situation, he became an active participator in it, when the stream of Rachel's filial devotion was diverted from that of her conjugal duties, it unconsciously assumed another aspect in his eyes. But not for worlds would he have put into words the annoyance he could not help feeling, and Rachel was entirely unconscious of his attitude. The devoted, uncritical affection for her father which had grown up with her life was in her mind so absolutely taken for granted as one of the foundations of existence, that it did not even occur to her that Rendel might possibly not look at it in the same light. She took for granted that he would share her attitude towards her father as he had shared her adoration for her mother. It was all part of her entire trust in Rendel, and the simple directness with which she approached the problems of life. She had, before her marriage, expressed an earnest wish, which Rendel understood as a condition, that even if her father did not wish to live with them, she might share in his life and watch over him, and Rendel had accepted the condition and promised that it should be as she wished. But it is obviously not the actual making of a promise that is the difficulty. If it were possible when we pledge ourselves to a given course for our imagination to show us in a vision of the future the innumerable occasions on which we should be called upon to redeem, each time by a conscious separate effort, that lightly given pledge of an instant, the stoutest-hearted of us would quail at the prospect. Rendel looked back with a sigh to those days, that seemed already to have receded into a luminous distance, when Rachel, alone with him in Scotland, with no divided allegiance, had given herself up, heart and mind, to the new happiness, the new existence, that was opening before her.

The danger of pouring life while it is still fluid into the wrong mould, of letting it drift and harden into the wrong shape, is an insidious peril which is not sufficiently guarded against. It is easy enough to say, Begin as you mean to go on; but the difficulty is to know exactly the moment when you begin, and when the point of going on has been arrived at; and of drifting gradually into some irremediable course of action from which it is almost impossible to turn back without difficulty and struggle. There had been a feeling that everything was somehow temporary during those first days at Cosmo Place, which extended into the weeks. Sir William held as a principle, and was quite genuine in his intention when he said it, that young people ought to be left to themselves. He would not, therefore, take up his abode under their roof, but still that he should do so eventually was felt by all concerned as a vague possibility which prevented in the young household a sense of having finally and comfortably settled down. Indeed, as it was, it was perhaps more unsettling to Rachel, and therefore to her husband, to have Sir William coming and going than it would have been to have him actually under the same roof. If he had been living with them his presence would have been a matter of course, and less constant companionship and diversion would probably have been considered necessary for him than they were when he dropped in at odd times. The advancing season and the grey dark mornings made the early rides impossible. Rachel in her secret soul did not regret them. Sir William had taken the habit of looking in at Cosmo Place on his way to Pall Mall and further eastward, and it always gave Rachel a pang of remorse if she found that by an unlucky chance she had been out of the way when he came. He would also sometimes come in on his way back, as has been said, in the obvious expectation of having a game of chess, of which Rendel, if he were at home, had not the heart to disappoint him. In these days there was not much occupation for him in the City. The excitement of starting and floating the "Equator" Company and the allotting of the shares to the eager band of subscribers had been accomplished some time since. The "Equator's" hour, however, had not come yet. The outlook in the City was not encouraging for those who knew how to read the weather chart of the coming days. The heart of the country was still beating fast and tumultuously after the emotions of the past two years; it needed a period of assured quiet to regain its normal condition. In the meantime the storm seemed to be subsiding. The great railway laying its iron grip on the heart of Africa was advancing steadily from the north as well as from the south: it was nearing the Equator. The country, its imagination profoundly stirred by the enterprise, watched it in suspense. But until the meeting of the two giant highways was effected, everything depended upon an equable balance of forces, of which a touch might destroy the equilibrium. German possessions and German forces lay perilously near the meeting of the two lines. At any moment a spark from some other part of the world might be wafted to Africa and set the fierce flame of war ablaze in the centre of the continent.

The General Election was coming within measurable distance; the Liberal Peace Crusade was strenuously canvassing the country in favour of coming to a definite understanding with certain foreign powers.

At the house in Cosmo Place it was no longer always possible, as on that first evening, to avoid the subject of politics.

"I must say," said Rendel one night with enthusiasm—Stamfordham had made a big speech the day before of which the papers were full—"Stamfordham is a great speaker, and a great man to boot."

"A great speaker, perhaps," Sir William said. "I don't know that that is entirely what you want from the man at the helm."

"Well, proverbially it isn't," said Rendel, with a smile, determined to be good-humoured.

"As to being a great man," continued Sir William, "anybody who knocks down everything that comes in his way and stands upon it looks rather big."

"Even admitting that," said Rendel, "it seems to me that the determination and courage necessary to knock down what is in your way, when it can't be got out by any other method, is part of what makes a great statesman."

"You speak," said Sir William, "as if he were a savage potentate."

"In some respects," said Rendel, "the savage potentate and civilised ruler are inevitably alike. The ultimate ground, the ultimate arbiter of their empire, is force."

"Empire!" said Sir William. "That is the cry! In your greed for empire you lose sight of everything but the aggrandisement of a dominion already so immense as to be unwieldy."

"Still," said Rendel, "as we have this big thing in our hands, it is better to keep it there than let it drop and break to pieces."

"I don't wish to let it drop," said Gore. "I wish to be content to increase it by friendly intercourse with the world, by the arts of peace and civilisation, and not by destruction and bloodshed."

"I am afraid," said Rendel, "that the savage, which, as you say too truly, still lurks in the majority of civilised beings, will not be content to see the world governed on those amiable lines."

"There I must beg leave to differ from you," said Sir William, "I believe that the majority of civilised human beings will, when it has been put before them, be on the side of peace."

"We shall see," Rendel said, with a smile which was perhaps not as conciliatory as he intended it to be.

"Yes, you will see when the General Election comes," said Gore. "And if it goes for us, and we have a Cabinet composed of men who are not the mere puppets in the hands of an autocrat, the destinies of the world will be altered."

"Father," said Rachel, "do you really think that is how the General Election will go?"

"Quite possibly," Gore said, with decision. Rendel said nothing.

"Oh, father!" said Rachel. "I wish that you were in Parliament! Suppose you were in the Government!"

"Ah, well, my life as you know, was otherwise filled up," said Sir William, with a sigh; "but in that case the Imperialists perhaps might not have found everything such plain sailing." And so much had he penetrated himself with the conviction of what he was saying, that he felt himself, as he sat there opposite Rendel, whose wisdom and sagacity in reality so far exceeded his own, to be in the position of the older, wiser man of great influence and many opportunities condescending to explain his own career to an obscure novice.

Rendel looked across at Rachel sitting opposite to him, listening to what her father said with her customary air of sweet and gentle deference, and then smiling at himself; and again he inwardly vowed that, for her sake, he would endure the daily pinpricks that are almost as difficult to bear in the end as one good sword-thrust.

"I must say it will be interesting to see who goes out as Governor of British Zambesiland," he said presently, looking up from the paper. "That will be a big job if you like."

"Let's hope they will find a big man to do it," said Sir William.

"I heard to-day," said Rendel, "that it would probably be Belmont."

"Well, he'll be a firebrand Governor after Stamfordham's own heart," said Gore. "It's absurd sending all these young men out to these important posts."

"That is rather Stamfordham's theory," said Rendel—"to have youngish men, I mean."

"If he would confine himself to theories," said Sir William, "it would be better for England at this moment."

"It might, however, interfere with his practical use as a Foreign Secretary," Rendel was about to say, but he checked the words on his tongue.

After dinner that evening he remained downstairs under pretext of writing some letters, while Rachel proposed to her father to give her a lesson in chess.

Rendel turned on the electric light in his study, shut the door, stood in front of the fire and looked round him with a delightful sense of possession, of privacy, of well-being. His new house—indeed, one might almost have said his new life—was still so recent a possession as to have lost none of its preciousness. He still felt a childish joy in all its details. The house was one of those built within the last decade which seem to have made a struggle to escape the uniformity of the older streets. The front door opened into a square hall, from the left side of which opened the dining-room, from the right the study, both of these rooms having bow windows, built with that broad sweep of curve which makes for beauty instead of vulgarity. The house, Rendel had told his wife with a smile when they came to it, he had furnished for her, with the exception of one room in it; the study he had arranged for himself. And it certainly was a room in which, to judge by appearances, a worker need never be stopped in his work by the paltry need of any necessary tool. Rendel was a man of almost exaggerated precision and order. Everything lay ready to his hand in the place where he expected to find it. A glance at his well-appointed writing-table gave evidence of it. The back wall of the study, opposite the window, was lined with books. On the wall over the fireplace hung a large map of Africa. Rendel looked intently at it as he thought of the stirring pages of history that were in the making on that huge, misshapen continent, of the field that it was going to be for the statesmen and administrators of the future: he thought of Lord Belmont, only two years older than himself, with whom he had been at Eton and at Oxford, and wondered what it felt like to be in his place and have the ball at one's feet. For Rendel in his heart was burning with ambition of no ignoble kind. He was burning to do, to act, and not to watch only; to take his part in shaping the destinies of his fellow-men, to help the world into what he believed to be the right path; and he would do it yet. In his mind that evening, as he stood upright, intent, looking on into the future, there was not the shadow of a doubt that he would carry out his purpose. He had come downstairs smarting under the impression of Sir William's last words when they were discussing the new Governor. Then he recovered, and reminded himself of the obvious truism that the man occupied with politics must school himself to have his opinions contradicted by his opponents, and must make up his mind that there are as many people opposed to his way of thinking in the world as agreeing with it. But it is one thing to engage in a free fight in the open field, and another to keep parrying the petty blows dealt by a persecuting antagonist. Day by day, hour by hour, as the time went on, Rendel had to make a conscious effort to keep to the line he had traced out for himself; he had to tighten his resolution, to readjust his burden. The yoke of even a beloved companionship may be willingly borne, but it is a yoke and a restraint for all that. But Rendel would not have forgotten it. He accepted the lot he had chosen, unspeakably grateful to Rachel for having bestowed such happiness on him, ready and determined to fulfil his part of the compact, to carry out, even at the cost of a daily and hourly sacrifice, the bargain he had made. And, after all, as long as he made up his mind that it did not signify, he could well afford, in the great happiness that had fallen to his lot, to disregard the minor annoyances. His life, his standards, should be arranged on a scale that would enable him to disregard them. If one is only moving along swiftly enough, one has impetus to glide over minor impediments without being stopped or turned aside by them. For Rachel's sake all would be possible, it would be almost easy. At any rate, it should be done. Rendel's will felt braced and strengthened by his resolve, and he knew that he would be master of his fate. There are certain moments in our lives when we stop at a turning, it may be, to take stock of our situation, when we look back along the road we have come—how interminable it seemed as we began it!—and look along the one we are going to travel, prepared to start onward again with a fresh impulse of purpose and energy. That night, as Rendel looked on into the future, he felt like the knight who, lance in rest but ready to his hand, rides out into the world ready to embrace the opportunity that shall come to him.

CHAPTER X

The opportunity that came that night was ushered in somewhat prosaically, not by the sound of a foeman's horn being wound in the distance, but by the postman's knock. There was only one letter, but that was an important looking one addressed to Rendel, in a big, square envelope with an official signature in the corner. It was, however, marked "private and confidential," and was not written in an official capacity. Rendel as he looked at it, saw that the signature was "Belmont." In an instant as he unfolded the page his hopes leapt to meet the words he would find there. Yes, Lord Belmont was going to be Governor of Zambesiland; that was the beginning. And what was this that followed? He asked Rendel whether, if offered the post of Governor's Secretary, practically the second in command, he would accept it and go out to Africa with him. The offer, which meant a five years' appointment, was flatteringly worded, with a mention of Lord Stamfordham's strong recommendation which had prompted it, and wound up with an earnestly expressed hope that Rendel would not at any rate refuse without having deeply considered it. Belmont, however, asked for a reply as soon as was consistent with the serious reflection necessary before taking the step. Rendel looked at the clock. It was half-past nine. He need not write by post that night, he would send round the first thing in the morning. That would do as well. At this particular moment he need do nothing but look the thing in the face. Serious consideration it should have, undoubtedly, though that was not needed in order to come to a decision. He was not afraid of gazing at this new possibility that had just swum into his ken. The moment that comes to those who are going to achieve, when the door in the wall, showing that glorious vista beyond, suddenly opens to them, is fraught with an excited joy which partakes at once of anticipation and of fulfilment, and is probably never surpassed when in the fulness of time the opportunities come even too fast on each other's heels, and it has become a foregone conclusion to take advantage of them. There is no moment of outlook that has the charm of that first gaze from afar, when the deep blue distances cloak what is lovely and unlovely alike and merge them all into one harmonious and inviting mystery. Rendel was in no hurry for that curtain of mysterious distance to lift: possibility and success lay behind it. He relished with an exquisite pleasure the sense of having a dream fulfilled. The crucial moment that comes to nearly all of us of having to compare the place that others assign to us in life with that which we imagined we were entitled to occupy, is to some fraught with the bitterest disappointment. The sense of having cleared successfully that great gulf which lies between one's own appreciation of oneself and that of other people is one of rapture. Rendel had been so short a time married, and had had so few opportunities during that time of being called upon for any decision, that it was an entirely new sensation to him to remember suddenly that this was a thing which concerned somebody else as well as it did himself. But the thought was nothing but sweet; it meant that there was somebody now by his side, there always would be, to care for the things that happened to him; and Rachel, too, would be borne up on the wave of excitement and rejoicing that was shaking Rendel, to his own surprise, so strangely out of his usual reserved composure. He sat down mechanically at his writing-table and drew a sheet of writing-paper idly towards him, wondering how he should formulate his reply. To his great surprise and somewhat shamefaced amusement, he found that his hand was shaking so that he could not control the pen. He would go up before writing and tell Rachel. Then, as he went upstairs, he was conscious of a secret annoyance that a third person should just at this moment be between them.

A profound silence reigned as he opened the drawing-room door. Rachel and her father were poring intently over the chess-board. Rachel looked up eagerly as her husband came in.

"Oh, Francis," she said, "I am so glad. Do come and tell me what to do."

"Yes, I wish you would," Sir William said, with some impatience. "Look what she is doing with her queen."

"Is that a letter you want to show me?" said Rachel, looking at the envelope in Rendel's hand.

"All right. It will keep," he said quietly, putting it back in his breast pocket.

Sir William kept his eyes intently fixed upon the board. He would not countenance any diversion of fixed and rigid attention from the game in hand.

"That is what I should do," said Rendel, moving one of Rachel's pawns on to the back line.

"Oh! how splendid!" said Rachel. "I believe I have a chance after all."

Sir William gave a grunt of satisfaction. "That's more like it," he said. "If you had come up a little sooner we might have had a decent game."

Rendel made no comment. The game ended in the most auspicious way possible. Rachel, backed by Rendel's advice, showed fight a little longer and left the victory to Sir William in the end after a desperate struggle. The hour of departure came. Rachel and her husband both went downstairs with Sir William. They opened the door. It was a bright, starlight night. Sir William announced his intention of walking to a cab, and with his coat buttoned up against the east wind, started off along the pavement. Rachel turned back into the house with a sigh as she saw him go.

"He is getting to look much older, isn't he?" she said. "Poor dear, it is hard on him to have to turn out at this time of night."

Rendel vaguely heard and barely took in the meaning of what she was saying. His one idea was that now he would be able to tell her his news.

"Come in here," he said, drawing her into the study. "I want to tell you something." And he made her sit down in his own comfortable chair. "I have had a letter this evening," he said.

"Have you?" said Rachel, looking up at him in surprise at the unusual note of joyousness, almost of exultation, in his tone. "What is it about?"

"You shall read it," he said, giving it to her. Her colour rose as she read on.

"Oh, what an opportunity!" she said, and a tinge of regret crept strangely into her voice. "What a pity!"

"A pity?" said Rendel, looking at her.

"Yes," she said. "It would have been so delightful."

"Would have been?" said Rendel, still amazed. "Why don't you say 'will be'? Do you mean to say you don't want to go?"

"I don't think *I* could go," Rachel said, with a slight surprise in her voice. "How could I?"

Rendel said nothing, but still looked at her as though finding it difficult to realise her point of view.

"How could I leave my father?" she said, putting into words the thing that seemed to her so absolutely obvious that she had hardly thought it necessary to speak it.

"Do you think you couldn't?" Rendel said slowly.

"Oh, Frank, how would it be possible?" she said. "We could not leave him alone here, and it would be much, much too far for him to go."

"Of course. I had not thought of his attempting it," said Rendel, truthfully enough, with a sinking dread at his heart that perhaps after all the fair prospect he had been gazing upon was going to prove nothing but a mirage.

"You do agree, don't you?" she said, looking at him anxiously. "You do see?"

"I am trying to see," Rendel said quietly. For a moment neither spoke.

"Oh, I couldn't," Rachel said. "I simply couldn't!" in a heartfelt tone that told of the unalterable conviction that lay behind it. There was another silence. Rendel stood looking straight before him, Rachel watching him timidly. Rendel made as though to speak, then he checked himself.

"Oh, isn't it a pity it was suggested!" Rachel cried involuntarily. Rendel gave a little laugh. It was deplorable, truly, that such an opportunity should have come to a man who was not going to use it.

"But could not *you* — —" she began, then stopped. "How long would it be for?"

"Oh, about five years, I suppose," said Rendel, with a sort of aloofness of tone with which people on such occasions consent to diverge for the moment from the main issue.

"Five years," she repeated. "That would be too long."

"Yes, five years seems a long time, I daresay," said Rendel, "as one looks on to it."

"I was wondering," she said hesitatingly, "if it wouldn't have been better that you should have gone."

"I? Without you, do you mean?" Rendel said. "No, certainly not. That I am quite clear about."

"Oh, Frank, I should not like it if you did," she said, looking up at him.

"I need not say that I should not." There was another silence.

"Should you like it very, very much?" she said.

"Like what?" said Rendel, coming back with an effort.

"Going to Africa."

There had been a moment when Rendel had told Lady Gore how glad he was that Rachel had no ambitions, as producing the ideal character. No doubt that lack has its advantages—but the world we live in is not, alas, exclusively a world of ideals.

"Yes, I should like it," he replied quietly. "If you went too, that is—I should not like it without you."

"Oh, Frank, it *is* a pity," she said, looking up at him wistfully. But there was evidently not in her mind the shadow of a possibility that the question could be decided other than in one way.

"Come, it is getting late," Rendel said. And they left the room with the outward air of having postponed the decision till the morning. But the decision was not postponed; that Rachel took for granted, and Rendel had made up his mind. This was, after all, not a new sacrifice he was called upon to make: it was part of the same, of that sacrifice which he had recognised that he was willing to make in order to marry Rachel, and which was so much less than that other great and impossible sacrifice of giving her up.

He came down early the next morning and wrote to Lord Belmont, meaning when Rachel came down to breakfast to show her the letter, in which he had most gratefully but quite decisively declined the honour that had been done him. He read the letter over feeling as if he were in a dream, and almost smiled to himself at the incredible thought that here was the first big opportunity of his life and that he was calmly putting it away from him. Perhaps when he came to talk it over with Rachel again she might see it differently. Might she? No. He knew in his heart that she would not. It was probable that Rendel's ambition, his determined purpose, would always be hampered by his old-fashioned, almost quixotic ideas of loyalty, his conception of the seemliness, the dignity of the relations between husband and wife. In a matter that he felt was a question of right or wrong he would probably without hesitation have used his authority and decided inflexibly that such and such a course was the one to pursue; but here he felt it was impossible. It would not be consistent with his dignity to use his authority to insist upon a course which, though it might be to his own advantage, was undeniably an infringement of the tacit compact that he had accepted when he married. With the letter in his hand he went slowly out of the study. Rachel was coming swiftly down the stairs into the hall, dressed for walking, looking perturbed and anxious.

"Frank," she said hurriedly, "I have just had a message from Prince's Gate, my father is ill."

"I am very sorry," Rendel said with concern.

"I must go there directly," she said.

"Have you breakfasted?" asked Rendel.

"Yes," she said. "At least I have had a cup of tea—quite enough."

"No," said Rendel, "that isn't enough. Come, it's absurd that you should go out without breakfasting."

"I couldn't really," Rachel said entreatingly. "I must go."

"Nonsense!" Rendel said decidedly. "You are not to go till you have had some breakfast." And he took her into the dining-room and made her eat. But this, as he felt, was not the moment for further discussion of his own plans. He saw how absolutely they had faded away from her view.

"I shall follow you shortly," he said, "to know how Sir William is."

"Oh, do," she said. "You can't come now, I suppose?"

"I have a letter to write first. I must write to Lord Belmont."

"Oh yes, of course," she said, with a sympathetic inflection in her voice. "Oh, Frank, how terrible it would have been if you had been going away now!" And she drew close to him as though seeking shelter against the anxieties and troubles of the world.

"But I am not," said Rendel quietly. And she looked back at him as she drove off with a smile flickering over her troubled face.

Rendel turned back into the house. There was nothing more to do, that was quite evident. He fastened up the letter to Belmont and sent it round to his house, also writing to Stamfordham a brief letter of thanks for his good offices and regrets at not being able to avail himself of them.

Later he went to Prince's Gate. Sir William was a little better. It was a sharp, feverish attack brought on by a chill the night before. It lasted several days, during which time Rachel was constantly backwards and forwards at Prince's Gate, and at the end of which she proposed to Rendel that her father should, for the moment, as she put it, come to them to Cosmo Place.

In the meantime Stamfordham, surprised at Rendel's refusal of the opportunity he had put in his way, had sent for him to urge him to reconsider his decision while there was yet time. Rendel found it very hard to explain his reasons in such a way that they should seem in the least valid to his interlocutor. Stamfordham, although he was well aware that Rendel had married during the spring, had but dimly realised the practical difference that this change of condition might bring into the young man's life and into the code by which his actions were governed. He himself had not married. He had had, report said, one passing fancy and then another, but they had never amounted to more than an impulse which had set him further on his way; there had never been an attraction strong enough to deflect him from his orbit. With such, he was quite clear, the statesman should have nothing to do.

"Of course," he said, after listening to what Rendel had to say, "I should be the last person to wish to persuade you to take a course contrary to Mrs. Rendel's wishes, but still such an opportunity as this does not come to every man."

"I know," said Rendel.

"I never was married," Stamfordham went on, "but I have not understood that matrimony need necessarily be a bar to a successful career."

"Nor have I," Rendel said, with a smile.

"Let's see. How long have you been married?"

"Four months," Rendel replied.

"As I told you, I am inexperienced in these matters," Stamfordham said, "but perhaps while one still counts by months it is more difficult to assert one's authority."

"My wife," said Rendel, "does not wish to leave her father, who is in delicate health. Sir William Gore, you know."

"Oh, Sir William Gore, yes," said Stamfordham, with an inflection which implied that Sir William Gore was not worth sacrificing any possible advantages for.

"I am very, very sorry," Rendel said gravely. "I would have given a great deal to have been going to Africa just now."

"Yes, indeed. There will be infinite possibilities over there as soon as things have settled down," said Stamfordham. And he looked at a table that was covered with papers of different kinds, among them some notes in his own handwriting, and said, "Pity my unfortunate secretaries! I don't think I have ever had any one who knew how to read those impossible hieroglyphics as you did."

"I don't know whether I ought to say I am glad or sorry to hear that," said Rendel, as he went towards the door.

"What are you going to do if you don't go to Africa?" Stamfordham said.

"Something else, I hope," said Rendel, with a look and an accent that carried conviction.

"Shan't you go into the House?" said Stamfordham.

"I mean to try," Rendel said. Then as he went out he turned round and said, "I daresay, sir, there are still possibilities in Europe, after all."

"Very likely," said Stamfordham; and they parted.

One of the most difficult tasks of the philosopher is not to regret his decisions. The mind that has been disciplined to determine quickly and to abide by its determination is one of the most valuable instruments of human equipment. But it certainly needed some philosophy on Rendel's part, during the period that elapsed between his refusal of Lord Belmont's offer and the departure of the newly appointed governor, not to regret that he himself was remaining behind. Day by day the papers were full of the administrators who were going out, of their qualifications, of their responsibilities. Day by day Rendel looked at the map hanging in his study and wondered what transformations the shifting of circumstances would bring to it.

Sir William Gore, in the meantime, had got better. He had slowly thrown off the fever that had prostrated him, although he was not able to resume his ordinary life. He had demurred a little at first to the proposal that he should take up his abode at Cosmo Place, then, not unwillingly, had yielded. In his ordinary state of health he would have been alive to the proverbial drawbacks of a joint household, but in his present state of weakness and depression he felt he could not be alone, and in his secret heart it was almost a relief to be away from Prince's Gate, its memories and associations. It had been in one of these moments of insight, of revelation almost, that suddenly, like a blinding flash of light shows us in pitiless details the conditions that surround us, that with intense self-pity he had said to himself that there was actually no one in this whole world with whom he was entitled to come first. Rachel's solicitude certainly went far to persuade him of the contrary; but in his secret soul he bitterly resented the fact that there should now be someone to share Rachel's allegiance, although Rendel might well have contended that he was divided in Sir William's favour.

CHAPTER XI

The Miss Pateleys, sisters of Robert Pateley, lived together. The death of their parents, as we have said, had taken place when their brother was already launched on his successful career as a journalist. They had at first gone on living in the little country town in which their father had been a solicitor. It had not occurred to them to do anything else. They were surrounded there by people who knew them, who considered them, towards whom their social position needed no explaining and by whom it was taken for granted. When they went shopping, the tradespeople would reply in a friendly way, "Yes, Miss Pateley,—No, Miss Jane. This is the stocking you generally prefer"; or, "These were the pens you had last time," with an intimate understanding of the needs of their customers, forming a most pleasing contrast to the detached attitude of the staff of big shops. The sisters had a very small income between them, eked out by skilful management, and also, it must be said, by constant help from their brother, who represented to them the moving principle of the universe embodied in a visible form. He it was who knew things the female mind cannot grasp, how to read the gas meter, what to do when the cistern was blocked, or when the landlord said it was not his business to mend the roof. These things which appeared so preoccupying to Anna and Jane seemed to sit very lightly on their brother Robert, and when they saw him shoulder each detail and deal with it with instant and consummate ease they admired him as much as they did when they saw him carrying upstairs his own big portmanteau which the united female strength of the house was powerless to deal with. After a time Robert, devoted brother though he was, found that it complicated existence to have to settle these matters by correspondence, still more to have suddenly to take a journey of several hours from London in order to deal with them on the spot. He proposed to his sisters that they should come and live in London. With many misgivings, and yet not without some secret excitement, they assented, and for a few months before our story begins they had been established in the same house as their brother, on the floor above the lodgings he inhabited in Vernon Street, Bloomsbury. Vernon Street, Bloomsbury, was perhaps a fortunate place for them to begin their London life in, if London life, except as a geographical term, it can be called, for two poor little ladies living more absolutely outside what is commonly described by that name it would be hard to find. Indeed, if it had not been for the courage and adventurous spirit of Jane, the younger of the two, their hearts might well have failed them during those first months in which the autumn days shortened over the district of Bloomsbury. Since they knew no one, they had nobody to visit, and nobody came to see them. They were still not a little bewildered by London. There were, it was true, a great many sights of an inanimate kind; but how to get at them? They did not consider themselves justified in taking cabs, and omnibuses were at first, to two people who had lived all their lives in a tramless town, a disconcerting and complicated means of locomotion. However, as the time went on they shook down, they found their little niche in existence; they made acquaintance with the clergyman's wife and some of the district visitors, and when the first summer of their London life came round, the summer following Rachel's marriage, everything seemed to them more possible. London was bright, sunshiny, and welcoming, instead of being austere and repellent. Pateley had succeeded in obtaining a key of the square close to which they lived, and they sat there and revelled in the summer weather. The mere fact of having him so near them, of knowing that at any moment in the day he might come in with the loud voice and heartiness of manner which always cheered and uplifted them, albeit some of his acquaintants ventured to find it too audible, gave them a fresh sense of being in touch with all the great things happening in the world. Then came a moment in which, indeed, the larger issues of life seemed to present themselves to be dealt with. Pateley, under whose auspices the *Arbiter* had prospered exceedingly, and who had an interest in it from the point of view of a commercial enterprise as well as of a political organ, found himself one day the possessor of a larger sum of ready money than he had expected. He made up his mind that some of it should be given to his sisters, and that the rest should join their own savings invested in the "Equator," which seemed to present every prospect of succeeding when once the moment should come to work it. Pateley was altogether in a high state of jubilation in those days. The Cape to Cairo railway was actually on the verge of being completed. In a week more the gigantic scheme would be an accomplished fact. The excitement in London respecting it was immense. A small piece of German territory still remained to be crossed, but if no unforeseen incident arose to jeopardise the situation at the last moment all would yet be well. The rejoicings of Englishmen commonly take a sturdy and obvious form, and two days after the great junction was expected to take place, the *Arbiter* was to give a dinner at the Colossus Hotel in the Strand to the representatives of the Cape to Cairo Railway in London, after which the Hotel would be illuminated on all sides, and fireworks over the river were to proclaim to the whole town that Africa had been spanned. Pateley was to take the chair at the dinner. He had some shares in the railway himself, although the rush upon it had been too great for him to secure any large amount of them. He had golden hopes, however, in the future of the "Equator," when once the railway was at its doors. Anderson had gone back again to Africa, this time with an eager staff of companions, and was only waiting for his time to come.

"Now then," Pateley said jovially, one evening, as he went into the lodgings in Vernon Street and found his sisters sitting over their somewhat inadequate evening meal, "Times are looking up, I must tell you. I shouldn't wonder if you were better off before long. When the railway's finished, and if the "Equator" mine is all we believe it to be, you ought to get something handsome out of it—and I have got something for you to go on with which will keep you going in the meantime. So now I hope you will think yourselves justified in sitting down to a decent dinner every evening, instead of that kind of thing," and he pointed, with his loud, jovial laugh, to the cocoa and eggs on the rather dingily appointed table.

Jane's eyes sparkled and her cheeks flushed with an incredulous joy. Anna's breath came quickly. What a fairy prince of a brother this was!

"But, Robert, we had better not make much difference in our way of living at first, had we?" Anna said, timidly, calling to mind the instances in fiction of imprudent persons who had launched out wildly on an accession of fortune and then been overtaken by ruin.

"Well, I don't suppose you are either of you likely to want to cut a big dash," he said with another loud laugh. "At least, I don't see you doing it."

"It is a great responsibility," Anna said timidly. "I hope we shall use it the right way."

"Right way!" said Pateley. "Of course you will. Go to the play with it, get yourself a fur cloak, have a fire in your bedroom——"

"Oh!" said Jane.

"But, Robert," Anna said, "I don't feel it is sent to us for that."

"Sent!" said Pateley. "Well, that is one way of putting it."

But he did not enlarge upon the point. He accepted his sisters just as they were, with their limitations, their principles, and everything. He was not particularly susceptible to beauty and distinction, in the sense of these qualities being necessary to his belongings, and perhaps it was as well. Anna and Jane, though they looked undeniably like gentlewomen, had nothing else about them that was particularly agreeable to look upon. Nor were they either of them very strikingly ugly, or, indeed, strikingly anything. Jane was the better looking of the two. It was, perhaps, a rather heartless freak of destiny that life should have ordained her to live with somebody who was like a parody of herself, older, rounder, thicker, plainer. Living apart they might each have passed muster; living together they somehow made their ugliness, like their income, go further. But in the composite photograph it was Anna who predominated. It was a pity, for she was the stumpier of the two.

Long and earnest were the discussions the little sisters had that night after their splendid brother had departed, until by the time they went to bed they were prepared, or so it seemed to them, to launch their existence on a dizzy career of extravagance. They were going, as they expressed it, to put their establishment on another footing, which meant that instead of being attended by an inexperienced young person of eighteen they were to have an arrogant one of twenty-five. Their own elderly servant had declined to face the temptations of London, and had remained behind, living close to their old home. And, greatest event of all, they had at length—it was now summer, but that didn't matter, furs were cheaper—yielded to the thought which they had been alternately caressing and dismissing for months, and they were each going to buy a Fur Cloak. The days in which this all important purchase was being considered were to the Miss Pateleys days of pure enjoyment. Days of walks along Oxford Street, no longer so bewildered by the noise of London traffic, the discovery of some shop in an out of the way place whose wares were about half the price of the more fashionable quarters. The days were full of glorious possibilities.

It was two days after that evening visit of Pateley's to his sisters, which had so gilded and transformed their existence, that sinister rumours began to float over London, bringing deadly anxiety in their wake. Telegrams kept pouring in, and were posted all over the town, becoming more and more serious as the day went on: "Disturbances in South Africa. Hostile encounter between English and Germans. Cape to Cairo Railway stopped. Collapse of the 'Equator, Ltd.,'" until by nightfall the whole of England knew the pitifully unimportant incidents from which such tragic consequences were springing—that a group of travelling missionaries, halting unawares on German territory and chanting their evening hymns, had been disturbed by a rough fellow who came jeering into their midst, that one of the devout group had finally ejected him, with such force that he had rolled over with his head on a stone and died then and there; and that the Germans were insisting upon having vengeance. As for the "Equator, Ltd.," nobody knew exactly in what the collapse consisted. The wildest reports were circulated respecting it; one saying that it was in the hands of the Germans, another that they had destroyed the plant that was ready to work it, another again, and it was the one that gained the most credence, that there was no gold in the mine at all, and that the whole thing was a swindle. The offices of the "Equator" were closed for the night. They would probably be besieged the next morning by an angry crowd eager to sell out, but the shares would now be hardly worth the paper they were written upon. Pateley, in a frenzy of anxiety, in whichever direction he looked—for his sisters, for himself, for his party, for the Cape to Cairo Railway—spent the night at his office to see which way events were going to turn. In his unreasoning anger, as the day of misfortune dawned next morning, against destiny, against the far-away unknown missionaries, against all the adverse forces that were standing in the way of his wishes, there was one concrete figure in the foreground upon whom he could justifiably pour out his wrath: Sir William Gore, the Chairman of the "Equator," who, in the public opinion, was responsible for the undertaking. He would go to see Sir William that very day as soon as it was possible. In the meantime he would go round to his sisters to try to prepare them for the unfavourable turn that their circumstances after all might possibly take. As, sorely troubled at what he had to say, he came up into their little sitting-room, he found it bright with flowers; the fragrance of sweet peas filled the air. Anna, who had longed for flowers all her life and had welcomed with tremulous gratitude the rare opportunities that had come in her way of receiving any, had suddenly realised that it might not be sinful to buy them. The joy that she had in the handful bought from a street vendor was cheap, after all, at the price that might have seemed exorbitant if it had been spent on the flowers alone.

"Robert," said Jane, almost before he was inside the room, "guess what we are going to do?"

"Something very naughty, I'm afraid," Anna said, excited and shy at the same time. She was generally less able than Jane to overcome the awe that they both felt of a relation so great and so beneficent, so altogether perfect, as their brother Robert, but at this moment she was intoxicated by the possession of wealth, by the sense of luxury, of well-being, by that fragrance of the spirit her imagination added to the fragrance of the flowers that stood near her. "We're each going to buy a fur cloak like that, look!" And she held out to him proudly the picture in the inside cover of the *Realm of Fashion*, representing a tall, slender, undulating lady, about as unlike herself as could well have been imagined, wrapped in a beautiful clinging garment of which the lining, turned back, displayed an exquisite fur. Pateley, as we have said, was not as a rule given to an excess of sensibility. He did not ridicule sentiment in others, but neither did he share it; that point of view was simply not visible to him. Suddenly, however, on this evening he had a moment of what felt to himself a most inconvenient access of emotion.

There was a plain and obvious pathos in this particular situation that it needed no very fine sensibilities to grasp, in the sight of his sister, her small, thickset little figure encased in her ugly little gown, looking up appealingly to him over her spectacles with the joy of a child in the toy she was going to buy. It was probably the first, the very first time in her life, that she had had that particular experience. Added to the joy of getting the thing she coveted was the sense of having looked a conscientious scruple in the face, and seen it fly before her like an evil spirit before a spell. She had routed the enemy, pushed aside the obstacle in front of her, and, excited, and flushed with victory, was looking round on a bigger world and a fairer view. Pateley, to his own surprise, found himself absolutely incapable of putting into words what he had come to say, not a thing that often happened to him. In wonder at his not answering at once, Anna, misinterpreting his very slight pause, caught herself up quickly and said anxiously—

"That is what you suggested, isn't it, Robert? You are quite sure you approve of it?"

"Yes, yes, I approve," he said heartily, recovering himself. "Of course. Go ahead."

"You must not think," she went on, reassured, "that we mean to spend all our money in things like this, but of course a fur cloak is useful; it is a possession, isn't it? and it is, after all, one's duty to keep one's health."

"Of course it is," Pateley said. "No need of any further argument."

"I am so glad," she said, "so glad you approve!" and she smiled again with delight.

Again Pateley felt an unreasoning fury rising in his mind that people who were so easily satisfied should not be allowed to have their heart's desire. Perhaps after all, it was not true about the "Equator"; perhaps things might be better than they seemed. At any rate, he would not say anything to his sisters until he had seen Gore. And with some hurried explanation of the number of engagements that obliged him to leave them, he strode out.

CHAPTER XII

In the meantime Lord Stamfordham, watching the situation, felt there was not a single instant to lose. There is one moment in the life of a conflagration when it can be stamped out: that moment passed, no power can stop it. Stamfordham, his head clear, his determination strong and ready, resolved to act without hesitating on his own responsibility. He sent a letter round to Prince Bergowitz, the German Ambassador, begging him to come and see him. Prince Bergowitz was laid up with an attack of gout which unfortunately prevented his coming, but he would be glad to receive Lord Stamfordham if he would come to see him.

It was a little later in the same day that Rendel, alone in his study, was standing, newspaper in hand, in front of the map of Africa looking to see the exact localities where the events were happening which might have such dire consequences. At that moment Wentworth, passing through Cosmo Place, looked through the window and saw him thus engaged. He knocked at the hall door, and, after being admitted, walked into the study without waiting to be announced.

"Looking at the map of Africa, and I don't wonder," he said. "Isn't it awful?"

"It's terrible," said Rendel, "about as bad as it can be."

"Look here, why aren't you over there to help to settle it?" said Wentworth.

"Well, I should not have been there, in any case," said Rendel. "That is where I should have been—look," with something like a sigh.

"You would have been nearer than you are now," said Wentworth. "Upon my word, I haven't patience with you. The idea of throwing up such a chance as you have had!"

"How do you know about it?" Rendel said.

"How do I know?" said Wentworth. "Everybody knows that you were offered it and refused."

"After all," said Rendel, "there are some things one leaves undone in this world. It does not follow that because people are offered a thing they must necessarily accept it."

"I don't say I am not in favour of leaving things undone," Wentworth said, "on occasion."

"So I have observed," said Rendel.

"But really, you know," Wentworth went on, "this is too much. What do you intend to do?"

"What do I intend to do?" Rendel said, with a half smile, then unconsciously imparting a greater steadfastness into his expression, "broadly speaking, I intend to do—everything."

"Oh! well, there's hope for you still," Wentworth said, "if that is your intention. It's rather a large order, though."

"Well, as I have told you before," Rendel said, "I don't see why there should be any limit to one's intentions. The man who intends little is not likely to achieve much."

"That's all very well, and plausible enough, I dare say," said Wentworth, "but the way to achieve is not to begin by refusing all your chances."

"This is too delightful from you," said Rendel, "who never do anything at all."

"Not at all," said Wentworth. "It is on principle that I do nothing, in order to protest against other people doing too much. I wish to have an eight hours' day of elegant leisure, and to go about the world as an example of it. It would be just as inconsistent of me to accept a regular occupation as it is of you to refuse it."

"I have a very simple reason for refusing this," said Rendel more seriously, and he paused. "I am a married man."

"To be sure, my dear fellow," said Wentworth, "I have noticed it."

"My wife didn't want to go to Africa," said Rendel, "and there was an end of it."

"Oh, that was the end of it?" said Wentworth.

"Absolutely," said Rendel. "She did not want to leave her father."

"Ah, is that it?" said Wentworth, feeling that he could not decently advance an urgent plea against Sir William. "Poor old man! I know he's gone to pieces frightfully since his wife died—still, couldn't some one have been found to take care of him?"

"Hardly any one like Rachel," Rendel said.

"Naturally," said Wentworth.

"You know he is living with us?" Rendel said.

"Is he?" said Wentworth surprised. "Upon my word, Frank, you are a good son-in-law."

Rendel ignored the tone of Wentworth's last remark and said quite simply—

"Oh! well, there was nothing else to be done. He's been ill, you know, really rather bad; first he had a chill, and then influenza on the top of it. He's frightfully low altogether."

"But I rather wonder," said Wentworth, "as Mrs. Rendel had her father with her, that you didn't go to Africa without her. Wouldn't that have been possible?"

"No," said Rendel decidedly. "Quite impossible."

"I should have thought," said Wentworth, "that in these enlightened days a husband who could not do without his wife was rather a mistake."

"That may be," said Rendel. "But I think on the whole that the husband who can do without her is a greater mistake still."

"It is a great pity you were not born five hundred years ago," said Wentworth.

"I should have disliked it particularly," said Rendel. "I should have been fighting at Flodden, or Crécy, or somewhere, and I should have been too old to marry Rachel, even in these days of well-preserved centenarians. It is no good, Jack; I am afraid you must leave me to my folly."

"Well, well," said Wentworth, agreeing with the word, and thinking to himself that even the wisest of men looks foolish at times when he has the yoke of matrimony across his shoulders; "after all there is to be said—if we are going to have another war on our hands in Africa, which Heaven forfend, the time of the statesmen over there is hardly come yet."

At this moment the door opened and the two men turned round quickly as Rachel came in.

"Frank," said Rachel. "Should you mind——" Then she stopped as she saw Wentworth. "Oh, how do you do, Mr. Wentworth? I didn't know you were here. Don't let me interrupt you."

"On the contrary," said Wentworth, "it is I who am interrupting your husband."

"I only came to see, Frank, if you were very busy," she said.

"I am not at this moment. Do you want me to do anything?"

"Well, presently, would you play one game of chess with my father? I am not really good enough to be of much use; it doesn't amuse him to play with me."

"Yes," said Rendel. "I have just got one or two letters to write and then I'll come."

"I think it would really be better," said Rachel, "if he came in here. It is rather a change for him, you know, to come into a different room after having been in the house all day."

"Just as you like," said Rendel, without much enthusiasm, but also without any noticeable want of it.

"Well," said Wentworth, "I'm not going to keep you any longer, Frank. I just came in to—give you my views about things in general."

"Thank you," said Rendel, with a smile. "I am much beholden to you for them."

"Perhaps you would come up and see my father, Mr. Wentworth," said Rachel, "before you go away?"

"I shall be delighted," Wentworth said. His feeling towards Sir William Gore was kindly on the whole, and the kindliness was intensified at this moment by compassion, although he could not help resenting a little that Gore should have been an indirect cause of Rendel's refusing what Wentworth considered was the chance of his friend's life. He shook hands with Rendel and prepared to follow Rachel. At this moment a loud, double knock resounded upon the hall door with a peremptoriness which must have induced an unusual and startling rapidity in the movements of Thacker, Rendel's butler, for almost instantly afterwards he threw open the study door with a visible perturbation and excitement in his demeanour, saying—

"It's Lord Stamfordham, sir, who wants particularly to see you." And to Rendel's amazement Lord Stamfordham appeared in the doorway. He bowed to Wentworth, whom he knew slightly, and shook hands with Rachel. She then went straight out, followed by Wentworth. As the door closed behind them, Stamfordham, answering Rendel's look of inquiry and without waiting for any interchange of greetings, said hurriedly—

"Rendel, I want you to do me a service."

"Please command me," Rendel said quickly, looking straight at him. He felt his heart beat as Stamfordham paused, put his hat down on the table, took his pocket-book out of his breast pocket and a folded paper out of it.

"I want you," he said, "to transcribe some pencil notes of mine."

"You want *me* to transcribe them?" said Rendel, with an involuntary inflection of surprise in his tone.

"Yes, if you will," said Stamfordham. "The fact is, Marchmont, the only man I have had since you left me who can read my writing when I take rough pencil notes in a hurry, has collapsed just to-day, out of sheer excitement I believe, and because he sat up for one night writing."

"Poor fellow!" said Rendel, half to himself.

"Yes," said Stamfordham drily; and then he went on, as one who knows that he must leave the sick and wounded behind without waiting to pity them. "These," unfolding the paper, "are notes of a conversation that I have just had at the German Embassy with Bergowitz." Rendel's quick movement as he heard the name showed that he realised what that juxtaposition meant at such a moment. "Every moment is precious," Stamfordham went on, "and it suddenly dawned on me as I left the Embassy that you were close at hand and might be willing to do it."

The German Embassy was at the moment, during some building operations, occupying temporary premises near Belgrave Square.

"I should think so indeed," Rendel said eagerly.

"The notes are very short, as you see," said Stamfordham. "You know, of course, what has been happening. I needn't go into that." And as he spoke a boy passed under the windows crying the evening papers, and they distinctly heard "Panic on the Stock Exchange." The two men's eyes met.

"Yes, there is a panic on the Stock Exchange," Stamfordham said, "because every one thinks there will be war—but there probably won't."

"Not?" said Rendel. "Can it be stopped?"

Stamfordham answered him by unfolding the piece of paper and laying it down before him on the table. It was a map of Africa, roughly outlined, but still clearly enough to show unmistakably what it was intended to convey, for all down the map from north to south there was a thick line drawn to the west of the Cape to Cairo Railway—the latter being indicated, but more faintly, in pencil—starting at Alexandria and running down through the whole of the continent, bending slightly to the southward between Bechuanaland and Namaqualand, and ending at the Orange River. East of that line was written ENGLAND, west of it GERMANY, and below it some lines of almost illegible writing in pencil.

Rendel almost gasped.

"What?" he said; "a partition of Africa?"

"Yes," said Stamfordham. Then he said with a sort of half smile, "The partition, that is to say, so far as it is in our own hands. But," speaking rapidly, "I will just put you in possession of the facts of the case and give you the clue. We abandon to Germany everything that we have a claim to west of this line. It does not come to very much," in answer to an involuntary movement on Rendel's part; and he swept his hand across the coast of the Gulf of Guinea as though wiping out of existence the Gold Coast, Ashanti, Sierra Leone, and all that had mattered before. "Germany abandons to us everything that she lays claim to on the east of it, including therefore the whole course of the Cape to Cairo Railway."

"But has Germany agreed?" said Rendel, stupefied with surprise.

"Germany has agreed," said Stamfordham. "We have just heard from Berlin."

Rendel felt as if his breath were taken away by the rapid motion of the events.

"That means peace, then?" he said.

"Yes," Stamfordham said; "peace."

"Then when is this going to be given to the world?" said Rendel.

"Some of it possibly to-morrow," said Stamfordham. "The Cabinet Council will meet this evening, and the King's formal sanction obtained. Of course," he went on, "the broad outlines only will be published—the fact of the understanding at any rate, not necessarily the terms of the partition. But it is important for financial reasons that the country should know as soon as possible that war is averted."

"Of course, of course," said Rendel. "Immeasurably important."

Stamfordham took up his hat and held out his hand with his air of courtly politeness as he turned towards the door.

"I may count upon you to do this for me immediately?"

"This instant," said Rendel, taking up the papers. "Shall I take them to your house as soon as they are done?"

"Please," said Stamfordham. "No, stay—I am going back to the German Embassy now, then probably to the Foreign Office. You had better simply send a messenger you can rely upon, and tell him to wait at my house to give them into my own hand, as I am not sure where I shall be for the next hour. Rendel, I must ask you by all you hold sacred to take care of those papers. If that map were to be caught sight of before the time— —"

Rendel involuntarily held it tighter at the thought of such a catastrophe.

"Good Heavens!—yes," he said. "But that shan't happen. Look," and he dropped the paper through the slit in the closed revolving corner of his large writing-table, a cover that was solidly locked with his own key so that, though papers could be put in through the slit, it was impossible to take them out again without unlocking the cover and lifting it up. "This is the only key," he said, showing his bunch. "Now then, they are perfectly safe while I go across the hall with you."

Stamfordham nodded.

"By the way," he said, pausing, "you are married now, Rendel...."

"I am, yes, I am glad to say," Rendel replied.

"To be sure," said Stamfordham, with a little bow conveying discreet congratulation. "But—remember that a married man sometimes tells secrets to his wife."

"Does he, sir?" said Rendel, with an air of assumed innocence.

"I believe I have heard so," said Stamfordham.

"On the other hand," said Rendel, "I also have heard that a married man sometimes keeps secrets from his wife."

"Oh well, that is better," said Stamfordham.

"From some points of view, perhaps," said Rendel. Then he added more seriously, "You may be quite sure, sir, that no one—*no one*—in this house shall know about those papers. I would give you my word of honour, but I don't suppose it would make my assertion any stronger."

"If you said nothing," said Stamfordham, "it would be enough;" and Rendel's heart glowed within him as their eyes met and the compact was ratified. "By the way, Rendel, there was one thing more I wanted to say to you. There will probably be a vacancy at Stoke Newton before long; aren't you going into the House?"

"Some time," said Rendel. "When I get a chance."

"Well, there is going to be a chance now," said Stamfordham. "Old Crawley is going to resign. I hear it from private sources; the world doesn't know it yet. It is a safe Imperialist seat, and in our part of the world."

"I should like very much to try," said Rendel, forcing himself to speak quietly.

"Suppose you write to our committee down there?" said Stamfordham. "That is, when you have done your more pressing business—I mean mine."

"That shall come before everything else," Rendel said. "I will do it at this moment."

He turned quickly back into his study after Stamfordham had left him, and unlocked and threw up the revolving cover of the writing-table hastily, for fear that something should have happened to the paper on which the destinies of the civilised world were hanging. There it was, safe in his keeping, his and nobody else's. He took it in his hand and for a moment walked up and down the room, unable to control himself, trying to realise the tremendous change in the aspect of his fortunes that had taken place in the last half-hour. Then he had seemed to himself in the backwater, out of the throng of existence. He had been trying to reconcile himself to the idea that he was "out of it," as he had put it to himself—left behind. And now he shared with the two great potentates of the world the knowledge of what was going to take place; it was his hand that should transcribe the words that had decided it; he was a witness, and so far the only one. Then with an effort he forced himself to be calm. Every minute was of importance. He sat down at the writing-table, took up the paper, and pored over it to try to disentangle the strange dots, scratches, and lines which, flowing from Stamfordham's pen, took the place of handwriting. Some ill-natured people said that Stamfordham was quite conscious of the advantage of having writing which could not be read without a close scrutiny. It was no doubt possible. However, having the clue to what the contents of the paper were, Rendel, to his immense relief, found that he could decipher it. As he was writing the first word of the fair copy the door of the study opened slowly, and Sir William Gore appeared on the threshold, a newspaper in his hand.

CHAPTER XIII

Sir William, who had not been able to come downstairs for a month, may be forgiven for unconsciously feeling that the occasion was one which demanded from his son-in-law a semblance of cordial welcome at any rate, if not of glad surprise. It is an extraordinarily difficult thing to learn that we are not looking each of us at the same aspect of life as our neighbour, especially our neighbour of a different time of life from ourselves. We appeal to him as a matter of course, and say, "Look! see how life appears to me to-day! see what existence is like in relation to myself!" But unfortunately the neighbour, who is standing on the outside of that particular circle, and not in its centre, does not see what we mean. Sir William had been shut up for a month in the room that he inhabited on the drawing-room floor of the house in Cosmo Place. He had simply not had mental energy to care about what was happening beyond the four walls of that room. If he had been asked at that moment what the universe was, he would have said that it was a succession of days and nights in which the important things of life were the hours and compositions of his meals, the probable hour of the doctor's visit, and the steps to be made each day towards recovery and the resumption of ordinary habits.

Rachel had of course devoted herself to him. It was she who went up with his breakfast, who read to him during the morning, who tried to remember everything that happened out of doors to tell him on her return; it was she who had done many hundreds of patiences in the days when he was not well enough to play at chess. He was hardly well enough now, but he had set his heart upon the first day when he should come down and play chess with Rendel as a sort of pivot in his miserable existence. And now the moment had come. How should he know that for all practical purposes his son-in-law was a different being from the young man who had come upstairs to see him the day before? For yesterday Rendel had come up and talked to him about indifferent things, not telling him, lest he should be excited, of the evil rumours that were filling the air, and had gone downstairs again himself with a miserably unoccupied day in front of him—a day in which to remember and overcome the fact that, instead of being in the arena of which the echoes reached him, he was doomed to be a spectator from afar, who could take no part in the fray. But so much Sir William had not known. How should we any of us know what the inward counterpart is to the outward manifestation? know that the person who comes into the room may be, although appearing the same, different from the one who went out? He knew only that the Rendel of this morning had said with a smile, "I am looking forward to the moment when you will checkmate me again." And Sir William had a right to expect that, that moment having come, Rendel should feel the importance and pleasure of it as much as he did himself. But it was not the same Rendel who sat there, it was not the unoccupied spectator ready to join his leisure to that of another; it was a resolute combatant who had been suddenly called into a front post, and for whom the whole aspect of the world had changed. It was an absolute physical effort to Rendel, as the door opened and he saw Sir William, to bring his mind back to the conditions of a few hours before. The fact of any one coming in at that moment called him back to earth again, turned him violently about to face the commonplace importunities of existence. Sir William had probably not formulated to himself what he had vaguely expected, but it certainly was not the puzzled, half-questioning look, the indescribable air of being taken aback, altered at once by a quick impulse into something that tried not to look forbidding, and more strange and tell-tale than all the quick movement by which Rendel drew a large sheet of blotting-paper over what he was writing. Sir William's whole being was jarred, his rejoicing in the small occasion of being on another stage towards recovery was gone; nobody cared, not one. Rachel was not in the house, and who else was there to care? Nobody: there never would be again. Could it be possible that for the rest of his life he was doomed to be in a world so arranged that his comings and goings were not the most important of all? He stood still a moment, then tried to speak in his usual voice.

"I am not in your way, am I, Rendel?"

Rendel also made a conscious effort as he replied, rising from his chair as he spoke—

"Oh no, Sir William, please come in. I have some writing to finish, if you don't mind."

"Pray go on," said Sir William; "I won't disturb you. I'll sit down here and read the paper till you are ready"; and he sat down with his back to the writing-table and the window, in the big chair which Rendel drew forward.

"Thank you," Sir William said. "I took the liberty of bringing in your afternoon paper which was outside."

"Certainly," Rendel replied, too absorbed for the moment in the thing his own attention was concentrated upon to realise the bearing of what Gore was saying. "Of course," and went back to his writing.

Gore leant back, idly turning over the pages of the *Mayfair Gazette*; then he started as his eye fell on the alarmist announcements. What was this? What incredible things were these that he saw? The letters were swimming before him; he could only vaguely distinguish the black capitals and the headlines; the rest was a blur. All that stood out clearly was: "Cape to Cairo Railway in Danger," and then beneath it: "Sinister Rumours about the 'Equator, Ltd.'"

"Rendel!" he said, half starting up. Rendel turned round with a start, dragging his mind from the thing it was bent upon. "How awful this is!" said Sir William, holding up the paper with a shaking hand. Rendel began to understand. But, that he should have to look up for one moment, for the fraction of a second, from those words that he was transcribing!

"Yes, yes, it is terrible," he said, and bent over his writing again. Sir William tried to go on reading. What was this about Germany? War would mean the collapse of everything—private schemes as well as all others.

"War! Do you think it can possibly mean war?" he said. "Can't Germany be squared?"

"War!" said Rendel without looking up. "Who can tell?" And again he felt the supreme excitement of standing unseen at the right hand of the man who was driving the ship through the storm. Sir William laid down the paper on his knee and tried to think, but all he could do was to close his eyes and keep perfectly still. Everything was vague ... and the worst of it—or was it the best of it?—was that nothing seemed to matter.

At the same moment a brief colloquy was being exchanged outside the hall door. Stamfordham's brougham had drawn up again, and Thacker, who was standing hanging about the hall with a secret intention of being on the spot if tremendous things were going to happen, had instantly rushed out.

"Is Mr. Rendel in?" said Lord Stamfordham hurriedly as Thacker stood at the door of the brougham.

"Yes, my lord."

"Ask him to come and speak to me."

Thacker was shaken into unwonted excitement; he opened the door of the study quickly and went in. Sir William started violently. Any sudden noise in the present state of his nerves threw him completely off his balance.

"Can you come and speak to Lord Stamfordham, sir?"

Rendel sprang up; then with a sudden thought turned back and pulled down the top of his writing-table, which shut with a spring, and rushed out without seeing that Sir William had begun raising himself laboriously from his chair as he said—

"Don't let me be in your way, Rendel."

"His lordship is not coming in, Sir William," said Thacker.

Sir William sank back into his chair. Thacker, after waiting an instant as though to see whether Gore had any orders for him, went quietly out, closing the door after him.

Rendel had madly caught up a hat as he passed, and flown down the steps, not seeing in his haste a burly personage who was coming along the pavement dressed in the ordinary garb of the English citizen, with nothing about him to show that his glowing right hand held the thunderbolts which he was going to hurl at the head of Gore. It is unnecessary to say that Robert Pateley knew Stamfordham's carriage well by sight; and it was with pleasure and satisfaction that he found that Providence had brought him on to the pavement at Cosmo Place in time to see one of the moves in the great game which the world was playing that day. It was better on the whole that he should not accost Rendel. There was no need at that moment for Stamfordham to be aware of his presence, although, after all, there was no reason why he should not be. But seeing Rendel standing speaking to Stamfordham at the door of the brougham he conceived that he was probably coming in again directly, and made up his mind to go in and see Gore at any rate if possible. He went up the steps, therefore, and into the house, the front door being open. It happened neither Rendel nor Stamfordham saw him enter, the former having his back turned and blocking the view of the latter. Thacker, with intense interest, was watching the development of affairs from the dining-room window, and did not see Pateley go in either.

"Have you done the thing?" said Stamfordham quickly.

"All but," Rendel said.

"Well, I want you to add this," said Stamfordham. "Get in and drive back with me, will you? I have so little time."

Rendel jumped in, and the brougham moved past the window just as Sir William Gore, who had painfully pulled himself out of his chair, looked out, petrified with surprise at the unexplained crisis that seemed to have come upon the household. "Stamfordham!" he said to himself, "and Frank! What are the Imperialists hatching now, I wonder?" and he mechanically looked round him at Rendel's writing-table. It was, however, closed and forbidding, save for a little corner of white paper that was sticking out under the revolving flap. By one of those strange, almost unconscious impulses which may suddenly overtake the best of us at times, Gore put out his hand and pulled out the paper. It was quite loose and came away in his hand. What was it? He looked at it vaguely. Then gradually it became clear. A map?... yes, it was a rough map, with a thick line drawn from the top to the bottom down the middle of it; names to the right and the left. England? Germany? And what were those words written underneath? *What?* Was that how Germany was going to be 'squared?' And sheer excitement gave him strength to grasp more or less the meaning of what he saw. If Africa were going to be divided, if Germany and England were agreeing to that division, it meant Peace. There was no doubt of it. But had the Imperialists suddenly gone on to the side of peace? Had they snatched that trump card from their adversaries and were they going to play it? Sir William stood gazing at the paper. Then as he heard some one at the door of the room he suddenly realised what he had done. He instinctively clutched the paper in the hand which held the *Mayfair Gazette,* the newspaper concealing it. As he turned and looked towards the door an unexpected sight greeted his eyes—no other than Pateley, who, finding himself in the hall unheralded, had made up his mind to come into Rendel's study and there ring the bell for some one who should bring word to Sir William Gore of his presence. But he was surprised to find Sir William downstairs instead of in his room as he had expected. He paused for a moment, shocked at the change in Gore's appearance. He looked thin, listless, bent: his upright figure, his spring, his energy were gone. Pateley's heart smote him for a moment. Would it be possible to call this feeble, suffering creature to account? Then his heart hardened again as he thought of his sisters.

"Pateley!" said Gore, advancing with the remains of his usual manner, but curiously shaken for the moment, as Pateley said to himself, out of his usual self-confidence.

The state of nervousness of the older man was painfully perceptible. Added to his general weakness, which made the mere fact of seeing some one unexpectedly a sudden shock to him, he had besides at that moment an additional and very definite reason for uneasiness in the thing which he held in his hand. He endeavoured, however, to pull himself together as he shook hands with Pateley.

"I have not seen you for a long time," he said, pointing to a chair and sinking back into his own.

"No," Pateley replied. "I was very sorry to hear that you had been ill. You are looking rather bad still."

"And feeling so," Sir William said wearily. "The worst of influenza is that one feels just as bad when one is supposed to be getting better as when one is supposed to be getting worse. It is a most annoying form of complaint."

"So I have understood," said Pateley, "though I have not learnt it by personal experience."

"No, you don't look as though you suffered from weakness," said Sir William, with a faint smile and a consciousness that this was not a person from whom it would be very easy to extract sympathy for his own condition.

Pateley paused. He felt curiously uncomfortable and hesitating, a sensation somewhat novel to him. Sir William leant back in his chair, trying to control the trembling of his hands, of which one held the *Mayfair Gazette*, the smaller paper still concealed underneath it.

"I see," Pateley said, "you are reading the evening paper. Not very good reading, is it? Things look pretty bad."

"They do indeed," said Sir William.

"It looks uncommonly like war with Germany," Pateley said; "prices are tumbling down headlong on the Stock Exchange. I believe there is going to be something very like a panic."

"Is there?" said Gore uneasily; "that's bad."

"Yes, it is very bad," Pateley went on. "I suppose you have heard that there are ugly rumours about the 'Equator.'"

"I saw something," Sir William said, forcing himself to speak. "What is it exactly that they say?"

"Well, the last thing they say," Pateley replied with a harder ring in his voice, "is that it is not a gold mine at all."

"What?" said Sir William, grasping the arms of his chair.

"And that the whole thing, therefore, is going to pieces with every penny invested in it."

"Is it—is it as bad as that?" said the other, tremulously. "No, no, it can't be. Surely it can't be."

"Do you mean to say you don't know?" said Pateley.

"I know nothing," said Sir William. "I have heard nothing about it, up to this moment."

"One can't help wondering," said Pateley, "that a man in your responsible position towards it," the words struck Sir William like a blow, "should not have known, should not have inquired — —"

"I have been ill, you know," Sir William said nervously, "I have not been able to look into or understand anything. I have not been out of the house yet. I could not go to the City or do any business."

"Yes, I see that," said Pateley, "and I am sorry to be obliged to thrust a business discussion upon you now — —"

Sir William looked up at him quickly, anxiously.

"But the fact is, at this moment the business won't wait. If you remember, when the 'Equator' Company was first started, I, like many others, invested in it, having asked your opinion of it first, and having heard from you that you were going to be the Chairman of the Board of Directors."

"I believed in it, you know," Sir William said, with eagerness; "I put a lot of money into it myself."

"I know you did, yes," said Pateley, "but *you* fortunately had a lot to do it with, and also a lot of money to keep out of it. Every one is not so happily situated. I blame myself, I need not say, acutely, as well as others." And as Sir William looked at him sitting there in his relentless strength, he felt that there was small mercy to be expected at his hands.

"I don't know," Sir William said, trying to speak with dignity, "that I was to blame. I believed in it, as others did."

"No doubt," Pateley said. "But I am afraid that will hardly be a satisfactory explanation for the shareholders. The shares at this moment are absolutely worthless."

"But what can I do?" said Sir William. "What would you have me do?"

"It seems to me there is a rather obvious thing to be done," said Pateley. "It is to help to make good the losses of the people who, through you, will be" — and he paused — "ruined."

"Ruined!" Sir William repeated, "No, no — it cannot be as bad as that. It is terrible," he muttered to himself. "It is terrible."

"Yes, it is terrible," said Pateley, "and even something uglier."

"But," Sir William said miserably, "I don't know that I can be blamed for it. Anderson, who is absolutely honest, reported on the thing, and believed in it to the extent of spending all he had in getting the rights to work it."

"That is possible," Pateley said, "but Anderson was not the chairman of the company. You are."

"Worse luck," Sir William said bitterly.

"Yes, worse luck," Pateley said. "Your name up to now has been an honourable one." Sir William started and looked at him again. "I am afraid," Pateley went on, "after this it may have," and he spoke as if weighing his words, "a different reputation."

Sir William cleared his throat and spoke with an effort.

"Pateley," he said, "you won't let *that* happen? You will make it clear...? You have influence in the Press— —"

"I am afraid," Pateley said, "that my influence, such as it is, must on this occasion be exerted the other way. Of course there is a good deal at stake for me here," he went on, in a matter of fact tone which carried more conviction than an outburst of emotion would have done. "I care for my sisters, and I am afraid I can't sit down and see them—swindled, or something very like it."

"Not, swindled!" said Gore angrily.

"Well," Pateley said, "that is really what it looks like to the outsider, and that is what, as a matter of fact, it comes to."

"Heaven knows I would make it right if I could," said Sir William, "but how can I?"

"Well, of course, on occasions of this kind," Pateley said, still in the same everyday manner, as though judicially dealing with a fact which did not specially concern him, "it is sometimes done by the simple process of the person responsible for the losses making them good—making restitution, in fact."

"I have told you," said Sir William, "that I'm afraid that is impossible."

"Ah then, I am sorry," Pateley said, in the tone of one determining, as Sir William dimly felt, on some course of action. "I thought some possible course might have suggested itself to you."

"No, I can suggest nothing," Sir William said, leaning back in his chair, and feeling that neither mind nor body could respond at that moment to anything that called for fresh initiative.

"I thought that you might have other possibilities on the Stock Exchange even," said Pateley, "though I must say I don't see in what direction. There is bound to be a panic the moment war is declared."

There was a pause. Sir William lay back in his chair looking vaguely in front of him. Pateley sat waiting. Then Gore felt a strange flutter at his heart as the full bearing of Pateley's last sentence dawned upon him.

"Supposing," he said, trying to speak steadily, "there were no war?"

"That is hardly worth discussing," said Pateley briefly, as he got up. "War, I am afraid, is practically certain. Then do I understand, Sir William," he continued, "that you can do nothing to help me in this matter? If so, I am sorry. I had hoped I might have spared you some discomfort, but since you can do nothing— —" He broke off and looked quickly out of the window, then said in explanation, "It is only a hansom stopping next door; I thought it might be Rendel coming back. But I was mistaken."

Sir William realised that every instant was precious.

"Pateley," he said, "look here. If you could wait a day or two longer...."

"Do you mean," said Pateley, "that if I were to wait there would be a chance of your being able to do something?"

"I don't know," said Sir William, "I am not sure, but there might be a turn in public affairs; the panic might be over, there might be a chance of peace."

"If that is all," Pateley said quite definitely, "I am afraid that prospect is not enough to build upon. I can't afford to wait on that security."

Sir William got up and spoke quickly with a visible effort.

"Look here, listen... I have a reason for thinking that is the way things may be turning."

"A reason?" said Pateley, turning round upon him.

"Yes," said Sir William.

"What is it?" said Pateley.

Sir William felt his courage failing him in the desperate game he had begun to play. It was no good pausing now. He stood facing Pateley, holding a folded paper in his hand, no longer hidden by the newspaper which had slid from his grasp on to the ground. He looked at the paper in his hand mechanically. Mechanically Pateley's eye followed his. The conviction suddenly came to him that Gore was not speaking at random.

"Sir William," he said, "time presses," and unconsciously they both looked towards the window into the street. At any moment Rendel might draw up again. "If you have any reason for what you are saying, tell me—if not, I must leave you to see what can be done."

"I have a reason," said Sir William, "the strongest, for believing that there will be peace."

Pateley looked at him. "Give me a proof?" he said, with the accent of a man who is wasting no words, no intentions.

Sir William's hand tightened over the paper. "If I gave you a proof," he said, "would you swear not to take any proceedings against the 'Equator' Company?"

"If you gave me a proof, yes—I would swear," said Pateley.

"And you will keep the things out of the papers," Sir William went on hurriedly, "till I have had time to see my way?"

"Yes," said Pateley again.

"And my name shall not appear in the matter?"

"No—no," Pateley said, in spite of himself breathlessly and hurriedly, more excited than he wished to show. Sir William paused and looked towards the window. "All right," said Pateley, "you have time. Quick! What is it?"

"There is going," Sir William said, "I am almost certain, to be an understanding, an agreement between England and Germany about this business in Africa."

"Impossible!" said Pateley.

"Yes," said Sir William, hardly audibly.

"Give me the proof," Pateley said, coming close to him and in his excitement making a movement as though to take the paper out of Gore's hand.

"Wait, wait!" Sir William said. "No, you mustn't do that!" and he staggered and leant back against the chimneypiece. Pateley had no time to waste in sympathy.

"Look here, if you don't give it to me, show me what it is."

"Yes, yes, I will show it you," Sir William said, "only you are not to take it, you are not to touch it."

Pateley signed assent, and Sir William unfolded the map of Africa and held it up with a trembling hand.

"What!" said Pateley, at first hardly grasping what he saw. Then its full significance began to dawn upon him. "Africa—a partition of Africa between Germany and England! Do you mean to say that is it?"

"Yes," Sir William said. "But for Heaven's sake don't touch it, don't take it out of my hand," he said again, nervously conscious that his own strength was ebbing at every moment, and that if the resolute, dominant figure before him had chosen to seize on the paper, nothing could have prevented his doing so.

"Well, at any rate, let me have a good look at it," Pateley said, "the coast is still clear," and as he went to the window to give another look out, he took something out of his breast pocket. "Now then," he said, turning back to Sir William, "hold it up in the light so that I can have a good look at it;" and as Sir William held it in the light of the window, Pateley, as quick as lightning, drew his tiny camera out of his pocket. There was a click, and the map of Africa had been photographed. Pateley unconsciously drew a quick breath of relief as he put the machine back. Sir William, as white as a sheet, dropped his hands in dismay.

"Good Heavens! What have you done? Have you photographed it?"

"Yes," said Pateley, trying to control his own excitement, and recovering his usual tone with an effort. "That's all, thank you. It is much the simplest form of illustration."

"Illustration! What are you going to do with it?" Sir William said, aghast.

"That depends," said Pateley. "I must see how and when I can use it to the best advantage."

"You have sworn," Sir William said tremulously, "that you won't say where you got it from."

"Of course I won't," Pateley said, gradually returning to his usual burly heartiness. "Now, may I ask where *you* got it from?"

"I got it out of there," Sir William said, pointing to the table. "A corner of it was sticking out."

"Might I suggest that you should put it back again?" said Pateley.

"Good Heavens, yes!" said Gore. "I had forgotten." And he nervously folded it up and dropped it through the slit of the table.

"Ha, that's safer," said Pateley, with a short laugh. "You should not lose your head over these things," and he gave a swift look down the street again. "Now I must go. I am going straight to the City, and I'll tell you what I shall do," and his manner became more emphatic as he went on, as though answering some objection. "I'm going to buy up the whole of the 'Equator' shares on the chance of a rise, and perhaps some Cape to Cairo too, and then we'll see. Now, can't I do something for you too? Won't you buy something on the chance of a rise?"

Sir William had sunk into a chair. He shook his head.

"I am too tired to think," he said. "I don't know."

"Well, you leave it to me," Pateley said, "and I'll do something for you—and if things go as we think, by next week you will be in a position to make good the losses of all London two or three times over. I'll let you know what happens, and what I've been able to do."

"Thank you," Sir William said again feebly.

"The news will soon pick you up," said Pateley heartily, as he shook him by the hand. "No, don't get up; I can find my way out. Goodbye." And a moment later he passed the window, striding away towards Knightsbridge.

CHAPTER XIV

Sir William remained lying back in his chair, looking up at the ceiling, too much exhausted by the excitement of the last few minutes to realise entirely what had happened, but with a vague, agonised consciousness that he had done something irrevocable, something that mattered supremely. But to try even to conceive what might be the consequence of it so made his heart throb and his head whirl that all he could do was to put it away from him with as much effort as he had strength to make. It was so that Rachel found him, when she came gaily in a few minutes later from a shopping expedition in Sloane Street, eager to tell him of all her little doings, and of some acquaintances she had met in the street. He looked at her and tried to smile.

"Father—father—dear father!" she said in consternation. "What is it? Are you not so well?"

"Yes, yes," he said nervously, trying to speak in something like his ordinary voice. "I am—tired, that's all."

"You have been up too long," she said anxiously.

"I don't think it's that," he said.

"But where is Frank?" asked Rachel. "I thought, of course, that he was with you. That was why I went out. I had no idea you would be alone."

"Lord Stamfordham came," said Sir William, feeling like one who is forced to approach something that horrifies him, and who dares not look it in the face. "Frank went out with him."

"Lord Stamfordham! Again!" said Rachel amazed.

"Yes," said Sir William, leaning back with his eyes closed, as though unable to expend any of his feeble strength on surprise or wonder, much less on attempts at explanation. And as Rachel looked at him her solicitude overcame every other thought.

"Darling," she said, "do come back to your own room. Let's go upstairs now."

"No, no," said Sir William quickly, feeling, even though he thought of Rendel's return with absolute terror, that it would be better to know the worst at once without waiting in suspense for the blow to fall. "I'll wait till Rendel comes in."

"But he shall go up to you at once," Rachel urged. "Do come up now, dear father."

At that moment, however, the question of whether they should wait or not for Rendel's return was settled for them, for his latchkey was heard turning in the front door. He came into the room with such an air as a winged messenger of victory might wear, unconscious of his surroundings and of the road he traverses as he speeds along. Rachel looked at him, and forbore to utter either the inquiry that sprang to her lips or any appeal for sympathy about her father's condition.

"I've got to finish some writing," Rendel said, bringing back his thoughts with visible effort. And he went quickly to the writing-table, opening it with the key of his watch-chain. Sir William dared not look. He tried to remember what had happened when he so hurriedly put the paper back; he wondered whether it had stuck in the slit, or if it had gone properly through and fallen straight among the others. There was a pause during which he sat up and gripped the arms of his chair, listening as if for life. Nothing had happened apparently. Rendel had drawn up his chair and was writing again busily. Sir William fell back again and closed his eyes as a flood of relief swept over him, Rachel sitting by him quietly, her hand laid gently on his. Rendel went on writing, transcribing from some more rough pencil notes he had brought in in his hand, then, having quickly rung the bell, he proceeded to do the whole thing up in a packet and seal it securely.

"I want this taken to Lord Stamfordham at once," he said, as the servant came into the room. "And, Thacker, I should like you to go with it yourself, please. It's very important, and I want it to be given into his own hand. If he isn't in, please wait."

"Yes, sir," said Thacker, taking the precious packet and departing, with a secret thrill of wondering excitement.

Rendel pulled down the lid of the table, drawing a sort of long breath as he did so, like one who has cleared the big fence immediately in front of him, and is ready for the next. Sir William's breath was coming and going quickly.

"I'm afraid you don't look very fit for chess, Sir William," he said kindly, struck with his father-in-law's look of haggard anxiety and illness.

"No," Sir William said feebly, "not to-day, I'm afraid."

"I'm sorry to see you like this," Rendel said. "Let me help you upstairs. What have you been doing with yourself since I left you? You don't look nearly so well as when you came down."

"I feel a little faint," Sir William said. "It would be better for me to go and rest now, perhaps." And leaning on Rendel's arm, and followed solicitously by Rachel, he went upstairs.

CHAPTER XV

The night passed slowly and restlessly for Sir William Gore, although he slept from sheer exhaustion, and even when he was not sleeping was in a state of semi-coma, without any clear perception of what had happened. But in his dreams he lived through one quarter of an hour of the day before, over and over and over again, always with the same result, always with the same sense of some unexpected, horrible, shameful catastrophe, that was to lead to his utter humiliation. That was the impression that still remained when at last the morning came, and he finally awoke to the life of another day. Over and over again he went over the situation as he lay there, Pateley's words ringing in his ears, his looks present before him. Again he felt the sensation of absolute sickness at his heart that had gripped him at the moment he had realised that the map had been photographed, passing as much out of his own power as though he had given it to a man in the street. Does any one really acknowledge in his inmost soul that he has on a given occasion done "wrong," without an immeasurable qualifying of that word, without a covert resentment at the way other people may label his action? There is but one person in the world who even approximates to knowing the history of any given deed. The very fact of snatching it from its context puts it into the wrong proportion, the fact of contemplating it as though it were something deliberate, separate, complete in itself, apart from all that has led up to it, apart from the complication and pressure of circumstance. Sir William went over and over again in his mind all that had happened the day before, trying to realise under what aspect his actions would appear to others—over and over again, until everything became blurred and he hardly knew under what aspect they appeared to himself. He felt helplessly indignant with Fate, with Chance, that had with such dire results made him the plaything of a passing impulse. Then with the necessity of finding an object for his anger, his thoughts turned first to Rendel, who had primarily put him in the position of gaining the knowledge he had used to such disastrous effect, and then to Pateley, who had taken it from him.

It is unpleasant enough for a child, at a time of life generally familiar with humiliation and chastisement, to see the moment nearing when his guilt will be discovered: but it is horrible for a man who is approaching old age, who is dignified and respected, suddenly to find himself in the position of having something to conceal, of being actually afraid of facing the judgment and incurring the censure of a younger man. And at that moment Gore felt as if he almost hated the man whose hand could hurl such a thunderbolt. Then his thoughts turned to Pateley, to the probable result of his operations in the City. In the other greater anxiety which he himself had suddenly imported into his life, that first care, which yet was important enough, of the "Equator," had almost sunk out of sight. Would the mine turn out to be a gold mine after all? What would Pateley be able to do? Would he be able to make enough to cover his liabilities? and his head swam as he tried to remember what these might amount to.

In the meantime Rendel, in a very different frame of mind from that of his father-in-law, or, indeed, from that of his own of the night before, filled with a buoyant thrill of expectation, with the sense that something was going to happen, that everything might be going to happen, was looking out into life as one who looks from a watch tower waiting on fortune and circumstances, waiting confident and well-equipped without a misgiving. The day was big with fate: a day on which new developments might continue for himself, the thrill of excitement of the night before, the sense of being in the foreground, of being actually hurried along in the front between the two giants who were leading the way. The dining-room was ablaze with sunshine as he came into it, and in the morning light sat Rachel, looking up at him with a smile when he came into the room.

"What an excellent world it is, truly!" said Rendel, as he came across the room.

"I am glad it is to your liking," she answered.

"You look very well this morning," said Rendel, looking at her, "which means very pretty."

"I don't feel so especially pretty," said Rachel, with something between a smile and a sigh.

"Don't you? Don't have any illusions about your appearance," said Rendel. "Don't suppose yourself to be plain, please."

"I am not so sure," said Rachel, as she began pouring out the tea.

"What is the matter with you?" said Rendel. "What fault do you find with the world, and your appearance?"

"I am perturbed about my father," she said, her voice telling of the very real anxiety that lay behind the words. "I don't think he is as well as he was yesterday."

"Don't you?" said Rendel, more gravely. "I am very sorry. What is the matter?"

"I can't think," Rachel answered. "He may have done too much yesterday afternoon."

"He certainly looked terribly tired," said Rendel.

"Terribly," said Rachel, "but I can't imagine why. He had been so absolutely quiet all the afternoon."

"Well, you take care of him to-day," said Rendel, unable to eliminate the cheerful confidence from his voice.

"I shall indeed," said Rachel.

"Oh, he'll come all right again, never fear," said Rendel. "You mustn't take too gloomy a view."

"You certainly seem inclined to take a cheerful one this morning," said Rachel, half convinced in spite of herself that all was well.

"Well, I do," said Rendel. "I must say that in spite of the prevalent opinion to the contrary, I feel inclined this morning to say that the scheme of the universe is entirely right; it is just to my liking. The sunshine, and my breakfast, and my wife——"

"I am glad I am included," she said.

"And the day to live through. What can a man wish for more?"

"It sounds as though you had everything you could possibly want, certainly," said Rachel, smiling at him.

"I don't know," said Rendel, reflecting, "if it is that quite. The real happiness is to want everything you can possibly get. That is the best thing of all."

"And not so difficult, I should think," said Rachel.

"I am not sure," said Rendel. "I am not sure that it is quite an easy thing to have an ardent hold on life. Some people keep letting it down with a flop. But I feel as if I could hold it tight this morning at any rate. I do not believe there is a creature in the wide world that I would change places with at this moment," he went on, the force of his ardent hope and purpose breaking down his usual reserve.

"You are very enthusiastic to-day, Frank," she said.

"Well, one can't do much without enthusiasm," said Rendel, continuing his breakfast with a satisfied air, "but with it one can move the world."

"Is that what you are going to do?" said Rachel.

"Yes," said Rendel nodding.

"Frank, I wonder if you will be a great man?"

"Can you doubt it?" said Rendel.

"Supposing," she said, "some day you were a sort of Lord Stamfordham."

"That is rather a far cry," he replied. "By the way, I wonder where the papers are this morning? Why are they so late?"

"They will come directly," Rachel said. "It is a very good thing they're late, you can eat your breakfast in peace for once without knowing what has happened."

"That is not the proper spirit," said Rendel smiling, "for the wife of a future great man."

"The only thing is," said Rachel, "that if you did become a great man, I don't think I should be the sort of wife for you. I am very stupid about politics, don't you think so? I don't understand things properly."

"I think you are exactly the sort of wife I want," said Rendel, "and that is enough for me. That is the only thing necessary for you to understand. I don't believe you do understand it really."

"Then are you quite sure," she said, half laughing and half in earnest, "that you don't like politics better than you do me?"

"Absolutely certain," said Rendel, with a slight change of tone that told his passionate conviction. "I wish you could grasp that in comparison with you, nothing matters to me."

"Nothing?" she repeated.

"There is nothing," said Rendel, looking at her, "that I would not sacrifice to you—my career, my ambitions, anything you asked for."

"I am glad," she said, "that you like me so much, but I don't want you to make sacrifices," and she spoke in all unconsciousness of the number of small sacrifices, of an unheroic aspect perhaps, that Rendel was daily called upon to make for her sake.

At this moment Thacker came in with the morning papers, which he laid on the table at Rendel's elbow.

"Now then you are happy," said Rachel lightly. "Now you can bury yourself in the papers and not listen to anything I say."

"I wonder if there is anything about Stoke Newton and old Crawley's resignation," said Rendel, quite prepared to follow her advice. "I don't suppose he takes a very jovial view of life just now, poor old boy. Oh, how I should hate to be on the shelf!"

"I don't think you are likely to be, for the present," said Rachel.

And then Rendel, pushing his chair a little away from the table, opened the papers wide, and began scanning them one after another, with the mild and pleasurable excitement of the man who feels confidently abreast of circumstances. Then, as he took up the *Arbiter*, his eye suddenly fell upon a heading that took his breath away. What was this? He dropped the paper with a cry.

"What is it, Frank?" said Rachel startled.

"Good Heavens! what have they done that for?" he said, springing to his feet in uncontrollable excitement.

"Done what?" said Rachel.

"Why, they have announced—they have put in something that Lord Stamfordham——" He snatched up the paper again and looked at it eagerly. "It is incredible! and the map too, the very map, at this stage! Well, upon my word, he has made a mistake this time, I do believe." And he still gazed at the paper as though trying to fathom the whole hearing of what he saw.

At this moment the door opened, and Thacker came in.

"Sir William wished me to ask you for some foolscap paper, ma'am, please," he said, "with lines on it."

"Foolscap paper? What is he doing?" said Rachel anxiously.

"He is writing, ma'am," said Thacker. "He seems to be doing accounts."

"Oh, I wish he wouldn't!" Rachel said. "I must go and see. I'll bring the foolscap paper myself, Thacker. Frank, there is some in your study, isn't there?"

"What?" said Rendel, who, still absorbed in what he had just seen, had only dimly heard their colloquy.

"Some foolscap paper," she repeated. "There is some in your study?"

"Yes, yes, in my writing-table," he said absently.

Rachel went quickly out of the room. At that moment the hall door bell rang violently. Rendel started and went to the window. In the phase of acute tension in which he found himself, every unexpected sound carried an untold significance, but he was not prepared for what this one betokened: Lord Stamfordham in the street, dismounting from his horse. Stamfordham was accustomed to ride every morning from eight till nine, alone and unattended. Thacker hurried out to hold the horse. Rendel followed him and met Stamfordham on the doorstep. He led the way quickly across the hall into his study and shut the door. They both felt instinctively that greetings were superfluous.

"Have you seen the *Arbiter*?" Stamfordham said.

"Yes," said Rendel, looking him straight in the face with eager expectation.

"So have I," said Stamfordham, "at the German Embassy. I had not seen it before leaving home, but I saw a poster at the corner, and I went straight to Bergowitz to ask him what it meant; he is as much in the dark as I am."

"In the dark!" said Rendel, looking at him amazed. "What! but—was it not you who published it?"

"*I* publish it?" said Stamfordham. "Do you mean to say you thought I had?"

"Of course I did! who else?" said Rendel.

"Who else?" Stamfordham repeated. "I have come here to ask you that."

"To ask *me*?" said Rendel, bewildered. "How should I know? I have not seen those papers since I gave the packet sealed to Thacker to take it to you."

"And I received it," said Stamfordham, "sealed and untampered with, and opened it myself, and it has not been out of my keeping since."

"But at the German Embassy," said Rendel, "since it was telegraphed...?"

"The substance of the interview was telegraphed," said Stamfordham, "but not the map—*not the map*," he said emphatically. "That map no one has seen besides Bergowitz, you, and myself. Bergowitz it would be quite absurd to suspect, he is as genuinely taken back as I am—I know that it didn't get out through me, and therefore——" he paused and looked Rendel in the face.

"What!" said Rendel, with a sort of cry. A horrible light, an incredible interpretation was beginning to dawn upon him. "You can't think it was through *me*?"

"What else can I think?" said Stamfordham—Rendel still looked at him aghast—"since the papers after I gave them into your keeping were apparently not out of it until they passed into mine again? I brought them to you here myself. Of course I see now I ought not to have done so, but how could I have imagined— —"

Rendel hurriedly interrupted him.

"Lord Stamfordham, not a soul but myself can have had access to those papers. I went out of the room, it is true," and he went rapidly over in his mind the sequence of events the day before, "for a short half-hour perhaps, when you came back here and I went out with you, but before leaving the room I remember distinctly that I shut the cover of my writing-table down with the spring, and tried it to see that it was shut, and then unlocked it myself when I came back."

"Was any one else in the room?" said Stamfordham.

"Yes," said Rendel, and a sudden idea occurred to him, to be dismissed as soon as entertained, "Sir William Gore."

"Gore?" said Stamfordham, looking at Rendel, but forbearing any comment on his father-in-law.

"It was quite impossible," Rendel said decidedly, answering Stamfordham's unspoken words, "that he could have got at the papers; for, as I told you, when I came back again they were exactly where I had left them, and the thing locked with this very complicated key, and he showed it hanging on his chain."

"It is evident," Stamfordham repeated inflexibly, "that some one must have got hold of it with or without your knowledge. I warned you yesterday, you remember, about taking your—any one in your household into your confidence."

"And I did not," Rendel said, grasping his meaning. "My wife did not even know that I had the papers to transcribe. She does not know it now."

Stamfordham paused a moment. He could not in words accuse Rendel's wife, whatever his silence might imply. Then he spoke with emphatic sternness.

"Rendel," he said, "by whatever means the thing happened, we must know how. I must have an explanation."

Rendel was powerless to speak.

"For you must see," Stamfordham went on, "what a terrible catastrophe this might have been—the danger is not over yet, in fact, although I may be strong enough for my colleagues to condone the fact that the public has been told of this before themselves, and the country may be strong enough for foreign Powers to do the same. But, as a personal matter, I must know how it got out, and I repeat, I must have an explanation. For your own sake you must explain."

Rendel felt as if the ground were reeling under his feet.

"I will try," he said, still feeling as if he were in some wild dream.

"When you have made inquiries," Stamfordham said, still speaking in a brief tone of command, "you had better come and tell me the result. I shall be at the Foreign Office till twelve."

"Till twelve. Very well," said Rendel, feeling as if there was a dark chasm between himself and that moment. Mechanically he let Lord Stamfordham out, and stood as the latter mounted and rode away. Then he turned back into the house.

CHAPTER XVI

He went into the dining-room first—Rachel was still upstairs—and picked up the *Arbiter* again, looking at it with this new, terrible interpretation of what he saw in it. There it was, as damning evidence as ever a man was convicted upon, the map that no one but himself and the two principals had seen, reproduced, roughly it is true, but still unmistakably, from the paper that he alone in the house had had in his possession. He turned hurriedly to the brief but guarded commentary evolved at a venture by Pateley, but nevertheless very near the truth. Pateley had played a bold game indeed, but he was playing it as skilfully and watchfully as was his wont. Rendel threw down the paper with a gesture of despair, then clenched his hands. If he had been a woman he would have wept from sheer misery and agitation. But it was of no good to clench his hands in despair; every moment that passed ought to be used to find out the truth of what had happened, to clear himself from that nightmare of suspicion.

He went hurriedly across the hall to his study with the instinct of one who feels that on the spot itself there may be some suggestion to help discovery. His writing-table was locked. He tried it, shook it. The key, one of a peculiar make, hung always on his watch-chain. It was quite impossible that, save by one who had the key, the table should have been opened. What had he done yesterday? What had happened? And he sat down and buried his face in his hands, concentrating his thoughts, trying to recall every incident. The first time that Stamfordham had come in and given him the rough notes and the map, he, Rendel, had been alone. There was no doubt of that. After that who came in? Rachel? No, Rachel had not been in the room with the papers except just at the end when Rendel was sealing up the packet. Besides, if Rachel had had a hundred secrets in her possession, they would have been as safe as in his own. Then he caught himself up—in his own! after all, he was suspected—so the impossible idea, apparently, could be entertained. Then the thought of Sir William Gore came into his mind, but only to be instantly dismissed, for since the papers were locked up in Rendel's writing-table they must have been as inaccessible to Sir William as though they had been separated from him by the walls of several apartments. And there was one thing pretty certain: Gore, supposing him to be capable of using it, had not got a duplicate key. "Even he," Rendel found himself thinking, "would not do that." He heard Rachel's step swiftly descend the stairs and go into the dining-room, then she came quickly across the hall to the study.

"Oh, there you are, Frank," she said. "My father is— —" then she broke off as she saw that he was apparently buried in painful thought from which he roused himself with a start as she spoke. "Is anything the matter?"

"I will tell you," said Rendel, speaking with an effort.

"May I just ask you something first?" said Rachel hurriedly. "I want some foolscap paper for my father. He is so restless this morning, so impatient."

"It is in there—I told you, didn't I?" said Rendel, turning round and pointing to one of the drawers at the side of his table.

"In that drawer!" said Rachel. "How very stupid of me! I didn't think of that. I thought it was in the top part, and I could only get one sheet out of there."

"The top? Wasn't the top locked?" said Rendel quickly, his whole thought concentrated on the problem before him, and the part of the table must have played in the drama that affected him so nearly.

"Yes, it was," said Rachel smiling, "and I couldn't open it, but there was a little tiny corner of ruled paper sticking out, so I pulled it, and out it came."

Rendel started and looked at her.

"It is sweetly simple," she added.

"Yes," said Rendel, with an energy that surprised her. "It would come out quite easily, of course."

"Frank," she said, surprised, "what is it? You didn't mind my pulling it out, did you?"

"Of course not; I don't mind your doing anything—only—I didn't realise that things could be got out of my writing-table in that way."

"Well, you must be sure to poke them in further next time," Rachel said lightly, shutting again the side drawer to which she had been directed, and out of which she had got some sheets of foolscap. "I will be back directly."

"Wait one moment," said Rendel. "Lord Stamfordham has been here."

"Lord Stamfordham! Since I went upstairs?" said Rachel, standing still in sheer surprise.

"Yes," said Rendel. "Some secret information that—I knew about, has got into the paper and is published this morning."

"Oh, Frank, how terrible!" said Rachel. "How did it happen? Do they mind?"

"Yes, they mind," Rendel said.

"Was that what you saw in the paper," Rachel said, "that excited you so much?"

"Yes," said Rendel.

"I don't wonder," Rachel said, standing with her hand on the handle of the door, an attitude of all others least inviting of confidence. "Who let it out?"

"That is what we want to know," said Rendel. "That is what Lord Stamfordham came here to ask."

"Well, he doesn't think it was you, I suppose," said Rachel, smiling at the absurd suggestion.

"It is quite possible," Rendel said, with a dim idea that he would lead up to the statement, "that he might—that he does."

"What!" said Rachel, opening her eyes wide. "Frank! how absurd!"

"So it seems to me," said Rendel sombrely.

"Too ridiculous!—I'll come down in one moment," Rachel said apologetically. "I don't want to keep my father waiting."

"Don't say anything to him," said Rendel, "of what I have just been saying to you."

"Oh, no, I won't indeed," Rachel said. "He ought not to have anything to excite him to-day," and she went rapidly upstairs.

Rendel, as the door closed behind her, felt for the moment like a man who, shipwrecked alone, has seen a vessel draw near to him and then pass gaily on its way without bringing him help. What was to be done? Again he took hold of the situation and looked it in the face. But now a new light had been thrown upon it by Rachel. If a paper could be taken out in the way that she had shown him, it was possible that Gore might have obtained the map in the same way, though it still seemed to Rendel exceedingly unlikely that, granted he had done so, he would have been able, given the condition he was in, to act upon it soon enough for it to appear this morning. He hesitated a moment, then he made up his mind to wait no longer. He took up the *Arbiter* and went upstairs to Sir William's room. He met Rachel coming out.

"Oh, thank you," she said, as she saw the paper. "I was just coming down to fetch that. Father would like to see it."

"I thought I would bring it up," Rendel said. "I want to speak to him a moment."

Rachel looked alarmed.

"Frank, you will be careful, won't you?" she said. "He really is not in a fit state to discuss anything this morning."

"I am afraid what I have to say won't wait," Rendel said. "I think I had better speak to him alone." And he quite unmistakably waited for Rachel to go her way before he went into Sir William's room and shut the door. Sir William, wrapped in his dressing-gown, was sitting up in an easy chair. On the table near him were sheets of foolscap paper covered with figures, and lying beside them a letter with a bold, splotchy writing, which he quickly moved out of sight as Rendel came in, a letter that had told him of certain successful financial operations undertaken in the City on his behalf. His face was pale and haggard. He looked up, as he saw Rendel come into the room, with an expression almost of terror, dashed however with resentment. In his mind at that moment, his son-in-law was the embodiment of the fate that, in some incredible way, had, as it were, turned him, Sir William Gore, who had hitherto spent his life in the sunshine of position, of dignity, of the deserved respect of his fellow-creatures, out into a chill storm of circumstances, absolutely alone, into some terrible world where, instead of walking upright among his fellow-men, he was, by no fault of his own, he kept repeating to himself, hurrying along with a burden on his back, crouching, fearing observation, fearing detection. That burden was almost intolerable. He had been trying to distract his thoughts and seek some cold comfort by making calculations based upon the letter he had received from Pateley, but all the time, behind it lay ice-cold and immovable the thought of the price at which Pateley's co-operation had been bought, of the moment of reckoning with Rendel that must come when the sands should have run out their appointed time. So much had he suffered, so much had he been dominated by this thought, that when the door opened and Rendel finally came in, the moment brought a sort of relief. Rendel, on the other hand, when he saw Sir William looking so old, so white and feeble, suddenly felt his purpose arrested. It was impossible, surely, that this old man, with the worn, handsome face and pathetically anxious expression, could have had a hand in a diabolical machination, and the thought that it was unlikely came to him with a gleam of comfort. Then as quick as lightning came a reaction of wonderment as to what hypothesis was to take the place of this one. At any rate, there was only one thing to be done: to tell Gore the story without a moment's further delay.

"Good morning, Sir William," he said. "I am sorry to hear you are not well this morning."

"Not very," Gore said, trying to speak calmly, and involuntarily looking at the newspaper in Rendel's hand.

"I hear you were asking for the *Arbiter*," Rendel said.

"Yes, I should like to see it," Gore replied, "when you have done with it."

"I want you to see it," Rendel said. "There is something in it which matters a great deal." Gore felt a sudden grip at his heart. He said nothing. "Here it is," said Rendel, and he handed him the paper, folded so as to show the startling headings in big letters and the rough facsimile of the map. Gore looked at it. The whole thing swam before his eyes; he held it for a moment, trying desperately to think what he had better say, but he could find no anchorage anywhere.

"That is very surprising," he said finally. "As far as I can see, it's—it's a partition of Africa between England and Germany? Is that it? I can't see very well this morning."

"That is it," said Rendel.

"Yes, that is very important," Gore said, leaning back and letting the paper slide from his grasp. "Most important," and he was silent again, waiting in an agony of suspense for what Rendel's next words would be. Rendel, scarcely less agitated, was trying to choose them carefully.

"I am very sorry," he began, "to have to tire and worry you about this when you are not well, but I have a particular reason for talking to you about it."

"Pray go on," Gore managed to say under his breath.

"I have a special reason," said Rendel, "for wanting to remember what happened in my study yesterday afternoon."

"Yesterday afternoon?" said Gore. "Did anything particular happen?"

"That is what I want to know," said Rendel, trying to speak calmly and quietly. "You will oblige me very much if you will try to remember exactly what happened all the time, from the moment you came into the room until you left it."

Gore made an effort to pull himself together. There was no difficulty, alas! for him in remembering every single thing that had taken place—the difficulty was not to show that he remembered too well.

"When I came in," he said, endeavouring to speak in an ordinary tone, "you were at your writing-table."

"I was," said Rendel, watching him.

"And then I sat down in an armchair and read the *Mayfair Gazette*——" and he stopped.

"Yes. All that," Rendel said, "I remember, of course. Thacker came in telling me Lord Stamfordham was there, and I rushed out, shutting the roller top of my writing-table, which closes with a spring. I was especially careful to shut it, as it had valuable papers in it."

"Indeed?" said Sir William, almost inaudibly.

"Yes, and among them," Rendel said, watching the effect of his words, "a map—that map of Africa which is reproduced this morning in the *Arbiter*."

"In your writing-table?" Gore said, with quivering lips.

"Yes, in my writing-table, out of which it must have been taken."

"That is very serious," Gore forced himself to say.

"It is very serious," said Rendel, "as you will see. When I came back and had finished my work on the papers I did them up myself in a packet and sent them to Lord Stamfordham."

"Your messenger was not trustworthy, apparently," said Gore, recovering himself.

"My messenger was Thacker," Rendel said, "who is absolutely trustworthy. Lord Stamfordham himself told me that he had received the packet with my seal intact."

"Still," said Gore, "servants have been known to sell State secrets before now."

"But not Thacker," said Rendel. "However, of course I shall ask him; I must ask every one in the house, for it must have been by some one here that the thing was done, that the map was got out."

"I thought you said the table was locked?"

"It was locked, yes," said Rendel, "but I have learnt this morning that papers can be pulled out from under the lid. Rachel got a piece of foolscap paper for you in that way."

"Did she?" said Gore, feeling that he had unwittingly supplied one link in the chain of evidence.

"There was only one person, so far as I know," said Rendel, "in the room while that paper was in my desk, who could have pulled it out and looked at it, and apparently made an unwarrantable use of it." The question that he expected to hear from Gore did not follow. Rendel waited, then he went on, "That person was—you."

"What do you mean?" said Gore, sitting up, his colour going and coming quickly.

"My words, I think, are quite plain," Rendel said. "I mean that all the evidence, circumstantial, I grant, points—you must forgive me if I am wronging you—to your having taken out the map."

"Will you please give me your reasons for this extraordinary accusation?" said Gore.

"Yes," said Rendel, "I will." And he spoke more and more rapidly as, his self-control at length utterly broken down, and his emotion having gained entire possession of him, he felt the fierce joy of those who, habitually watchful of their words, yield once or twice in their lives to the impulse of letting them flow out unchecked in an overwhelming flood. "You alone were in the room with the papers; your prepossessions are all against us; you spoke yourself just now of the value of a State secret sold in the proper quarter; things are looking ugly about the 'Equator.'"

"Do you mean to hint— —" said Gore.

Rendel interrupted him quickly. "No, not to hint," he said; "hinting is not in my line. I dare to say it out. I dare to say that in one of those moments of aberration, of deviation, whatever you choose to call it, that sometimes descend upon the most unlikely people, you pulled that paper out, from idle curiosity, I daresay, and finding out what it was you sent it to the *Arbiter*."

"You did well," said Gore bitterly, "to keep your wife out of the room while you were accusing me. I am old and defenceless," he said, with lips trembling, and again an immense self-pity rushing over him. "I can't answer; I can't reply to a young man's violence."

"I have no intention," Rendel said, still speaking with a passion which intoxicated him, "of being violent, but I must go on with this, for Lord Stamfordham won't rest until it is sifted to the bottom, and he is not a man to be trifled with. And as to your being defenceless, good God! your best defence is Rachel's trust in you and devotion to you. It is because of it that I wanted to spare her the knowledge of what we have been saying. Her faith in your infallibility has always seemed to me so touching that for her sake I have respected it. I have tried—Heaven knows I have tried!—all this time to be to you what she wished me to be." Gore stirred; he was quite incapable of speaking. "This is not the moment," Rendel went on, almost unconscious of his words, which poured out in a flood, "to keep up a hollow mockery of trust and friendship, and it is more honest to tell you fairly that I have not entirely shared her faith in you. I have always thought that, like the rest of us after all, you were neither better nor worse than most other fallible people in this world, and that you may be, as I daresay we all are, fashioned by circumstances, or even by temptation. And I tell you frankly that I believe that you did this thing that I accuse you of. How, I demand to know. That, at any rate, is not more than one man may ask of another."

Sir William winced and writhed helplessly under Rendel's words. The intolerable discomfort and misery that he felt as the moment of discovery drew near had given place gradually to a furious resentment at what he was being made to endure at the hands of one who ought not to have presumed to criticise him. As Rendel stood there, his clearly cut face hard and stern, pouring out accusations and reproach, Gore felt as if the younger man embodied all the adverse influences of his own life. It was through Rendel that the fatal opportunity had come of his getting himself into this terrible strait, Rendel: who, most unjustly in the scheme of things, was daring to tax Gore with it. It was too horrible to bear longer. He too felt that the time had come when that with which his heart and soul were overflowing must find vent in speech. As he heard Rendel's words of stern impeachment ringing in his ears, "I tell you frankly that I believe that you did this thing," he rose desperately to his feet.

"Well," he said, casting with a kind of horrible relief all restraints and prudence to the winds, "what if I had?"

Rendel turned pale.

"If you had?" he said. "You did it, then?"

"If I had," Gore went on quickly, "it wouldn't have been a crime. You can't know how easy it was for the thing to happen. I am not going to tell you—I am not going to justify myself——" And he went on with a passionate need of self-vindication, drawing from his own words the conviction that he had hardly been at fault.

"Sir William," Rendel said hurriedly, "tell me——"

"It is easy enough," said Gore, "for you to talk of faith and trust. You need not grudge my child's faith in me. I have nothing else left now." And as the two men looked at each other each in his soul had a vision of the gracious presence that had always been by Sir William's side: of one who would have believed in him, justified him, if the whole world had accused him. Rendel suddenly paused as he was going to speak.

"Life is very easy for you," Gore went on in a rapid, trembling voice. Oh, the relief of saying it all!

"It is all quite plain sailing for you, you with whom everything succeeds, you who are young and have your life before you. You have time for the things that happen to you to be made right."

"Don't let us discuss all that now," said Rendel, with an effort. "We are talking of something else that matters more than I can say. You only can tell me——"

"I will tell you nothing," said Gore loudly, excited and breathless, speaking in gasps. "One day when you are old and alone—and both of these things may come to you as well as to other people—you will understand what all this means to me."

"Father, dear father!" cried Rachel, coming in hurriedly. Anxious and wretched at Rendel's interview with her father being so unduly prolonged, she had wandered upstairs again, and when she heard the excited and angry voices she could bear the suspense no longer. "What is it?"

Gore sank back trembling into his chair as she came in, making signs to her that for the moment he was unable to speak. A glance at him was enough to show that it actually was so.

"Oh, Frank!" she cried, "what have you done? I asked you not to excite him."

"Wait, Rachel, wait!" said Rendel, trying to speak calmly, feeling that everything was at stake. "Sir William, can you not tell me——?"

Gore feebly shook his head.

"Frank!" cried Rachel, amazed at his persistence. "Oh, don't! Let me implore you not to ask him anything more. Frank! do you mind leaving him now? Oh, you must, you must, really. Look at him!"

Sir William, white and exhausted, was leaning back in his chair with his eyes closed. Rendel looked at her face of quivering anxiety as it bent over her father, then turned slowly and left the room.

CHAPTER XVII

Rendel came downstairs, hardly conscious of what he was doing, a wild conflict of emotion raging in his mind. He shut himself into his study, and tried to distinguish clearly the threads of motive and conduct that had become so hideously entangled. It sounds a simple thing, doubtless, as well as a praiseworthy one, to discover the doer of an evil deed, to convict him, to bring home to him what he has done, and to prove the innocence of any other who may be suspected. Such a course, when spoken of in general terms, gives a praiseworthy and sustaining sense of a duty accomplished towards society. But it is in reality a much more complicated operation than we are apt to think. The evildoer, unfortunately for our sense of righteousness in prosecuting him, is not always one who has unmixed evil instincts, and nearly every contingency of human conduct becomes, as we contemplate it, many-sided enough to be very confusing. And it was beginning to dawn upon Rendel that, although it may fulfil the ends of abstract justice that the guilty should be exposed and the innocent acquitted, such an act takes an ugly aspect when the eager pursuer is himself the innocent man who is to be vindicated, and the guilty one a weaker and defenceless person who is to be put in his place. "And yet," he said to himself bitterly, as he tried to think of it impartially, "if it were a question of any one else's reputation and not of my own I should be bound to say who the guilty man was." What was he to do? What could he do? He did not know how long he had been sitting there when Rachel came quickly in.

"Oh! Frank," she said, with a face of alarm, "he's very ill. I'm sure he is. I've sent for Dr. Morgan to come at once. He fainted after you left, and he's only just come round again. Oh! I am terribly anxious," and she looked at him, her lips quivering, then put her hands before her eyes and burst into tears.

Rendel's heart smote him. Everything else, as he looked at her, faded into the background. The thing that mattered was Rachel was the woman he loved. It was he who had brought this grief upon her.

"Darling," he said, "I'm so sorry."

She shook her head and tried to smile.

"Oh," she said, trying to suppress her tears, "I ought not to have left him. I daresay you didn't know, but it has done him the most terrible harm. Did you tell him, then, about—about—the thing you told me of, that you had been suspected—of telling something—what was it?" and she passed her hand over her forehead as if unable to think.

"No," said Rendel, "I didn't tell him that *I* had been accused of it. I daresay he guessed I had. I told him it had happened."

"But, Frank, why did you?" she said. "I implored you not."

"Rachel," he said, "do you realise what it means to me that I should be accused of a thing like this?"

"Of course, yes, of course," she said, evidently still listening for any sound from upstairs. "But still a thing like that, that can be put right in a few minutes, cannot matter so much as life and death...."

And again her voice became almost inaudible.

"There are some things," said Rendel in a low voice, "that matter more to a man than life and death."

"Do you mean to say," said Rachel, "that it matters more that you should be supposed to have done something that you have not done, than that my father should not get well?"

"Supposing your father had been wrongfully accused of something underhand and dishonourable," said Rendel, "would not that matter more to him than—than—anything else?"

Rachel put up her hands with a cry as if to ward off a blow.

"My father!" she said, drawing away from Rendel. "You must not say such a thing. How could it be said?"

"You endure," said Rendel, "that it should be said about me."

"About you! That is different," she said, unable in the tension of her overwrought nerves to choose her words. "You are young, you can defend yourself; but it is cruel, cruel of you to say that it might happen to my father. You don't realise what my father is to me or you couldn't say such things even without meaning them. No, you can't know, you can't understand, or you couldn't, just for your own sake, have gone to him to-day when he is so ill and told him things that excited him."

"I think I do understand," Rendel said, forcing himself to speak calmly. "Of course I know, I have always known, perhaps not quite so clearly as to-day, that—that—he must come first with you."

"Oh! in some ways he must, he must," Rachel said, half entreatingly, yet with a ring of determination in her voice. "I promised my mother that I would, as far as I could, take her place, and while he lives I must. Frank, I would give up my life to save him suffering, as she would have done. Ah! there is Doctor Morgan," and she left the room hastily as a doctor's brougham stopped at the door.

Rendel stood perfectly still, looking straight before him, seeing nothing, but gazing with his mind's eye on a universe absolutely transformed—the bright, dancing lights had gone, it was overspread by a dark, settled gloom. There were sounds outside. He was mechanically conscious of Rachel's hurried colloquy with the doctor in the hall, of their footsteps going upstairs. Then he roused himself. What would the doctor's verdict be? But he could not remain now, he must hear it on his return from the Foreign Office, he must now go as agreed to Lord Stamfordham. But first, for form's sake, he rang for Thacker and questioned him, and through him the rest of the household, without result, except renewed and somewhat offended assurances from Thacker that the packet had been given by himself into Stamfordham's own hands and that, to his knowledge, no one but Sir William Gore had been in the study during Rendel's absence. But Rendel knew in his heart that there was no need to question any one further, and no advantage in doing so, since he knew also that he could not use his knowledge.

He drove rapidly along in a hansom, unconscious of the streets he passed through. Wherever he went he saw only Rachel's face of misery, heard the words, "just for your own sake," that had cut into him as deeply as his own into Gore. Was that it? he asked himself, was it just for his own sake, to clear himself, that he had accused Gore? Well, why else? Once Stamfordham knew that the thing had been done, the secret revealed, the name of the actual culprit would make no real difference. It would make things neither easier nor more difficult for Stamfordham to know that it had been done, not by himself, but by Sir William Gore. But there was one person besides himself and Gore for whom everything hung in the balance, and it was still with Rachel's face before him and her words in his ears, that he went into Lord Stamfordham's private room.

Lord Stamfordham had been writing with a secretary, who got up and went out as Rendel came in. How familiar the room was to Rendel! how incredible it was that day after day he should have come there—was it in some former state of existence?—valued, welcome.

"Well, what have you to tell me?" Stamfordham said quickly.

Rendel's lips felt dry and parched; he spoke with an effort.

"I am afraid," he said in a voice that sounded to him strangely unlike his own, "that I have ... nothing."

"What?" said Stamfordham. "Have you not made any inquiries? Haven't you asked every one in your house?"

"I have made inquiries, yes," said Rendel.

"And do you mean to say that there is nothing that can throw any light upon it, no possible solution?"

"I can throw no light," said Rendel.

"But...." said Stamfordham. "Is this all you are going to say? Have you thought of no possibility? Have you no suggestion to offer?"

"I am afraid," said Rendel again, "that I can offer none."

Lord Stamfordham sat silent for a moment, absolutely bewildered. Part of his exceptional administrative ability was the almost unerring judgment he displayed in choosing those he employed about him, and it was an entirely new experience to him to have to suspect one of them, or to impugn the ordinary code of honourable conduct. He found it extremely difficult, autocrat as he was, to put it into words. He was sore and angry at the grave indiscretion, if not something worse, that had been committed, most of all that it should have been himself, the great officer of state, in whom it was unpardonable to choose the wrong tool, who had put that immeasurably important secret into the hands of a man who had somehow or other let it escape from them; so much could not be denied. It certainly seemed difficult to conceive that it should be Rendel himself who had betrayed it, or that if he had betrayed it he would not admit the fact. And yet—could it be?—there was something in Rendel's demeanour now that made it more possible than it had been an hour ago to credit him with the shameful possibility. The pause during which all this had rushed through Stamfordham's mind seemed to Rendel to have lasted through untold ages of time, when Stamfordham at last spoke again.

"Rendel," he said, "I have a right to demand that you should give me more satisfaction than this. You say you have learnt nothing, and can tell me nothing, but this I find impossible to believe." Rendel made a movement. "I am sorry, but I say this advisedly, since this disclosure *must* have taken place in your house," and he underlined the words emphatically. "I can't think it possible that a man of your intelligence should not have found some clue, some possible suggestion."

"I am very sorry," said Rendel. "I'm afraid I have not."

"Then, of course, it is obvious what conclusion I must come to," said Lord Stamfordham. "That it is not that you cannot give any explanation, but that you decline to give it."

Rendel, to his intense mortification, felt that he was changing colour. Stamfordham, looking at him earnestly, felt absolutely certain that he knew.

"Rendel," he said, gravely, "take my advice before it is too late. Don't let a wish to screen some one else prevent you from speaking. If you have had the misfortune to—let the secret escape you, don't, to shelter the person who published it, withhold the truth now. But I must remind you also," and his words fell like strokes from a hammer, "that I am asking it for my own sake as well as yours. When I brought you those papers, I trusted you fully and unreservedly, and now that this catastrophe has happened in consequence of my confidence in you I am entitled to know what has happened."

"Yes," Rendel said. "I quite see your position, and I know that you have a right to resent mine, but all I can say is that—" he stopped, then went on again with firmer accents, "I don't suppose I can expect you to believe me, but as a matter of fact I can't begin to conceive the possibility of knowingly handing on to some one else such a secret as that."

"Knowingly," said Stamfordham, "perhaps not," and he waited, to give Rendel one more chance of speaking. But Rendel was silent. Then Stamfordham went on in a different tone and with a perceptibly harsher note in his voice. "My time is so precious that I am afraid if you have nothing further to tell me there is no good in prolonging the interview."

"Perhaps not," said Rendel, who was deadly white, and he made a motion as though to go.

"Do you realise," said Stamfordham, "what this will mean to you?"

"Yes," said Rendel, "I do."

"Of course," said Stamfordham, "what I ought to do is to insist on the inquiry being continued until the matter is cleared up and brought to light."

A strange expression passed over Rendel's face as there rose in his mind a feeling that he instantly thrust out of sight again, that supposing—supposing—Stamfordham himself investigated to the bottom all that had happened, and that without any doing of his, Rendel's, the truth were discovered? Then with horror he put the idea away. Rachel! it would give Rachel just as great a pang, of course, whoever found it out. The flash of impulse and recoil had passed swiftly through his mind before he woke up, as it were, to find Stamfordham continuing—

"But I am willing for your sake to stop here."

Rendel tried to make some acknowledgment, but no words that he could speak came to his lips.

"It might, as I told you before," Stamfordham went on, standing up as though to show that the interview was over, "have been a national disaster. That, however, has, I hope, been averted, and we shall simply have done now something we meant to do a few days hence. But that does not affect the point we have been discussing," and he looked at Rendel as though with a forlorn hope that at the last moment he might speak. But Rendel was silent still. "You understand, then," Stamfordham said, looking him straight in the face, an embodiment of inexorable justice, "what this means to a man in your position?"

"Yes," said Rendel again.

"I owe my colleagues an explanation," said Stamfordham. "Since one is not to be had, I must repeat to them what has passed between us."

"Of course," said Rendel. And he went towards the door.

"There is another thing I must ask you," Stamfordham said, speaking with cold courtesy. "I have a letter here about Stoke Newton. It will have to be settled." And he waited for Rendel to answer the question which had not been explicitly asked.

"I shall not stand," said Rendel.

"That is best," said Stamfordham quietly. "Will you telegraph to the Committee, then?"

"I will," said Rendel, and with an inclination of the head, to which Lord Stamfordham responded, he went out.

CHAPTER XVIII

Rendel up to this moment had been accustomed, unconsciously to himself perhaps, to live, as most men of keen intelligence and aspirations do live, in the future. The possibilities of to-day had always had an added zest from the sense of there being a long, magnificent expanse stretching away indefinitely in front of him, in which to achieve what he would. In his moments of despondency he had been able to conceive disaster possible, but it was always, after all, such disaster as a man might encounter, and then, surmounting, turn afresh to life. But of all possible forms of disaster that would have occurred to him as being likely to come near himself, there was one that he would have known could not approach him: there was one form of misery from which, so far as human probabilities could be gauged, he was safe. He had never imagined that he could in his own experience learn what it meant, according to the customary phrase, to "go under" because he could not hold his head up: to disappear from among the honourable and the strenuous, to be dragged down by the weight of some shameful deed which would make him unfit to consort with people of his own kind. As he walked home he was not conscious, perhaps, of trying to look his situation in the face, of trying to adjust himself to it. And yet insensibly things began falling into shape, as particles of sand gradually subside after a whirlwind and settle into a definite form. Then Stamfordham's words rang in his ears: "I must tell my colleagues." It was a small fraction of the world in number, perhaps, that would thus know how it happened, but they were, to Rendel, the only people who mattered—the people, practically, in whose hands his own future lay. He realised now as he had never done before in what calm confidence he had in his inmost heart looked on that future, and most of all how much, how entirely he had always counted on Lord Stamfordham's good opinion of his integrity and worth. It was all gone. What should he do? How should he take hold of life now?

As he waited at a corner to cross the road, he saw big newspaper boards stuck up. The second edition of the other morning papers was coming out with the news eagerly caught up from the *Arbiter*. There it was in big letters, people stopping to read it as they passed: "Startling Disclosure. Unexpected

Action of the Government." No power on earth could stop that knowledge from spreading now. How it would turn the country upside down—what a fever of conjecture, what storms of disapproval from some, of jubilation from others. What frantic excitement was in store for the few who, with vigilance strained to the utmost, were steering warily through such a storm! Rendel involuntarily stopped and read with the others.

Some people he knew drove by in a victoria, two exquisitely dressed women who smiled and bowed to him as they passed—chance acquaintances whom he met in society, and to whom under ordinary circumstances he would have been profoundly indifferent.

Rendel could almost have stood still in sheer terror at realising some numbing sense that was stealing over him, some horrible change in his view of things that was already beginning. For as they bowed to him with unimpaired friendliness, he felt conscious of a distinct sensation of relief, almost of gratitude, that in spite of what had happened they should still be willing to greet him. Good God! was *that* what his view of life, and of his relations with his kind was going to be? No! no! anything but that. He would go away somewhere, he would disappear... yes, of course, that was what "they" all did. He remembered with a shudder a man he had known, Bob Galloway, who, beginning life under the most prosperous auspices, had been convicted of cheating at cards. He recalled the look of the man who knew his company would be tolerated only by those beneath him. He realised now part of what Galloway must have gone through before he went out of England and took to frequenting second-rate people abroad.

He looked up and found that he had mechanically walked back to Cosmo Place. He was recalled from his absorption to a more pressing calamity, as he recognised, with an acute pang of self-reproach, the doctor's brougham still standing before the door. He entered the house quickly. There was a sense of that strange emptiness, of the ordinary living rooms of the house being deserted, that gives one an almost physical sense that life is being lived through with stress and terrible earnestness somewhere else. He heard some words being exchanged in a low tone on the upper landing, and then a door shutting as Rachel turned back into her father's room. Rendel met Doctor Morgan as he came down the stairs. Morgan's face assumed an air of grave concern as he saw Sir William's son-in-law coming towards him, and Rendel read in his face what he had to tell. There are moments in which the intensity of nervous strain seems to make every sense trebly acute, in which, without knowing it, we are aware of every detail of sight and sound that forms the material setting for a moment of great emotion. As he looked at Doctor Morgan coming towards him, Rendel, without knowing it, was conscious of every detail that formed the background to that figure of foreboding: of the sunlight glancing on the glass of a picture, of its reflection in the brass of a loose stair rod that had escaped from its fastenings, and of which, even in that moment, Rendel's methodical mind automatically made a note.

"I am afraid I can't give you a very good account," he said in answer to Rendel's hurried inquiries. "He has had another and more prolonged fainting fit, and I think it possible that his heart may be affected."

"Do you mean, then," said Rendel, "that—that—you are really anxious about the ultimate issue?" and he tried to veil the thing he was designating, as men instinctively do when it is near at hand.

"Yes, I am," Doctor Morgan answered. "Unless there is a great change in the next few hours, there certainly will be cause for the gravest anxiety."

Rendel was silent, his thoughts chasing each other tumultuously through his brain.

"Does my wife know?" he said.

"I think she does," Morgan said. "I have not told her quite as clearly as I have said it to you, but she knows how much care he needs and how absolutely essential it is that he should be quiet. It is his one chance. No talk, no news, no excitement."

"What has brought on this attack, do you think?" said Rendel, feeling as if he were driven to ask the question.

"I can't tell," said Morgan. "He looked to me like a man who had been excited about something. Do you know whether that is so?"

"Yes," said Rendel; "he got excited this morning about something that was in the paper."

"Ah! by the way, yes, I don't wonder," said Morgan, who was an ardent politician. "It was a most astonishing piece of news, certainly."

"It was, indeed," said Rendel, brought back for a moment to the unendurable burthen he had been carrying about with him.

"The Imperialists are safe now to get in," said Morgan. "We look to you to do great things some day," and without waiting for the polite disclaimer which he took for granted would be Rendel's reply to his remark, without seeing the swift look of keen suffering that swept over Rendel's face, he hurried away.

Rendel was bowed down by an intolerable self-reproach. He could have smiled at the thought that he had actually been seeking solace in the idea that he had, at any rate, done a fine, a noble thing, that he had done it for Rachel, that, if she ever knew it, she would know he had sacrificed everything for her. And now, instead, how did his conduct appear? How would it appear to her, since she knew but the outward aspect of it? To her? Why, to himself, even, it almost appeared that wishing to insist on screening himself at the expense of some one else, he had, in defiance of her entreaties, appealed to her father, and brought on an attack that might probably cause his death.

He stood for a moment as the door closed behind Morgan, and waited irresolutely, with a half hope that Rachel would come downstairs to him. But all was silent, desolate, forlorn; it was behind the shut door upstairs that the strenuous issues were being fought out which were to decide, in all probability, other fates than that of the chief sufferer who lay there waiting for death. The chief sufferer? No. Rendel, as he turned back sick at heart, after a moment, into his own study, thought bitterly within himself that death to the man who has so little to expect from life is surely a less trial than dying to all that is worth having while one is still alive. That was how he saw his own life as he looked on into the future, or rather, as he contemplated it in the present—for the future was gone, it was blotted out. That was the thought that ever and anon would come to the surface, would come in spite of his efforts to the contrary, before every other. Then the thought of Rachel's face of misery rose before him, haunted him with an additional anguish. With an effort he pulled himself together, sat down to the table, and wrote a letter to the committee of Stoke Newton, stating briefly that he had relinquished his intention of standing, directed it, and closed the envelope with a heavy sigh. One by one he was throwing overboard his most precious possessions to appease the Fates that were pursuing him. Where would it end? What would be left to him? The one precious possession, the turning-point of his existence still remained: Rachel, his love for her, their life together. But, after all, those great goods he had meant to have in any case, and the rest besides. The door opened. It was the servant come to tell him that luncheon was ready; the ordinary bell was not rung for fear of disturbing Sir William. Luncheon? Could the routine of life be going on just in the same way? Was it possible that a morning had been enough to do all this? He went listlessly into the dining-room. Rachel was not there. He went upstairs, and as he went up met her coming out of her father's room. Her startled and almost alarmed look, as at the first moment she thought that he was going back into her father's room, smote him to the heart.

"You had better not go in, Frank," she said hurriedly. "The doctor said he was to be quite quiet. Please don't go in again," and the intonation of the words told him how much lay at his door already.

"I was not going in," he said quietly. "I was coming to fetch you to have some luncheon."

"I don't think I could eat anything," she said.

"You must try, darling," he said gently. "It is no good your being knocked up at this stage. You look pretty well worn out already."

And indeed she did. The last twenty-four hours had made her look as though she herself had been through an illness, and the nervous strain added to her own condition made her appear, Rendel felt as he looked at her, quite alarmingly ill. She suffered herself to be persuaded to eat something, then wandered wretchedly back to her father's room to remain there for the rest of the day.

Rendel did not leave the house again. He sat downstairs alone, trying to realise what this world was that he was contemplating, this landscape painted in shades of black and grey. Was this the prospect flooded with sunshine that he had looked upon that very morning? The afternoon went on: the streets of London were full of a gay and hurrying crowd. Was it Rendel's imagination, the tense state of his nerves, that made him feel in the very air as it streamed in at his window the electric disturbance that was agitating the destinies of the country? Everyone looked as they passed as though something had happened; men were talking eagerly and intently. The afternoon papers were being hawked in the streets. One of them actually had the map, all had the news, given with the same comments of amazement, and, on the part of the Imperialists, of admiration at the feat that had been so cleverly performed. So the day wore on, the long summer's day, till all London had grasped what had happened—while the man through whom London knew was sitting alone, an outcast, with Grief and Anxiety hovering by him.

These two same dread companions, seen under another aspect, were with Rachel as she sat through the afternoon hours in her father's darkened room, listening to his breathing, with all her senses on the alert for any sound, for any movement.

Sir William moved and opened his eyes; then, looking at Rachel, who was anxiously bending over him, he rapidly poured out a succession of words and phrases of which only a word here and there was intelligible. "Frank," he said once or twice, then "Pateley," but Rachel had not the clue that would have told her what the words meant. She tried in vain to quiet him: he was not conscious of her presence. Then suddenly his voice subsided to a whisper, and a strange look came over his face. An uncontrollable terror seized upon Rachel. She ran out on to the stairs; and as, unsteady, quivering, she rushed down, meaning to call her husband, she caught her foot on the loose stair-rod and fell forward, striking her head with violence as she reached the bottom. It was there that Rendel, aghast, found her lying unconscious as he hurried out of his study to see what had happened. The sickening horror of that first moment, when he believed she was dead, swallowed up every other thought. It made the time that followed, when Doctor Morgan, instantly sent for, had pronounced that she had concussion of the brain, from which she would recover if kept absolutely quiet, a period almost of relief.

And so Rachel was spared the actual moment of the parting she had been trying to face. For though Sir William rallied again from the crisis which had so alarmed her, he sank gradually into a state of coma from which he was destined never to wake, and from which, almost imperceptibly, he passed during the evening of the next day.

Rendel, tossed on a wild storm of clashing emotions, the great anxiety caused by Rachel's accident and possible peril added to all he had gone through, had in truth little actual sorrow to spare for the loss of Sir William Gore. But Gore's death meant in one direction the death of all his own remaining hopes. When he knew the end had come, and that he would have to tell Rachel, when she was able to bear it, that her father was dead, he then began to realise how, unconsciously to himself almost, he had built upon some possibility of Sir William doing something to put things right. What, he had not formulated to himself; but he had had vague visions of a possible admission of some sort, of an attempted reconciliation, atonement, confession, such as he had read of in fiction, by which means the truth would have come out, and he would have been absolved without any effort on his own part. But those half-formulated dreams had vanished almost before he had realised them. Sir William Gore had gone to his eternal rest, and, as far as Rendel knew, no one but himself knew exactly what had happened. And now there was nothing in front of him but that miserable blank.

Rachel was not told of what had happened until two days after her father's funeral. She received the news as though stunned, bewildered; as if it were too terrible for her to grasp. Gradually she came back to life again, but she was not the same as before. Her recovery would be, the doctor explained, a question of time. The accident that had befallen her, following the great strain and anxiety she had gone through, had completely upset her nervous system, and appeared—a not uncommon result after such an accident—to have completely obliterated the time immediately preceding her fall. The moment when Rendel, seeing her gradually recovering, first ventured on some allusion to Stamfordham and to what had taken place the day her father was taken ill, he saw a puzzled, bewildered look in her face, as though she had no idea of what he was saying, and he was seized by a fear almost too ghastly to be endurable.

"Lord Stamfordham?" she said, puzzled. "When? I don't know about it."

But the doctor reassured him, and told him that all would come right: she would be herself again, even if she never regained the memory of what had happened before her fall.

"It is a common result of an accident of this kind," he said, "and need give you no special cause for anxiety. I have known two or three cases in which men who have completely recovered in other respects have never regained the memory of what immediately preceded the accident. That girl who was thrown in the Park a month ago, you remember—her horse ran away and threw her over the railings—although she got absolutely right, does not remember what she did that morning, or even the night before. And after all," he added, "it does not seem to me so very desirable that Mrs. Rendel should remember those two particular days she may have lost."

Rendel gave an inward shudder. If he could but have forgotten them too!

"They were full, as I understand, of anxiety and grief about her father's condition."

"They were," said Rendel. "It would be much better if she did not remember them."

"That's right, keep your heart up, then," said Morgan, all unconsciously; "and above all, no excitement for her, no anxiety, no irritation. Change of scene would be good for her, perhaps, and seeing one or two people. If

I were you, I should take her to some German baths. On every ground I should think that would be the best thing for her."

See people? Rendel felt, with the sense of having received a blow, what sort of aspect social intercourse presented to him now. But as the days went on Doctor Morgan insisted more strongly on the necessity that Rachel should go for a definite 'cure' somewhere, and recommended a special place, Bad-Schleppenheim.

"Bad-Schleppenheim," he said, "is on the whole as good a place as you could go to."

"But isn't it thronged with English people?" said Rendel.

"Not unduly," said Morgan. "At any rate, I think it is worth trying."

"I wonder if my wife would like it," said Rendel doubtfully.

"I wouldn't tell her," said the doctor, "till it's all settled. That's the way to deal with wives, I assure you."

And with a cheery laugh, Dr. Morgan, who had no wife, went out.

CHAPTER XIX

Rachel, however, even after the move abroad so strongly recommended by her doctor had been made, did not all at once regain her normal condition. She appeared to be better in health; she was calmer, her nerves seemed quieter; but a strange dull veil still hung between her mind and the days immediately preceding the great catastrophe. To what had happened the day before her father's death she never referred; she had not asked Rendel anything more about the accusation brought against him. Once or twice she had spoken of her father as if he were still there, then caught herself up, realising that he was gone. Was this how it was always going to be? Rendel asked himself. Would he not again be able to share with her, as far as one human being can share with another, his hopes and his fears, or rather his renunciations? Would she never be able to take part in his life with the sweet, smiling sympathy which had always been so ineffably precious to him? Those days that she had lost were just those that had branded themselves indelibly into his consciousness: the afternoon that Stamfordham had come with the map, the morning following when it had appeared in the newspaper, the scenes with Gore, with Stamfordham,—all those days he lived over and over again, and lived them alone. There was some solace in the thought that if that time were to be to Rachel for ever blurred, she would never be able to recall what had passed between herself and her husband after Rendel had brought on Gore's illness by taxing him with what he had done. And while he struggled with his memories—would he always have to live in the past now instead of in the future?—Rachel, who had been told to be a great deal in the fresh air, passed her time quietly, peacefully, languidly, lying out of doors. They had deemed themselves fortunate in securing in the overcrowded town a somewhat primitive little pavilion belonging to one of the big hotels, of which the charm to Rachel was that it had a shady garden. Rendel, whose time even during the period in which he had had no regular occupation had always been fully occupied, reading several hours a day, making notes on certain subjects about which he meant to write later, became conscious for the first time in his life that the hours hung heavy on his hands. It was with a blank surprise that he realised that such a misfortune, which he had always thought vaguely could befall only the idlers and desultory of this world, should attack himself. Life is always laying these snares for us, putting in our way suddenly and unexpectedly some form of unpleasantness by which we may have seen others attacked, but from which unconsciously we have felt that we ourselves should be preserved by our own merits,—just as when we are in good health we hear of sciatica, lumbago, or gout, and accept them without concern as part of the composition of the universe, until one day one of these disagreeables attacks ourselves, and stands out quite disproportionately as something that after all is of more consequence than we thought. It unfortunately nearly always happens that we have to face the mental crises of life inadequately prepared. We think we have pictured them beforehand, and according to that picture we are ready, in imagination, with a sufficient equipment of fortitude and decision to enable us to encounter them. In reality we mostly do no better than a traveller who going to an unknown land and climate, guesses for himself beforehand what his outfit had better be, and then finds it deplorably inadequate when he gets there. Rendel, during those days of lonely agony in London that followed the revelations sprung on the public by the *Arbiter*, had endeavoured to school himself to face what the future might have in store for him; but he had thought that while he was abroad, at any rate, the horror that pursued him now would be in abeyance. He had never been to German baths, he had never been to a fashionable resort of the kind; he had no idea what it meant. All that he had vaguely pictured was that it would be some sort of respite from the thing that dogged him now, the fear—for there was no doubt that as the days went on it grew into a fear—of coming suddenly upon some one he knew, who would look him in the face and then turn away. And now that they were at the term of their journey, installed in their little foreign pavilion, he had become aware that at a stone's throw from him was a numerous cosmopolitan society, among whom was probably a large contingent from London. He did not try to learn their names; he would jealously keep aloof from them. Rachel had been advised to stay here for four weeks at least. Four weeks, no doubt, is not very long under ordinary circumstances: he had not imagined that it might seem almost unendurably long to a man who had been married less than a year to a wife that he loved. And yet, before he had been there three days, he was conscious that each separate hour had to be encountered, wrestled with, conquered, before going on to the next. He had meant to write: there was a point of administration upon which he had intended to say his say in one of the Reviews. But somehow in that sitting-room, with the windows opening down to the garden, the steady work, which in his own study would have been a matter of course, seemed almost impossible. Then he thought he would read. He read aloud to Rachel for part of the day; but he did not dare to choose anything that was much good to himself, as he had been told that the more inactive her mind was the better. Something he would have to do; he would have to organise his daily life in some way that would make the burden of it endurable. He made up his mind to take long walks—the hotel and pavilion lay on the outskirts of the town—to go into the outlying country and explore it on foot. But in the evenings when Rachel was gone to bed, and when, alone at last, he would try to concentrate his mind on the study or the writing to which he had been used so eagerly to turn, another thought that he had been keeping at bay by a conscious effort would rush at him again and overwhelm him.

In the meantime, at the other side of Bad-Schleppenheim, the hours were flying fast and gaily. From the moment when the visitors met together at an early hour in the morning to drink their glasses of Schleppenheim water, and onwards through the luncheon parties, excursions, walking up and down, listening to the band, seeing theatricals, or playing Bridge in the evening, there was never a moment in which they were not industriously engaged in the pursuit of something. It was mostly pleasure, though many of them imagined it was health. Many of the people who in London constituted Society were here, in an inner and hallowed circle, in the centre of which were many minor and a few major royalties out of every country in Europe; and revolving round them in wider circles outside, many other people who, at home just on the verge of being in Society, revelled in the thought that here, under altered conditions, and in the enforced juxtapositions of life in a watering-place, a special talent for tennis, a gift for Bridge, better clothes than other people, or a talent for private theatricals, would help them to be on the right side of the line they were so anxious to cross. Add to these, numbers of pretty girls anxious only to enjoy themselves, and swarms of young men who had come for the same reason, and it will be imagined that the atmosphere reigning in the brilliantly lighted Casino, in and around which the joyous spent their evenings singing, dancing, wandering in the grounds, was singularly different from that of the little isolated pavilion where Rendel sat trying to fashion the picture of his life into something that he could look upon without a shudder.

CHAPTER XX

The walls of the little town were placarded with the announcement of a great bazaar to be held for the benefit of the English Church in Bad-Schleppenheim. The economics of a fashionable bazaar are evidently governed by certain obscure laws, of which the knowledge is yet in infancy; for the ordinary laws of commerce are on these occasions completely suspended. That of supply and demand becomes inverted, since the vendors are seemingly eager to sell all that the buyers least want: the cost of production, of which statistics are not obtainable, the expenditure of money, time, and energy required to furnish the stalls is not taken into account at all. Loss and profit appear to be inextricably mingled; however much unsold merchandise remains on the stall at the end of the bazaar the seller is expected to hand over a substantial sum to the good object for which she is supposed to have been working. And yet there must be some advantage in this method of raising money, or even the female mind would presumably not at once turn to it as the simplest and most obvious way of obtaining funds for a given purpose.

These problems, however, did not exist for Lady Chaloner, one of the leaders of English Society in Schleppenheim. She took bazaars for granted, as she did everything else. She was one of the very pillars of the social fabric of her country. She was of noble blood, she was portly, she was decidedly middle-aged. She had been recommended to diet herself and to drink the waters of Schleppenheim, and as she did so in company with half the distinguished people in Europe, she was quite content to follow the course prescribed. In these days when everything is called into question, when social codes alter, and an undesirable fusion of human beings takes place in so many directions, it was positively refreshing to turn to Lady Chaloner, who not only did not know, but could not conceive that it mattered, what other people did in any layer of existence beneath her own. She had not at any time a keen eye to discrimination of character. Her judgment of those fellow-creatures whom she naturally frequented was based in the first instance on their degree of blood relationship with herself, then on their social standing: but she was but vaguely aware of the difference between the men and women, especially the women, who did not belong to that inner circle, and knew as little about them as a looker-on leaning from a window in a foreign town knows about the people who pass beneath him in the street. But there were times when she entirely recognised the usefulness in the scheme of creation of those motley crowds of well-dressed persons, even though they bore names she had never heard before. During her preparation for the bazaar, for instance, which she was getting up in the single-minded conviction that nothing better could be done for the institution she was trying to befriend, she had been more than willing to co-operate with Mrs. Birkett, the wife of the chaplain, and even to ask some of Mrs. Birkett's friends for their help. Mrs. Birkett, who approached the bazaar from the point of view from which she had artlessly imagined it was being undertaken, that of ensuring some sort of provision for the expenses of the chaplain who undertook the summer duty of Schleppenheim, received a series of shocks as she came face to face with the different points of view of the various stall-holders with whom she was successively brought into contact. Lady Chaloner—she looked on this as a great achievement—had succeeded in enrolling among the bazaar-workers the young Princess Hohenschreien, on the ground of her being a staunch Protestant. The Princess was half-English, half-German. Her mother had been a distant connection of Lady Chaloner. This relationship in some strange way entirely condoned in Lady Chaloner's eyes the fact that the Princess Hohenschreien had a good deal of paint on her face, and a good deal of paint in her manner, and that the loudness of her laugh and the boldness of her bearing were more pronounced than would have been permitted of the well-behaved ladies brought up within the walls of Castle Chaloner. However, Lady Chaloner's daughters were married to husbands of an excellent and irreproachable kind, and were out in the world; and Lady Chaloner felt no kind of responsibility about Madeline Hohenschreien, "Maddy," as she was called by her intimates. She expressed distinct approval of her, in fact, in the words, "Maddy has such a lot of go about her, hasn't she? It does one good to hear her laughin'." So when "Maddy" instantly and light-heartedly undertook to help the bazaar by performing at the Café Chantant, that was to go on at stated times all through the evening, Lady Chaloner felt that she was doing a distinctly good work. It was no small undertaking, however, marshalling her forces and trying to arrange that every one of the stallholders should not be selling exactly the same thing—namely, the small carved wooden objects, the staple commodity of Schleppenheim, made by the surrounding peasantry.

The bazaar was drawing near, and Lady Chaloner was very busy indeed. Indefatigably did she send for Mrs. Birkett several times every day, begging her to bring a pencil and paper that they might make lists. Mrs. Birkett's experience, however, was limited to sales of work under somewhat different conditions in England, and she was not of very much use, except as a moral support and outward material embodiment of the cause for which the bazaar was being undertaken. She sought comfort in her inmost soul in the thought of all the money that must surely flow into the coffers of the Church after this magnificent undertaking; but she was secretly out of her element and ill at ease, when Lady Chaloner pounced upon her to talk of the bazaar, at an hour when the most fashionable people in Europe, with their best clothes on, were walking up and down while the band was playing, or established at little tables exchanging intimate pleasantries with one another and greetings with the people that passed.

She was sitting by Lady Chaloner, in compulsory attendance upon that benefactress of the Church, a few days before the bazaar was to come off.

"Now, let me see," said Lady Chaloner, "what are you goin' to have on your stall?"

"On mine?" said Mrs. Birkett, rather taken aback.

"Yes," said Lady Chaloner, "aren't you goin' to have a stall?"

"You see," said Mrs. Birkett, "I have not any of the things here that—er—I generally use for the purpose," and she thought regretfully of a big box at home which contained a sort of rolling stock of hideous articles that travelled, so to speak, between herself and her friends from one bazaar to another, and reappeared, a sort of symbolical merchandise, a currency in a nightmare, at all the fancy sales held in the neighbourhood of Leighton Ham.

"The only thing is," said Lady Chaloner, "it is rather a pity, because, bein' for the Church, people will expect you to sell, you know. Perhaps you could sell at somebody else's stall. Mine's full, I think," she added prudently. "Let me see," and her ladyship ran quickly over the names of the half a dozen young women who, in the most beguiling of costumes, were going to trip about and sell buttonholes to their partners of the evening before. Lady Chaloner's solid good sense and long habit of the world kept things that should be separate perfectly distinct; she did not for a moment contemplate Mrs. Birkett tripping about and selling buttonholes. "Perhaps Mrs. Samuels hasn't got her number complete," she said, not realising this time, the thing being a little more out of her field of vision, that Mrs. Samuels, who had been spending her time, energy, and even money, in trying to be friends with Lady Chaloner, might quite possibly be in the same attitude towards Mrs. Birkett, if thrust upon her, as Lady Chaloner was to herself.

"I daresay, yes," said Mrs. Birkett, with some misgiving, as she saw Mrs. Samuels further down the alley, standing with a London manager in the centre of a group who were laughing and talking round them.

"Let me see, Mrs. Samuels is goin' to have the tea, isn't she?"

"Yes, the refreshment stall," said Mrs. Birkett, referring to her list.

"And Lady Adela Prestige the fortune tellin'—and Princess Hohenschreien, what did she say she would do? Oh! I remember, the Café Chantant. What has she done about it, I wonder? Do you know anything about that?"

"I am afraid I don't," said Mrs. Birkett. This, indeed, was quite beyond her competence.

"I wonder if she has got people enough. Ah! here she is. Madeline! Maddy!" she called out, as Princess Hohenschreien appeared at the end of the walk, a parasol lined with pink behind her, and her head thrown back as she laughed loud and heartily at something her companion had said.

"Yes, dear Lady Chaloner? Were you calling me?"

"I wanted to speak to you about the bazaar," said Lady Chaloner. "How do you do, M. de Moricourt," to the Princess's companion.

"The bazaar," said the young man in French, as he bowed, "what is that?"

"What is that?" said the Princess, with another burst of laughter. "But, *mon cher*, you are impossible! We have been talking of nothing else all the way down the alley."

"How?" said the young man. "I really beg your pardon, Princess, but I thought we were talking of the comedy we were going to act at the Casino."

"And what do you suppose that comedy is for," said the Princess, "if not for the bazaar?"

"How can I tell?" said Moricourt. "It might have been to please the public, or even to please the Princess Hohenschreien," with a little bow.

"Of course we shall please both," said the Princess. "And a bazaar gives us a reason. A charity bazaar, isn't it?"

"Ah! a charity bazaar," said Moricourt, "that is another thing. It doesn't matter how badly I shall act, then."

"Perhaps that is as well," said the Princess.

"Is it permitted to know the object of the charity we are going to assist so well?" said Moricourt.

Lady Chaloner, dimly aware that Mrs. Birkett was becoming very uncomfortable, although she did not clearly distinguish whether the peculiar expression to be observed on the latter's face came from irritation or embarrassment, hastily said—

"It is not a charity exactly. It is for the English Church at Schleppenheim. This is Mrs. Birkett, the wife of the clergyman," indicating Mrs. Birkett.

"Ah!" said Moricourt, "the English Church," and he bowed to Mrs. Birkett as though making the acquaintance of that honoured institution. Princess Hohenschreien also included herself in the introduction, and bowed with a good-natured smile of absolute indifference to Mrs. Birkett and to all that she represented.

"Well, now then, seriously," said Lady Chaloner, "do you undertake the Café Chantant, Madeline?"

"Not the whole of it, my dear lady," said the Princess. "That really is too much to ask. M. Moricourt and I will act a play."

"How long does the play last?" said Lady Chaloner.

"How long did we say it took?" said the Princess to her companion. "It depends upon how often Moricourt forgets his part. When we rehearsed it last night he waited quite ten minutes in the middle of it."

"I must remind you," said Moricourt, "that I was pausing to admire ... the beautiful feathers in your hat."

"Oh! well, that is different," said the Princess. "I think that explanation is satisfactory—but otherwise——" And she filled up the sentence with a telling glance, to which Moricourt replied with a look of fervent admiration.

"Well, how long does it take, then?" said Lady Chaloner, with a smile of strange indulgence, Mrs. Birkett thought, for a lady so highly placed, and of such solid dignity.

"Oh! about half an hour," said Moricourt; "perhaps three-quarters."

"Is that all?" said Lady Chaloner, in some consternation. "The Café Chantant goes on for how long did you say, Mrs. Birkett?"

This piece of statistics Mrs. Birkett was able to furnish.

"From six till ten, I think you said, Lady Chaloner," she said, reading from her list.

"Heavens!" said the Princess, "you don't expect us, I hope, to go on from six till ten. We had better do the Nibelungen Ring at once. I will be Brünnhilde—and I tell you what," turning to Moricourt, "you shall be the big lizard who comes in and says 'bow-wow,' or whatever it is. Mr. Wentworth!" and she called to Wentworth who was strolling along with an air of being at peace with himself and the universe. "What is it that lizards do?"

"If they are small," said Wentworth, "they run up a wall in the sun, or they run over your feet, and if they are big——"

"You fall over their feet, I suppose," said the Princess.

"But a lizard at a Café Chantant," said Moricourt, "what does he do?"

"At a Café Chantant? He sings, of course," said Wentworth.

"No no," said the Princess, with again her resonant laugh. "I don't know much about botany, but I am sure lizards don't sing."

"Then in that case," said Moricourt, "Wentworth must. He can sing; I have heard him."

"Can you, Mr. Wentworth? How well can you sing?" said the Princess with artless candour.

"Well," said Wentworth, "that is rather difficult to say. I don't sing quite as well as Mario perhaps, but a little better than ... a lizard."

"Oh, that will do perfectly," said the Princess. "For a charity, people are not particular."

"By the way, what is all this for?" said Wentworth.

"For the English Church here, you remember," said Lady Chaloner.

"Oh! to be sure, yes," said Wentworth. "I saw the placard."

"This is Mrs. Birkett," said Lady Chaloner.

Wentworth bowed and said politely, "I hope the bazaar will be a great success."

"I hope so, thank you," Mrs. Birkett said, feeling that if the bazaar were not a great success, she would have gone through a good deal for a very little. She longed to be allowed to go away, but she was not quite sure whether she would not be jeopardising the success of the bazaar by leaving at this juncture. Visions of having promised to meet her reverend husband to go for a walk at a given moment were haunting her. Finally, with a desperate effort, she said—

"I am afraid I have an appointment, Lady Chaloner, and must go now, unless there is anything more I can do."

"Oh, must you go?" said Lady Chaloner, "we had better meet in the morning, I think, and make a final list of the stalls."

"Certainly," said Mrs. Birkett, with a sigh of relief, and with a determined effort she tried to include the circle she was leaving in one salutation, and made away as fast as she could.

"I hope," said the Princess, "the poor lady is not shocked at having a Café Chantant in her Church bazaar."

"At any rate," said Wentworth, "she will be consoled when you hand over the results to her afterwards."

"What is the name of the piece you are going to do?" said Lady Chaloner, pencil in hand.

"*Une porte qui s'ouvre*," said Moricourt, with a glance at the Princess.

"Oh! if you think we'll have that one!" said the Princess. "Would you believe, Lady Chaloner, that he wants me to be the maid in it instead of the leading lady, because he kisses the maid behind the door!"

"My dear Maddy!" said Lady Chaloner, reprovingly.

"Don't look so shocked at me, dear Lady Chaloner," she said. "I am sure I am as shocked myself at the suggestion, as——"

"Mrs. Birkett," suggested Wentworth.

"Precisely," said the Princess.

"At any rate we'll put that piece on the list for the present," said Lady Chaloner. "Then there will be a song from Lady Adela——"

"And a song from Mr. Wentworth," said Moricourt.

"That's splendid," said Lady Chaloner. "The Café Chantant will do. The only thing I rather regret is about the stalls, that every one is goin' to sell the same thing."

"And who is going to buy?" said the Princess.

"That's another difficulty," said Lady Chaloner, "they'll all have to buy from one another."

"We had better have some autographs," said the Princess, "they always sell."

"Very good," said Lady Chaloner, putting it down on the list. "You had better get some."

"All right," said the Princess. "We'll have some of all kinds, I think. I will get some from those people too," nodding her head in the direction of the London manager.

"Everybody considers himself an autograph in these days," said Wentworth; "it is terrible what a levelling age we live in."

"We might sell photographs, of course," said the Princess, "instead of autographs."

"Or both," said Lady Chaloner, earnestly and anxiously, as though contemplating all sources of revenue. "Signed photographs."

"Excellent," said Wentworth.

"There ought to be people enough to buy, if they would only come," said Lady Chaloner, taking up a Visitors' List that lay beside her. "People like the Francis Rendels, for instance," putting her finger on the name, "or—"

"The Rendels? Are they here?" said Wentworth, with much interest.

"So it says here. What is she like?" said Lady Chaloner. "Would she help?"

"I am not sure," said Wentworth. "She's in mourning, and very quiet—but very charming."

"Thank you," said the Princess with a gay laugh. "I am sure that is a compliment *à mon adresse*. I know what you mean when you say that very quiet women are charming. Let us go away, Moricourt; we are too noisy for Mr. Wentworth."

"You are too bad, Maddy, really," said Lady Chaloner, smiling at this brilliant sally.

"*Ich bitte sehr*," said Wentworth to the Princess, with a little bow, as he took up the paper and looked for the address of the Rendels. "Pavillon du Jardin, Hôtel de Londres—I must go and look them up," he said.

"You might beat them up to come and buy, at any rate," said Lady Chaloner, "if they can't do anything else."

"I will do what I can," said Wentworth with a smile, reflecting as he walked off what a strange blurring of the focus of life there is when, everything being concentrated on to one particular purpose, whether it be a bazaar, an election, or the giving of a ball, all the human beings one encounters are considered from the point of view of their fitness to one particular end—in the aspect of a buyer or seller, as a voter, as a partner, as the case may be. There was no doubt that at this moment the whole of mankind were expected to fit somehow into Lady Chaloner's pattern: to be useful for the bazaar, or to be thrown away as useless.

As Wentworth turned away he exchanged greetings with a jovial important-looking personage coming in the other direction, no other than Mr. Pateley, exhaling prosperity as he came. The completion of the Cape to Cairo railway, and the reinstatement in public opinion of the 'Equator' Mine, proved to be of gold after all—let alone certain fortunate pecuniary transactions connected with that reinstatement—had given Pateley both political and material satisfaction. The *Arbiter* was advancing more triumphantly than ever, and its editor was a person of increasing consideration and influence.

"You seem very busy, Lady Chaloner," he said, as he looked at the sheets of paper on the table by her.

"We are gettin' up a bazaar," Lady Chaloner said. "Will you help us?"

"I shall be delighted," said Pateley obviously. "What do you want me to do?"

"Give us your autograph," said the Princess promptly, "and we will sell it for large sums of gold."

She had certainly chosen a skilful way of enlisting Pateley's co-operation. He revelled in the joy of being a political potentate, and every fresh proof that he received of the fact was another delight to him.

"I shall be greatly honoured," he said.

"We are going to have autographs of all the distinguished people we can find," said the Princess, continuing her system of ingratiation.

"I can tell you of an autograph who has just arrived," said Pateley. "I have just seen him driving up from the station; a very expensive autograph indeed—Lord Stamfordham."

"Lord Stamfordham?" said Lady Chaloner, the Foreign Secretary, like the rest of the world, falling instantly into his place in her kaleidoscope. "Certainly, if he would give us a dozen autographs we should do an excellent business with them."

"You had better make Adela Prestige ask him, then," said the Princess with a laugh.

"I wonder where Adela is?" said Lady Chaloner, considering the question entirely on its merits.

"That depends upon where Lord Stamfordham is," murmured the Princess to her companion. "By the way, Lady Chaloner, before we part, it is Tuesday, isn't it, that we make our expedition to Waldlust to lunch in the wood?"

"Tuesday?—let me see, this is Thursday. Yes, I think so," said Lady Chaloner. Then she gave a cry of dismay. "Oh! no, Maddy, Tuesday is the bazaar; that will never do."

"Oh, yes," said the Princess, "all the better. The bazaar doesn't open till half-past five after all, and we can lunch at half-past twelve. It will do us good to be in the fresh air before our labours begin; we shall look all the better for it."

"Very well," said Lady Chaloner dubiously. "But then what about the arrangements?"

"Can't those be made on Monday?" said the Princess; "and if there are any finishing touches required, Mrs. Birkett and her friends can do them on Tuesday. They won't want to look their best, I daresay," and she laughed again.

"Very well," said Lady Chaloner. "Tuesday, then, for Waldlust. I will ask Lord Stamfordham to come."

"And I will ask Adela," said the Princess.

"Come then, Moricourt," said the Princess, "if you want to rehearse that play before we act it."

"Pray do," said Lady Chaloner anxiously. "I am sure people who act always rehearse first."

"I am more than willing," said M. de Moricourt, throwing an infinity of expression into his voice and glance as he looked at the Princess.

"Some parts especially will require a great deal of rehearsing." And they departed together.

"She is so amusin'," said Lady Chaloner to Pateley. "I really don't know anybody that can be more amusin' when she likes."

Pateley gave a round, sonorous laugh of agreement, tantamount to a smile of assent in any one else. He wisely did not commit himself to any expression of opinion as to the accomplished wit of the Princess, which at all events as far as he had had opportunity of observing it, did not strike him as being of a very subtle character.

CHAPTER XXI

The echoes of the band which was enlivening the promenade we have just left penetrated to the pavilion where Rachel and her husband were sitting alone. A little path ran from the back of the pavilion straight up into the woods. At certain hours, when the fashionable world met to drink the waters, to listen to the band, or to talk at the Casino, the woodland path was almost deserted. At no time was it very crowded, as it was a short and rather steep short cut to a walk through the wood which could be reached by a more convenient access from the principal street in the town.

Rendel, although it had not occurred to him to look at a Visitors' List, and although he did not realise yet how many people he knew were at Schleppenheim, still had a strange, unpleasant feeling, horribly new to him, of shrinking from meeting any one he had ever seen before. He had seen the woodland path, and was wondering if he should go and explore it at this hour when presumably every one was listening to the band, of which the incessant strains heard in the distance were beginning to be maddening. As he looked up vaguely, the little door into the garden opened, and he saw the familiar figure of Wentworth appear. His heart stood still. Did Wentworth know? Was he coming out of compassion? And at the same moment that he thought it, further back somewhere in his mind he was conscious of the absurdity of Wentworth having become suddenly so important—Wentworth's opinion, his personality mattering, his representing one of the instruments of Fate. He stood, therefore, to Wentworth's surprise, absolutely still, waiting to see what his friend's attitude would be. But there was no mistake about that, about the unaffected heartiness and rejoicing with which Wentworth met him, in absolute unconsciousness of any possible cloud between them, any possible reason why Rendel should not be as glad to see him as he had been at any time since they had been at Oxford together.

"Frank!" he said, as he came forward, "what's all this about? Why are you hiding yourself here?" And he stopped in surprise at seeing as he spoke the words something in Rendel's whole bearing that made him feel as if he were speaking the truth in jest, as if the man before him really were hiding, really had something to conceal.

Then, after that first moment, Rendel realised that Wentworth knew nothing. That, at any rate, for the moment was to the good, and with an abounding sense of relief he held out his hand.

"Don't you like these quarters?" he said. "We think they are perfectly delightful."

"So do I," Wentworth said, "so do I. They are so quiet."

"My wife wants to be quiet," said Rendel, half indicating Rachel, who was lying back in a garden chair, some knitting in her hands.

"How are you, Mrs. Rendel?" said Wentworth, and he hastened forward to greet her.

She put out her hand with a smile and shook hands with him, apparently not surprised at seeing him, or particularly interested.

"You are certainly most delightfully cool here in the shade," he said. "It is awfully hot in that promenade."

"It must be," said Rachel.

"How long have you been here?" Wentworth went on, sitting down.

"How long is it?" said Rachel, with a slightly puzzled look, looking at Rendel. "Only a few days, isn't it?"

"Yes, not quite a week. My wife has not been well. We were recommended here that she might do the cure."

"I see," Wentworth said, somewhat relieved at finding himself on the way to an explanation. "Well, this is a splendid place, I believe, for the people that it cures," he added sapiently.

"No doubt," Rendel said.

There was another pause.

"Then that is why we have not seen you at the Casino," Wentworth said. "One can't avoid running up against people one knows at every turn here."

"Is that so?" said Rendel, a note of anxiety in his voice. "We have not run up against any one yet."

"Oh! dear me, yes," said Wentworth, unconscious that each of the names he might enumerate would represent to Rendel a possible inexorable judge. "Half London is here: Lady Chaloner, Pateley—all sorts of people."

"Pateley?" said Rendel, the blood rushing to his face at the association of ideas called up in his mind by that name.

"Of course," said Wentworth. "Pateley, flourishing like the bay-tree. They say he is making thousands, and he looks as if he were."

"Out of the *Arbiter*?" asked Rendel.

"The *Arbiter*, I suppose, or something else. But I have no doubt he would tell you if you asked him. He does not impress me as being one of the very reserved kind."

"I don't know," said Rendel. "I don't suppose Pateley ever says more than he means to say, with all his air of hearty communicativeness."

"Well, I daresay not," said Wentworth. "The man's very good company after all; and as long as none of our secrets are in his keeping, it doesn't matter particularly."

Rendel said nothing. He felt he could not meet Pateley face to face at this moment.

"What do you do, then, all day here," said Wentworth, "if you don't drink the waters, and don't go to the Casino, and don't play Bridge?"

"I don't know. I don't do very much," said Rendel, with an involuntary accent in the words that made Wentworth ponder over the undesirability of marrying a wife who is in mourning and depressed.

"You should go into the wood," said Wentworth, "as the Germans do. We found a lot of them the other day singing part-songs out of little books. There is a band of them here called the Society of the United Thrushes, composed of the most respectable and most middle-aged ladies of the district."

"That sounds charming," said Rendel.

"Look here," said Wentworth, "if you don't care to walk alone, do let's walk together. One can go up here and along the wood for miles. We'll have good long stretches as we used to at Oxford. What do you think, Mrs. Rendel? Don't you think it would be a good thing for him?"

"Very," said Rachel with a smile. "I think he ought to go and walk."

"That's capital," said Wentworth. "Let's do that to-morrow, shall we?"

"I should like it very much," said Rendel.

But the next day the weather broke, and was unsettled for three days. On the Tuesday morning, happily for the bazaar and the big tent in the grounds of the Casino, the sun shone out again, and everything was radiant as before. Wentworth turned up at the pavilion in the forenoon and persuaded Rendel to make a day of it. The two started off together through the wood, the scented air floating round them, and bringing to Rendel, as he strode along with a congenial companion, a sense of mental and physical relief as though the atmosphere of both kinds that he was breathing were as different from that which had weighed him down a fortnight ago as the scent of the aromatic pines was from the air of the London streets. Wentworth was full of talk, of a kind it must be confessed which left his hearer at the end without any very distinct impression of what it had been about, although it passed the time agreeably and genially. He had his usual detached air, which Rendel had always been accustomed to find a relief as opposed to his own strenuous attitude, of standing aloof as an amused spectator of human contingencies.

"I haven't seen you for ever so long," Wentworth was saying. "What became of you at the end of the season? You vanished somehow, didn't you?"

"We were in mourning, you know," Rendel replied.

"Ah, to be sure, yes, Sir William Gore died," said Wentworth, attuning his voice to what he considered a suitable key, on the assumption that Rendel would feel still more bound to be loyal to his father-in-law now than when, as he put it to himself, the "old humbug" was alive. "Poor Mrs. Rendel, she looks as if it had been a great blow to her."

"Yes," said Rendel, "it was; and she has been ill besides." And he told Wentworth briefly of what had happened to Rachel, and the condition she was in, and the reassuring hopes held out by the doctors that she would almost certainly recover her normal state.

"I am very glad to hear that," said Wentworth cheerily. "Then you must come to London and start life again, Rendel, now you are free. Sir William Gore was rather a responsibility, I daresay."

"Yes," said Rendel, "he was."

"Let me see," said Wentworth, "it was just about when he died, I suppose, that Stamfordham published that sensational agreement with Germany?"

"Yes," said Rendel, "it was the day before he died."

"Ah," said Wentworth, "the day before? Then of course you didn't realise the excitement it was. By Jove! of course you know I'm not 'in' all that sort of thing myself, but I must say I never saw such a fuss and fizz as it was. The way it was sprung on people too! It was an awfully bold thing to do, you know; but it turned up trumps after all, that's the point. Stamfordham isn't like any body else, and that's the fact."

"What's that place we are coming to through the trees?" said Rendel.

"Why, that's it," said Wentworth. "That's where we shall get luncheon. They always have something ready for people who drop in."

"It isn't crowded, is it?" said Rendel.

"My dear fellow," replied Wentworth, "there is never anybody. I have been there twice since I came; once there was a German doctor, and once there was nobody."

"All right," said Rendel.

"You are sure to get veal," Wentworth said. "In Germany, whatever else is wanting, you can always get a veal cutlet to slake your thirst with, after the longest and hottest walk."

"I shall be quite content," said Rendel.

They went on across the hollow, and up a slight ascent. They strolled idly round the woodland house, and saw, as they expected, in the agreeable little garden behind, a long table all ready for luncheon.

"This is capital," said Wentworth. "You see, as I told you, they always expect people," and a waiting maid appearing at that moment, Wentworth proceeded to order luncheon for himself and Rendel in the best German he could muster. Unfortunately, however, the proprietor of the establishment was engaged in his cellar on important business, and the dialect spoken by the red-handed and red-cheeked maiden who received them was not very intelligible. However, by dint of nodding of heads and pointing out items on the bill of fare, they came to an understanding, Wentworth taking for granted that something quite unintelligible that she had said about the table was an inquiry as to whether they would sit at it, which indeed it was. But it was further an inquiry as to whether they were of the party that was coming to sit at it, which he also quite cheerfully and unsuspectingly answered in the affirmative. He then pulled out his watch, and pointing to a given time at which he would return, he and Rendel went further away into the wood.

CHAPTER XXII

When they returned, half an hour later, the little garden was no longer empty. People were coming and going, the table was covered with food; Lady Chaloner was seated at it, and at a little distance from her Princess Hohenschreien, with M. de Moricourt inevitably in her wake. Lady Chaloner's readiness in the German tongue was not equal at this moment to her sense of injury. It was Princess Hohenschreien, therefore, who was charged with the negotiations, and who was discussing in voluble and amused German with the inn-keeper the heinousness of his crime in having promised two unknown pedestrians a seat at that very select table. The inn-keeper was full of apologies. Not having a nice discrimination of the laws that govern the social relations of our country, he had thought that if the strangers were English they were entitled to sit down with the others.

"What does he say, Maddy?" said Lady Chaloner. "Ask him if he can't put them somewhere else. Good Heavens! here they are!" she said *sotto voce* as two people came through the trees at the bottom of the garden, and then stopped in surprise at seeing how populous it had become. Then, as Lady Chaloner looked at them, she suddenly realised with relief that she knew them.

"What!" she cried, "is it you? Are you the two people who came in here and ordered luncheon in the middle of our party?"

"I am afraid we are, do you know," said Wentworth, as he came forward. "We didn't know how indiscreet we were being. We'll go somewhere else."

"Not at all, not at all," said Lady Chaloner. "How do you do, Mr. Rendel? I have not seen you for a long time. Of course you must lunch with us, so it all ends happily. Maddy, this is Mr. Francis Rendel—Princess Hohenschreien."

Rendel bowed. He had had one moment, as they came up into the garden and saw there were other people there, before Lady Chaloner had recognised them, to make up his mind as to what he would do. Then he had said to himself desperately that he would risk it. After all, he might be exaggerating the whole thing; Wentworth did not know, and so the others might not. Rendel had felt during the last hour one of those strange sudden lightenings of the burden of existence that for some unexplained reason come to our help without our knowing why. He was almost beginning to think life would be possible again. At any rate, here, at the present moment, he would not try to remember or realise what it was going to be, what it must be. He would sit here on this peerless day with these pleasant friendly people, and this one hour at any rate the sun should shine within and without.

"That's right," said Lady Chaloner, pointing to two places some way down the table at her left; "sit anywhere."

As Wentworth and Rendel stood opposite to the Princess and her attendant cavalier, the door of the house, which faced them, opened, and Lady Adela Prestige appeared in the doorway, with some more people behind her.

"How delightful this is!" Lady Adela cried, as she stepped out into the garden.

"Isn't it?" said Lady Chaloner. "Look how amusin'," she continued. "Mr. Wentworth and Mr. Rendel have come to luncheon too, quite by chance."

Lady Adela nodded to Wentworth, whom she was seeing every day, and bowed to Rendel, whom she knew slightly. Then, as Rendel looked beyond her, he saw who was coming out of the house in her wake—Lord Stamfordham, followed by Philip Marchmont. Stamfordham, coming out into the dazzling sunlight, did not at first see who was there. In that hurried, almost imperceptible interval, Rendel had time to grasp that here was the horrible reality upon him in the worst form in which it could have come. He had wild visions of saying something, doing something, he knew not what, instantly repressed by the Englishman's repugnance to a scene. Then he pulled himself together, and simply stood and waited. And as he waited he saw Stamfordham come up to the table with a pleased smile, prepared to sit down on Lady Chaloner's right hand, next the seat into which Lady Adela had dropped. Then Stamfordham suddenly saw the two men still standing on the other side of the table, and recognised in one of them Francis Rendel. A swift extraordinary change came over his face. The genial content of the man who, having deliberately put all his usual cares and preoccupations behind him was now, under the most favourable conditions, prepared to enjoy a holiday in genial society, suddenly disappeared. He involuntarily drew himself up, his face became hard and stern; he again looked as Rendel had seen him look the last time they had met. The mental agony of the younger man during that moment was almost unendurable. What was going to happen next? As in a dream he heard the comfortable voice of Lady Chaloner, who had never in her life, probably, spoken with any misgivings, whose calm confidence in the bending of contingency to her desires nothing had ever occurred to shake.

"Will you sit down there, Lord Stamfordham? We have two new recruits to our party, you see. I don't think I need introduce either of them."

Stamfordham remained standing for a moment; then he said quietly, but very distinctly—

"I am afraid, Lady Chaloner, that I can't sit down at this table."

A sort of electric shock ran through the careless happy people who were surrounding him. Rendel turned livid. Then he tried to speak. But no words could come; mentally and physically alike he could not frame them. He pushed his chair away from the table, and moved out behind it; then with his hands grasping the back of it, he bowed to Lady Chaloner without speaking, turned and went away by the little opening in the wood from which he and Wentworth had come. Wentworth, ready and light-hearted as he generally was, was for one moment also absolutely paralysed with amazement and concern, then saying hurriedly, "Forgive me, Lady Chaloner, I must go and see what has happened," he quickly followed. Lord Stamfordham drew up his chair to the table and sat down. His urbane, genial manner had returned, and he spoke as though nothing had happened; the rest instantly took their cue from him.

"What delightful quarters you have found for us, Lady Chaloner," he said. "I don't think I made acquaintance with this place when I was at Schleppenheim last year."

"Charmin', isn't it?" said Lady Chaloner. And quite imperturbably, at first with an effort, which became easier as the meal went on, the whole party went on talking and laughing as usual, with, perhaps, if the truth were known, an added zest of excitement, certainly on the part of some of its members, at "something" having happened. The two extra places that had been put were taken away again, and the rank closed up indifferently and gaily round the table, as ranks do close up when comrades disappear by the way.

In the meantime Rendel was madly hurrying away through the wood, going straight in front of him, not knowing what he was doing, what he proposed to do—his one idea being to get away, away, away from those smiling, distinguished indifferent people, hitherto his own associates, who now all knew the horrible fate that had overtaken him, who would from henceforth turn their backs upon him too. The thought of that moment when he had been face to face with Stamfordham, of those distinct, inexorable tones, of the words which judged and for ever condemned him, burnt like a physical, horrible flame from which he could not escape. He flung himself down at last, and buried his face in his hands, trying to shut out everything, as a frightened child pulls the clothes over its head in the darkness. Then, to his terror, he heard footsteps in the wood. Who was it? Was this some one else who knew? Would he have to go through it all over again? And he lifted his head in anguish as the steps drew nearer. The sight of the newcomer brought him no relief. It was Wentworth, who, anxious and bewildered, came stumbling along, having by some strange chance come in the direction that brought him to the person he was seeking. Rendel looked at him.

"Well?" he said, in a strained voice, as though demanding an explanation of Wentworth's intrusion.

The sight of his face completely bewildered Wentworth.

"Good God, Rendel!" he said, "what is it? What has happened?"

There was a pause. Then Rendel said, trying with very indifferent success to speak in a voice that sounded something like his own—

"Didn't you see what happened?"

"I saw that—that—Stamfordham——" Wentworth began, then he stopped.

"Yes," said Rendel curtly, "you saw it—you saw what Stamfordham did? Well, there's an end of it," and he looked miserably around him as though hemmed in by the powers of earth and heaven.

"But, Frank," Wentworth said, still feeling as if all this were some frightful dream, one of those dreams so vivid that they live with the dreamer for weeks afterwards, and sometimes actually go to make his waking opinion of the persons who have appeared in them, "tell me—what——"

"Jack," said Rendel, "it's no good talking about it. I'll tell you another time, I daresay, if I can. Leave me alone now, there's a good fellow—that's all I want."

"Look here, Frank," said Wentworth; "if it's anything—anything that Stamfordham thinks you've done—that—that you oughtn't to have done—well, I don't believe it, that's all!"

"You are a good friend, old Jack," said Rendel, looking at him. "I might have known you wouldn't believe it."

"Of course I don't," said Wentworth stoutly. "I don't know what it is, but I don't believe it all the same."

"Well," said Rendel slowly, "I'll tell you this for your comfort—you needn't believe it."

"Of course not," said Wentworth heartily, "and I don't care what it is, of course you didn't do it. And what's more, I know you can't have done anything to be ashamed of, and of course other people will know it too," he said sanguinely, carried along by his zealous friendship.

Rendel's face turned dark red again. "No," he said, "other people won't. Of course other people will think I have done it. Don't let's talk about it now. The fact is," mastering his voice with an effort, "I can't, Jack. Just go away, and leave me alone. I'll come back some time."

"But what are you going to do? You're not going to sit here all day, I suppose."

"I'll come later," Rendel said. "You must find your way back without me, there's a good fellow. By the way," he added, "I'm sorry to have spoilt your day; I'm afraid you've had no luncheon. But you'll be back in Schleppenheim in time to get some. Look here, would you mind saying to my wife that—that I've walked a little further than you cared to go, or something of that sort, and that I'll be back at dinner time?"

"Very well," said Wentworth, hesitatingly. "She is not likely to be anxious, is she?" he said dubiously. "I mean, at your being away so long. She won't be alarmed, will she?"

"Oh no," said Rendel. "That is to say, if you don't alarm her." And then looking up and seeing Wentworth's anxious expression, so very unlike the usual one, "And you needn't be alarmed yourself, Jack; I'm not going to do anything desperate," he said, forcing a smile; "that's not in my line."

"No, no, of course not," Wentworth said, with a sort of air of being entirely at his ease. And then reading in Rendel's face how the one thing he longed for was to be alone, he said abruptly, "All right, then, we shall meet later," and strode off the way he had come.

What a solution it would have been, Rendel felt, if he had indeed been able to make up his mind to the step that Wentworth evidently thought he might be contemplating—what an answer to everything! and as again that burning recollection came over him he felt that, in spite of the courage required for suicide, it would have required less courage to put himself out of the world, beyond the possibility of its ever happening again, than to remain in it and face what other agony of humiliation Fate might have in store for him. But he was not alone, unfortunately; his own destiny was not the only one in question. And if his words, his intention, his faith in the future had meant anything at all when he told Rachel that there was no sacrifice he would not be ready to make for her, he was bound to go on doggedly and meet the worst. He walked aimlessly through the wood, higher and higher, until he reached a sort of clearing from which he could see, far below him, the white road winding back again to Schleppenheim, and presently as he looked he saw driving rapidly back in the direction of the town the open carriages containing the people he had just left. Stamfordham must be in one of them. What were they saying about him, those people? Or, if not saying, what were they thinking? Could he ever look one of them in the face again? Not one. And again he had a wild moment of thinking that it would be possible to put the thing right, to establish his innocence, to insist upon knowing how it was that Sir William Gore had given the information to the *Arbiter*, on knowing what the arrangement was with Pateley on which that *coup de théâtre* had depended, and he sprang to his feet with the determination that he would go straight back into Schleppenheim, seek out Pateley and insist upon knowing what had happened. Then, just as before, the revulsion came. The principal thing, he had no need to ask Pateley. He knew, and that was the thing other people might not know. In a little while, he was told, Rachel would be herself again, and perhaps able to remember: she must not come back to the knowledge of something that must be such a cruel blow to her faith in her father, her adoring love for him. And yet as he turned downwards and strode hurriedly back along the woodland paths, across the shafts of sunlight which were growing longer as the day wore on, he felt how absurdly, horribly unequal the two things were that were at stake. On the one hand his own future, his success, his whole life, all the possibilities he had dreamt of; on the other, reprobation falling on one who was beyond the reach of it, one who had no longer any possibilities, who had nothing to lose, whose hopes and fears of worldly success, whose agitations had been for ever stilled by the hand of death. And Rachel? Would the suffering of knowing that her father's memory was attacked, of being rudely awakened from her illusions to find that in the eyes of the world he was not, and did not deserve to be, what he had been in hers, would that suffering be equal to that which he himself was encountering now? But even as he argued with himself, as he tried to prove that his own salvation was possible, he knew that when it came to the point he could do nothing. If it had been a question of another man, whom he himself could have saved by bringing the accusation home to the right quarter, he would have done it, he would have felt bound to do it: but as it was, he knew perfectly well that the thing was impossible. The fact is that, whether guided by supernatural standards or by those of instinct and tradition, there are very few of the contingencies in life in which the man accustomed to act honestly up to his own code is really in doubt as to what, by that code, he ought to do: and by the time that Rendel reached the little garden again which he had left in the company of Wentworth a few hours before, he knew quite well that he was going to do nothing, that he might do nothing, that he must simply again wait. Wait for what? There was nothing to come.

CHAPTER XXIII

Two of the occupants of the carriages that Rendel had seen going rapidly along the road knew the meaning of the scene that had taken place under their eyes; the others were in a state of simmering curiosity.

"I should be glad," said Stamfordham, as they approached Schleppenheim, "if nothing could be said about what happened."

He was sitting opposite to Lady Chaloner and Lady Adela in a landau. There was no need, of course, to explain to what he was referring.

"Of course, of course," said Lady Chaloner, not quite knowing what to say.

In the meantime Wentworth had got back, had been to see Rachel, and had told her that Rendel was going to extend his walk a little further and that he would be back without fail in time for dinner. He himself, he added, had been obliged to come back for an engagement. Rachel accepted quite placidly the fact that her husband would return later than she expected; she thanked Wentworth with the same sweet smile of old, asked where they had been, said the woods must have been delightful. Then, feeling that he could do nothing, Wentworth, with some misgiving, left her.

Rachel still felt the languor which succeeds illness,—not an unpleasant condition when there is no call for activity,—a physical languor which made her quite content to sit or lie out of doors most of the day, sometimes walk a little way, and then come back to rest again. She had accepted Rendel's unceasing solicitude for her with love and gratitude, she clung to his presence more than ever now that both her parents being gone she felt herself entirely alone: but for the rest she was strangely content to let the days go by in a sort of luxury of sorrow, while she recalled the happy time passed with those other two beloved ones who had made up her life. But there was no bitterness in the recollection; there was a sort of tender mystery over it still. At times she felt as if there were something more; she had some dim, confused recollection of her husband being connected with it all, and with Gore's illness; how, she could not remember. And she did not try. Deep down in her mind was the feeling that with a great effort it might all come back to her; but she shrank from making the effort.

After Wentworth left her, it had occurred to her that, since Rendel was not coming back again, she would venture outside the limits of their garden and go to where the band was playing. She did not at all realise what the surroundings of that band would be. The kind of life that she had led before, when they had come abroad with Lady Gore, had not been the sort of existence reigning at Schleppenheim. She strolled out, feeling that everything was very strange and new, in the direction of the music, following without knowing it a path which brought her into the very middle of the promenade into the centre of a gaily dressed throng of people, somewhat bewildering to one accustomed to pass all her days in solitude. Shrinking back a little she turned out of the stream, and, finding an unoccupied chair under a tree, sat down, looking timidly about her. Then finding that no one was paying any attention to her, or appeared to be conscious of the fact that she was venturing out alone, she gradually became amused at watching all that was going on round her. Presently two well-dressed women she did not know, an older and a younger one, Lady Chaloner and Lady Adela Prestige in fact, on their way to their bazaar, came along deep in talk, the older one stopping to speak with some emphasis whenever the interest of the conversation demanded it. One of these halts was made close by Rachel.

"I should like to know what it was," Lady Adela was saying.

"You may depend upon it," said Lady Chaloner, "that it was something very bad. He is not the man to do that sort of thing for nothing."

"I am quite sure of it," Lady Adela replied, with a little tremor of excitement. "One can't help feeling that it's something really bad; that it was not only that he had run away with his neighbour's wife or something of that kind. He must have done something that can't be condoned."

"I am sure of it," Lady Chaloner said seriously. "There is no doubt about that."

"Poor creature!" said Lady Adela. "Didn't he look awful?"

"Perfectly fearful!" said Lady Chaloner. "He looked like the villain in a play, who is found out—the man who has cheated at cards, or something of that sort."

"Perhaps that was it."

"I daresay," said Lady Chaloner. "I wonder if he has been playing Bridge?"

"Dear me, I wish I knew!" said Lady Adela.

This sounded very interesting, Rachel thought—exactly the kind of thing that happened in books at smart watering-places.

"Ah, there is Maddy," said Lady Adela. "I do wonder what she thought."

"By the way," said Lady Chaloner, "we must tell her not to say anything about it."

But the Princess had driven back in the company of M. de Moricourt and Mr. Marchmont, and had, therefore, not heard the warning given by Stamfordham to his companions in the other landau.

"Well," said the Princess eagerly, coming up to the others, "what did you think of that? Wasn't it amazing?"

"Yes," said Lady Adela. "What do you think it was, Maddy?"

"Something awful, you may depend upon it," said the Princess; "and I am sure little Marchmont knows. We tried to make him tell us on the way back, but he wouldn't. But I gathered somehow that Lord Stamfordham couldn't have done anything else."

Lord Stamfordham! Did they say Stamfordham? Rachel thought to herself wonderingly. Was he here? And she had some kind of queer, puzzled feeling that he was connected in her mind with something that had happened lately. What was it?

"And Pateley doesn't know anything about it either," said the Princess. "I met him just now and asked him."

"Did you?" said Lady Chaloner. "I don't think you ought to have done that. I was going to tell you that Stamfordham said it was not to be mentioned."

"Did he?" said the Princess, somewhat taken aback. "I asked Mr. Pateley because I thought he would be sure to know. But I made him promise not to tell anybody."

"I believe he did know, though," said Moricourt, who, though he spoke his own language, understood perfectly everything that was said in English. "I wonder what the quiet and charming wife that Wentworth admires so much thinks?"

"Poor thing!" said Lady Chaloner gravely.

"By the way," said Lady Adela with a sudden idea, "Wentworth was with him. Wentworth must know all about it, of course. He is sure to come to the bazaar. We'll ask him."

"Wentworth was with him?" said Rachel to herself with an involuntary movement, rising from her seat. Of whom were they speaking? What was it all about? She was unconscious that she was standing scrutinising the faces of the group near her as though trying to gather from them what their words might mean. They, deep in their conversation, did not notice her. Then, with a feeling of extraordinary relief—she hardly knew why—she saw a familiar, substantial person coming along the promenade with a sort of friendly swagger. She went forward to meet him, still feeling as though she were walking in her sleep.

"Mrs. Rendel!" said Pateley in his usual hearty tone, in which there was now an inflection of surprise and almost of anxiety.

Pateley had not met either of the Rendels since the day of his last interview with Sir William Gore, and he had carefully not investigated further the incident which had been of such great advantage to himself. But in the last half-hour, since, under the seal of profound secrecy, it had been confided to him what had happened at the luncheon, and he had been anxiously asked what was the cloud hanging over Rendel, he had pieced things together in a way which brought him pretty near the truth. It was beginning to be clear to him that Stamfordham had somehow visited upon Rendel the treachery into which he himself had practically led Gore. Stamfordham had asked Pateley at the time of the disclosure how the *Arbiter* had become possessed of the information. Pateley had apologetically declined to give an explanation. But the ardent support given by the *Arbiter* to Stamfordham's action in the matter and to all his subsequent policy had made it tolerably certain that Stamfordham would not bear him much malice. And, as a matter of fact, the whole affair had added to Stamfordham's reputation. The masterly way in which he had caught up the situation and dealt with it after the premature disclosure of the Agreement had added a fresh laurel to his crown.

As Pateley uttered the words, "Mrs. Rendel," the whole of the group who were standing near turned with a common impulse as if a thunderbolt had fallen into their midst, and he grasped at once that they had been talking within earshot of her of something she ought not to have heard. Lady Adela was the first to recover her presence of mind.

"Come," she said; "we must go and take our places. I mean to have some tea if we can get it before the opening," and she made a move in which the others joined.

Pateley, remaining by Rachel, lifted his hat to them as they strolled away. "How long have you been at Schleppenheim?" he asked. "I had no idea you were here."

"We have been here," said Rachel—"let me see—about a week."

She looked anxious and disturbed.

"And where are you staying?" said Pateley.

"In the little pavilion behind the Hôtel de Londres," and she pointed.

"Charming place," said Pateley. "And how is your husband?"

"He is very well, thank you," said Rachel. "He has been out for a long walk to-day; he went for an expedition to the woods with Mr. Wentworth."

And she looked as if something else that she did not say were on the tip of her tongue.

"It must have been delightful in the woods to-day," said Pateley, hardly knowing what he answered. He also was preoccupied by the story he had heard and wondering how much she knew of it. "Are you going home now?" he said, as Rachel turned away from the promenade in the direction she had pointed out.

"I think so. I am a little tired," said Rachel, holding out her hand.

"May I come and see you?" Pateley said.

"Please do," said Rachel.

"I certainly shall," Pateley said. "It will be delightful to get away for a little while from this seething mass of humanity."

And he again gave one of his loud laughs as he also went towards the tent, to plunge with the greatest zest into the seething mass whose company he had been contemning.

CHAPTER XXIV

Rachel turned in the other direction and walked slowly back to the pavilion. What had happened? What had she been hearing? The slightest mental exertion still made her head ache, but she was conscious that if she once let herself go and made the effort it would be possible for her to understand. But that moment had not come yet.

She had not been many minutes in her quiet shady garden when the little gate at the bottom of it was thrown open, and her husband came quickly in, looking round him with an anxious, hurried glance as though not knowing what he might find. What had he expected? He could hardly have told. But as he drew nearer and nearer he had been gradually nerving himself for the worst. He had been dreading to find he knew not what. Wentworth might be sitting with Rachel, the faces of both telling that Wentworth's would-be explanations had been of no avail; or Rachel herself might have been absent—she might have strolled out into the crowd and there unawares heard rumours of what he felt convinced must by this time be in every one's mind, on every one's lips. It was therefore for the moment an unmeasured relief to find that all seemed as usual, that Rachel was sitting there quiet and cool before her little tea-table.

"Ah!" he almost gasped, with a long sigh, as he sank into a chair and leant his head against the back of it with a weary, hunted look.

"Frank!" said Rachel anxiously, "what is the matter? What has happened?"

"What do you mean?" he said, sitting up, with again the startled, haggard expression on his face. "What should have happened?"

"I don't know," Rachel said, startled too at his look and manner. "You look so tired, so ill."

"Oh, I'm all right," he said, taking up and drinking eagerly the cup of tea that almost mechanically she had poured out and pushed towards him, and as he did so he realised that he had had no food since the morning. He ate and drank and then again lay back in his chair and was silent. As Rachel looked at him the absolute conviction swept over her—she knew not why—that he had been concerned in the terrible catastrophe of which she had heard the broken accounts. It began to dawn upon her that in some inconceivable way the thing had happened to him; that it was of him those women were speaking. She still heard Lady Adela saying: "Did you ever see any one look so awful?" And yet what could it be? What horrible misunderstanding was it? What horrible mistake could have been made?

She sat and waited. Not the least of her charms was that she knew, what many women do not know, how to sit absolutely quiet. She knew when to refrain from questioning, how to sit by her companion in so peaceful, so final a manner, as it were, that he did not feel that she was simply waiting for what he would do next.

The band blared out again with renewed vigour. Rendel leant his elbows on his knees, his face between his hands.

"Oh! that miserable noise!" he said. "Will it never leave off? The hideousness of it all!—those people, that band! Oh! to get away from it all!" he muttered half to himself.

"Frank," said Rachel entreatingly, touching his arm, "if you don't like it why shouldn't we go away from it? I think it is horrible, too. I went out of the garden to-day to where the people were walking."

Rendel looked up quickly.

"Did you? Did you see any one you knew?"

"Yes," said Rachel; "I saw Mr. Pateley."

"Pateley!" said her husband. "Did you have any talk with him? What did he say?"

"Hardly anything," said Rachel. "He was surprised to see me, and asked how long we had been here, and if he might come and see us. That was all."

"That was all," echoed Rendel, again with an inward shiver. "Coming to see us, is he?"

That encounter for the moment he must at any cost avoid.

"Frank, I wonder if we must go on staying here?" Rachel said.

"Of course we must," Rendel replied, trying to pull himself together again. "Dr. Morgan said that this was the very best place for you to come to, and that the waters would do you all the good in the world."

"I wonder if we need," said Rachel. "I am sure it is the kind of thing you hate."

"It is not for very long, after all," said Rendel, trying to smile.

He was gradually regaining possession of himself, but was still afraid to trust himself to utter any but the most commonplace and ordinary sentences.

"The moment I have done the cure," said Rachel, "we'll go back to London, won't we? And you can begin your work again, and do all the things you like. And then," she went on with an attempt at lightness of tone, "you can go back to your beloved politics, and think of nothing else all day." And she went on talking of their house, of their arrival, of what they would do, in a forlorn little attempt to show him that she meant to try to shoulder life valiantly, although it had been so altered. "You will stand for somewhere. You will go into the House."

Rendel thought of what the life might have been that she was sketching, and what it was going to be now. What he had gone through that day was an earnest probably of what awaited him many a time if he should try to lead his life as he used to lead it, among the people who were congenial to him.

"No," he said, "I'm not going to stand. I'm not going into the House. I shan't have anything to do with politics."

"What?" said Rachel, looking at him startled.

"All that, is at an end," he said firmly. Then with the relief of speaking, came the irresistible desire to go on, to tell her something at least of what his fate was, although he might not tell the thing that mattered most.

"Do you remember," he said, "something that I told you had happened——" he broke off, then began again. "Tell me," he said, impelled to ask, "how much you remember, if you remember anything, of those days when your father was so ill, at the end, just before he died, or is it still a blank to you?"

Rachel shuddered.

"No, I can't remember," she said. "The last thing I remember clearly is one afternoon when he was beginning to be worse and had to go upstairs again; and I remember nothing more after that till," and her voice trembled, "till—a day that I woke up in bed and wanted to go to him, and you told me that—that he was dead. The rest of that time is a blank."

"How extraordinary it is!" muttered Rendel to himself.

"I did not even know," said Rachel, "that I had fallen on the stairs, until the doctor told me days afterwards that I had caught my foot as I was running downstairs. He told me then it was no use trying to remember the time just before," she went on in a low, anxious voice, something stirring uneasily within her: "that it might not come back at all. It seems it doesn't sometimes to people who have that sort of accident."

Rendel, his eyes fixed on the ground, had been listening; he took in the meaning of her words and tried to realise their bearing on himself, but he was too far gone on the slope to stop. It was clear that she would not know what had happened, unless she were told by himself... and yet, who could tell how the awakening would come? it might even be in a worse form when she was able once more to mix with her kind.

"Rachel," he said. "I want to tell you something that happened the day before your father became worse, the day before you had that accident, the last day, in fact, that you remember." She looked at him with anxious eagerness. "Something tremendously important happened. Lord Stamfordham brought me some private notes of his own to decipher and copy."

"Of course," said Rachel, "that I remember. In your study downstairs."

"You remember?" said Rendel eagerly. Then instantly conscious, alas, that the evidence could do him no kind of good, "that I gave some papers to Thacker to take to Stamfordham?"

"Stop a minute," said Rachel. "Yes, I remember that too. My father wanted to play chess afterwards, but he was too tired."

"In those papers," said Rendel, "there was a very important secret, though it didn't remain a secret," he added, with a bitter little laugh, "for twenty-four hours. Those papers contained the notes of a conversation at the German Embassy at which that agreement was decided upon by which Germany and England divided Africa between them. It was *I* copied those papers from Stamfordham's notes. I copied the map of Africa with a line down the middle of it. The next morning, no one knew how or why, that map appeared in the *Arbiter*."

Rachel looked at him, still not understanding all that was implied.

"Do you see what that means for me?" Rendel said. "It was not Stamfordham published it, he did not mean to do so until the moment should come, and since I was the person who had had the original notes, he thought that I had published it; that I had let it out, somehow."

"You!" said Rachel, with wide-open eyes.

"Yes," said Rendel shortly. "That I had betrayed the great secret entrusted to me."

"Frank!" she cried. "But of course you didn't!"

"Of course I didn't," Rendel said quietly.

"And—then——?" said Rachel breathlessly.

"Then," Rendel said, shrinking at the very recollection, "Stamfordham told me he believed I had done it. Then of course,"—and the words came with an effort—"there was an end of everything, and I knew that there was nothing left for me to do but to go under, to throw everything up. I knew that people would turn their backs upon me, and I didn't see Stamfordham again until—until to-day. And to-day Wentworth and I went up to that place in the woods to lunch, and by chance, by the most horrible, evil fortune, we came upon a luncheon party at which Stamfordham was, and—and," he said trying to speak calmly, "when he saw me he refused to sit down at the same table with me." And as he spoke Rachel felt that things were becoming clear to her and that she was beginning to understand. The comments of the people who had stood by her and discussed the scene they had witnessed still rang in her ears, and she realised what the horror of that scene must have been.

"Frank!" she cried, with her tears falling. And she went to him and took his hand, then drew his head against her bosom as though to give him sanctuary. "Imagine believing that you, *you* of all people..." and the broken words of comfort and faith in him, of love and belief again gave him a moment of feeling that rehabilitation might be possible.

"Frank!" Rachel went on, "tell me this. Did my father know?"

"Know what?" Rendel said, starting up, the iron reality again facing him.

"That you were accused? That they could believe that you had done such a shameful thing?"

"Yes," said Rendel slowly. "At least he knew what had happened—and—and—he guessed that the suspicion would fall upon me."

"Oh!" cried Rachel, hiding her face in her hands and trying to steady her voice. "I am sorry he knew just at the end. I wonder if he realised?"

Rendel said nothing. Even now was Sir William Gore to stand between them?

"Perhaps he didn't," Rachel said, almost entreatingly, "as he was so ill. Because think what it would have been to him! Of course he would have known it was not true, but he was so fastidious, so terribly sensitive, the mere thought that you could have been suspected of such a thing even would have preyed upon him so terribly."

"Well," said Rendel, in a low voice—the last possibility of clearing himself was put behind him, and the darkness fell again—"he is beyond reach of it. It is I who must suffer now."

Rachel had walked to the other side of the garden, pressing her handkerchief to her eyes and trying to control herself. Now she came swiftly back, a sudden determination in her heart.

"Frank," she cried, "why must you suffer? We must find out who really did it."

"I can't," said Rendel.

"But have you tried?"

"Yes," he said. "As much as was possible."

"But it must be possible," she cried. And she came to him, her eyes and face glowing with resolve. "If the whole world came to me and said that you had done this I should not believe it. I remember so well my mother saying, the day that I came back from Maidenhead," and their eyes met in the recollection of that happy, cloudless time, "'what a man needs is some one to believe in him,' and I thought to myself that when—if—I married I would believe in my husband as she believed in my father."

At this moment one of the Swiss waiters came quickly through the pavilion into the garden.

"Monsieur Pateley," he said, "wishes to know if Madame is at home." Rachel and her husband looked at each other in consternation.

"I can't see him at this moment," Rendel said, going to the gate.

"Can't we send him away?" said Rachel, anxiously.

"Where is he?" addressing the waiter. But it was too late. The question answered itself, as Pateley's large form appeared behind that of the waiter, distinctly seen on every side of it. Rachel, trying to control her face into a smile of welcome, went forward to meet him as Rendel disappeared amongst the trees, from whence he could get round into the house another way.

CHAPTER XXV

We do not move unfortunately all in one piece. It would be much simpler if we did, and if our actions could be accounted for by saying, "He did this, being a generous man, or a forgiving man, or a curious man, or a remorseful man." Unhappily, and it makes our actions more difficult to account for, we are more complicated than this, and Pateley, when he finally felt impelled to make his way into Rachel's presence so soon after parting from her in the promenade, could not probably have said exactly what motive prompted him to seek her. To Rachel he arrived as the complement, the consolidation, of the resolve that she had made. She hardly tried to conceal her agitation as she shook hands with him and looked in his face. Her own wore an expression that had not been there an hour ago. Something new had come to life in it. So conscious were they both of something abnormal, overmastering, between them that there did not seem anything strange in the fact that for a moment, after the first greeting, they stood without thinking of any of the commonplaces of intercourse. Then Pateley, more accustomed to overlay the realities of life by the conventional outside, recovered himself and said in an ordinary tone, looking round him—

"What a delightful oasis! What charming quarters you are in here!"

"Yes, we like them very much," said Rachel, recovering herself; and they went towards the little table and sat down.

"No tea for me, thank you," said Pateley. "I have just been made to drink a liquid distantly resembling it at the bazaar."

"At the bazaar?" said Rachel. "It was German tea, I suppose?"

"I imagine so. It has been well said," said Pateley, "that no nation has yet been known great enough to produce two equally good forms of national beverage. We have good tea, but our coffee is abominable: the Germans have good coffee, but their tea is poison. The Spaniards, I believe, have good chocolate, but that I have to take on hearsay. I have never been to Spain. I mean to go some day, though."

"Do you?" Rachel said, dimly hearing his flow of words while she made up her mind what her own were to be. She had had so little time to form her plan of action, to piece together all that she had been hearing during the afternoon, that it was not yet clear to her that from the circumstances of the case Pateley must necessarily be concerned in it; and at the moment she began to speak she simply looked upon him as some one who knew Rendel in London, who had known her father and mother, who had a general air of bluff and hearty serviceability, and had presented himself at a moment when she had no one else to turn to.

"Mr. Pateley," she said, and at the sudden ring of resolution in her tone Pateley's face changed and his smiling flow of chatter about nothing came to a pause. "There is something I want very much to ask you about," she went on, "something I want your help in."

"I am at your orders," said Pateley, with a smile and bow that concealed his surprise.

"It is something that matters very, very much," Rachel went on. "Something you could find out for me."

Pateley said nothing.

"I don't know if you know," she went on hurriedly—"if you heard, of what happened to me in London just before my father died? I had an accident. It seemed a slight one at the time. I fell down on the stairs one evening that he was worse when I ran down quickly to fetch my husband, and I had concussion of the brain afterwards and was unconscious for forty-eight hours. And since, I have not been able to remember anything of what happened during those days."

Pateley made a sort of sympathetic sound and gesture.

"But," Rachel said, "I have heard to-day—not until to-day—of something that happened during that time, something terrible. I am going to tell it to you, in the greatest confidence. You will see when I tell you that it matters very, very much. First of all,—this I remember—on the day my father began to be worse, Lord Stamfordham brought my husband some papers to copy for him in which was the Agreement with Germany, and told him no one was to know about them, and my husband told no one, and sent them back, when they were done, to Stamfordham, in a sealed packet."

Pateley, as he listened, sat absolutely impenetrable, with his eyes fixed on the ground.

"But somebody got hold of them," she went on—"somebody must have stolen them, because they were published the next morning in the paper, in the *Arbiter*." And as the words left her lips she suddenly realised that the man in front of her was the one of all others in the world who must know what had happened. The *Arbiter* was embodied in Pateley, it was Pateley: that, everybody knew, everybody repeated. Pateley would, he must, be able to tell her.

"Oh," she cried, "the *Arbiter* is your paper!"

"Yes," said Pateley, looking at her.

"Then," she said, "you know—you must know."

"Know what?" he said calmly.

"You must know," she said, "who it was told the *Arbiter* what was in those papers."

Pateley sat silent a moment. Then he said—

"It can and does happen occasionally that things are brought to the *Arbiter* of which I don't know the origin, in fact of which the origin is purposely kept a secret."

She waited for him to add something to this sentence, to add a *but* to it, but he remained silent. Being unversed in diplomatic evasions, she accepted his words as a disclaimer.

"But still," she said, "even if you don't know this you could find it out. It matters terribly. I don't want to say to any one else, it is not a thing to be told, how horribly it matters, but I must tell *you*, that you may see. Lord Stamfordham thought that my husband had betrayed the secret—he told him so then. And to-day—it was too terrible!—he was at a luncheon to which Frank and Mr. Wentworth went, not knowing——" A sudden involuntary change in Pateley's face made her stop and say, "But perhaps you were there? Were you at the luncheon?"

"No," said Pateley. "I was not there."

"But you heard about it?" she said.

"Yes," he said after a pause. "I heard about it."

"It's too horrible!" said Rachel, covering her face with her hands. "Of course you heard about it—everybody will hear about it: how Lord Stamfordham insulted him and refused to sit down with him, because of the unjust accusation that was brought against him. Now do you see," she said excitedly, and Pateley, as he looked at her, was amazed at the fire that shone from her eyes, at the glow of excitement in her whole being—"now do you see how much it matters? how if we don't find out the truth, if we don't get to know who did it, this is the kind of thing that will happen to him? You see now, don't you? You will help me?"

Pateley had got up and restlessly paced to the end of the garden and back, his eyes fixed on the ground, Rachel breathlessly watching him. He was moved at her distress, he felt the stirrings of something like remorse at the fate that had overtaken Rendel. But in Pateley's Juggernaut-like progress through the world he did not, as a rule, stop to see who were the victims that were left gasping by the roadside. As long as the author of the mischief drives on rapidly enough, the evil he has left behind him is not brought home to him so acutely as if he is compelled to stop and bend over the sufferer. But a brief moment of reflection made him pretty clear that neither himself nor the *Arbiter* had anything to fear from the disclosure. He had nothing particularly heroic in his composition; he would not have felt called upon for the sake of Francis Rendel, or even for the sake of Rendel's wife, to sacrifice his own destiny and possibilities if it had been a question of choosing between his own and theirs; but fortunately this choice would not be thrust upon him. He looked up and met Rachel's eyes fixed upon him.

"Yes," he said. "I will help you."

"Oh, thank you!" she cried, her heart swelling with relief. "Will you, can you find out about it?"

"Yes," said Pateley again. He paused a moment, then came back and stood in front of her. "I have no need to find out," he said slowly. "I know who did it."

Rachel sprang up.

"What?" she cried, quivering with anxiety. "Do you mean that you know now, that you can tell Frank, that you can tell Lord Stamfordham? Oh, why didn't you say so?"

Pateley paused.

"I didn't know," he said, "that Stamfordham had accused your husband of it, and so I kept—I was rather bound to keep—the other man's secret."

"The other man?" Rachel repeated, looking at him.

"Yes," said Pateley. "The man who did it."

Rachel started. Of course, yes—if her husband had not done it some one else had, they were shifting the horrible burden on to another. But that other deserved it, since he was the guilty man.

"Yes," she said lower, "of course I know there is some one else!—it is very terrible—but—but—it's right, isn't it, that the man who has done it should be accused and not one who is innocent?"

"Yes," said Pateley, "it is right."

"You must tell me," she said, "you must!—you must tell me everything now, as I have told you. Is it some one to whom it will matter very much?"

Pateley waited.

"No," he said at length, "it won't matter to him."

Rachel looked at him, not understanding.

He went on, "Nothing will ever matter to him again. He is dead."

"Dead, is he?" said Rachel, but even in the horror-struck tone there rang an accent of glad relief. "Then it can't matter to him. And it is right, after all, that people should know what he did. It is right, it is justice, isn't it?" she repeated, as though trying to reassure herself, "not only because of Frank?"

"Yes," said Pateley, "I believe that it is right, that it is justice." Then as he looked at her he suddenly became conscious of an unwonted difficulty of speech, of an almost unknown wave of emotion rising within him, of shrinking from the words he was now clear had to be said.

"Mrs. Rendel," he said at last, "I am afraid it will be very painful to you to hear what I am going to say."

She looked at him bewildered. He waited one moment, almost hoping that the truth might dawn upon her before he spoke, but she was a thousand miles from being anywhere near it. "Those papers which I published in the *Arbiter* the next morning were shown to me on the afternoon your husband had them to copy, by—" again the strange unfamiliar perturbation stopped him, and he felt he had to make a distinct effort to bring the name out—"your father, Sir William Gore."

Rachel said absolutely nothing. She looked at him with dilated eyes, incredulous amazement and then horror in her face, as she saw in his that he was telling her the truth.

"My father?" she said at last, with trembling lips.

"Yes," Pateley said. The worst was over now, he felt, and he had recovered possession of himself.

"No, no, it can't be!" she said miserably. "It's not possible...."

"I fear it is," said Pateley. "They were shown to myself, you see, so it is an absolute certainty."

"But when was it?" said Rachel, bewildered. "When did he have them?"

"They were left," Pateley said, "in the study where he was, when your husband went down to speak to Lord Stamfordham. During that time I happened to go in."

And as Rachel listened to his brief account of what had taken place she knew that there was no longer any doubt as to the culprit. For the moment, as the idol of her life fell before her in ruins the discovery she had made swallowed up everything else. Pateley made a move.

"Wait, wait!" she said. "Don't go away. Only wait till I see what I must do. It is all so horrible! I see nothing clearly yet."

He walked away to the other end of the little garden.

She leant back in her chair, her eyes fixed, seeing nothing, trying to make up her mind. Gradually what she must do became more and more distinct to her, more and more inevitable. The sheer force of her agitation and emotion were carrying her own. If she acted at once, within the next half-hour, anything, everything might be possible. She would not wait to think, she would do it now, while it was still possible to pronounce the name, the dear name that she had hardly been able to bring to her lips during these last weeks in which every day, every hour, she had been conscious of her loss. She would go to the person who must be told, and who alone could remedy the great evil that had been done. She got up, a despairing determination in her face.

Pateley looked at her, his face asking the question which he did not put in words.

"I am going to Lord Stamfordham," she said. "I am going to tell him."

"You?" said Pateley. "Are you going to tell him yourself?"

"Yes," she said, "it is I who must tell him. I have quite made up my mind." She turned to him appealingly as though taking for granted he would help her. "I want to go now, while I feel I can, and before Frank knows anything about it. Can you help me—would you help me to find Lord Stamfordham?"

"Certainly," said Pateley, with a new admiration for Rachel rising within him, but with some misgivings, however, as to the possibility or the desirability of running Stamfordham to earth among his present surroundings.

"Do you know where he is?" Rachel said.

"I should think probably at the bazaar," said Pateley, and as he reflected on the scene he had just left, Stamfordham surrounded by a bevy of attractive ladies beseeching him to give them an autograph, to buy a buttonhole, to drink their tea, to put into their raffles, and to have his fortune told, he felt still more dubious as to the mission he was engaged upon. Fortunately Rachel realised none of these things.

"Come, then, let us go," she said, with a vibrating anxiety and excitement, at strange variance with the usual atmosphere that surrounded her, and he followed her out of the garden in the direction of the Casino.

CHAPTER XXVI

Pateley, who had been caught up in some measure into the excitement of Rachel's emotion, was brought back to earth again with a run, as he passed with her through the brightly coloured hangings which drooped over the portals of the bazaar and found themselves in the gay crowd within. His misgivings grew as he felt more and more the incongruity of the errand they were bent upon to the preoccupations of the people who surrounded them. There was no doubt that, whatever the ultimate result as far as Mrs. Birkett and the needs she represented were concerned, the bazaar, that subsidiary consideration apart, was being very successful indeed. The sound of voices and laughter filled the air, and the gloomy previsions Lady Chaloner had felt as to the lack of buyers were apparently not realised, since the whole of the available space surrounded by the stalls was filled with people engaged in some sort of very active and voluble commercial transactions with one another which, financial result or not, were of a most enjoyable kind, to judge by the bursts of laughter they necessitated. Rachel, pale, strung up, with the look of determination in her face called up in the usually timid by an unwonted resolve, was making her way, or rather trying to do so, in Pateley's wake, bewildered by the sights and sounds around her. Pateley at each step was beset by some laughing vendor from whom he had much ado to escape, and indeed in most cases did not succeed in doing so without having paid toll. By the time he had gone half along the room he was the possessor of three tickets for raffles, for each of which he had paid a sum he would have grudged for the unneeded article that was being raffled. He had bought several single flowers, each one on terms which should have commanded an armful of roses, and he had had three dips into a bag from which fortunately he had emerged with nothing more permanent than sawdust. Rachel also had been accosted by a vendor as soon as she came in, a moment of poignant embarrassment for all parties concerned—herself, her escort, and the fascinating seller who had offered her wares, for Rachel, looking at her with startled eyes, felt in her pocket as though at last seeing what was wanted of her, and then stammered, "I'm so sorry, I have no money with me." Pateley knew the vendor; it was no other than Mrs. Samuels, who had emerged from behind her stall, and was making the round of the bazaar with a basket of most attractive-looking cakes. His eye met hers in hurried and involuntary misgiving, mutely telling her that Rachel was not a suitable customer, and that she had better carry her wares elsewhere. She at once responded to the unconscious confidence and returned to himself.

"Now, Mr. Pateley," she said ingratiatingly, "you, I know, never refuse a cake. Look, these are what you had when you came to tea with me the other day. Now, I'll choose you the very best."

"Of course, if you will choose one for me," said Pateley gallantly.

"Oh, but one is not enough," she said, "you must have two—you really must. Five marks. Thank you so much!" and she tripped off.

Pateley, who had already, as we have seen, spent a good deal of time and of the money which is supposed to be its equivalent in the bazaar before going to see Rachel, began to be conscious that before he got round it again he would have spent a sum large enough to have kept him another week in Schleppenheim. "However," he said to himself with a sigh, "it is all part of the story, I suppose." In his inmost soul he felt the conviction that he was altogether, in his strange progress through the joyous crowd with that pale, anxious companion, going through a sufficient penance to make amends for the misfortune of which he was the primary cause.

"Where is Lord Stamfordham?" whispered Rachel anxiously. "Do you see him?"

"Not at this moment," said Pateley, looking vainly in every direction. The difficulties of his quest, and the still worse difficulties that would certainly face him when the object of that quest should be attained, loomed with increased terror before him.

The names of the stallholders, of the performers, waved above their respective quarters. In the corner of the great tent was a mysterious-looking enclosure, of which the entrance was closed by a curtain, and above which hung the legend, "Oriental Fortune-telling. Lady Adela Prestige." Lady Adela Prestige! That was probably the most likely place to try for. "I think he may be over there," he said, and without a word, hardly conscious of the people who were passing through, Rachel followed him.

"Hallo, Pateley, is that you?" said a cheery voice. He turned round and saw Wentworth, a packet of tickets in his hand. "Would you like to have a ticket for the performing dog?" said Wentworth, not seeing who Pateley's companion was.

"No," said Pateley, almost savagely, thankful to be accosted by some one whom he need not answer by a smile and a compliment. "I don't want any fooling of that sort now."

"My dear fellow," said Wentworth, amazed, "what have you come here for, then?" and as he spoke he saw Rachel behind Pateley, and realised that something was happening that had no connection with the business of the bazaar.

"Look here," Pateley said aside to him, "do you know where Stamfordham is?"

"Over there," said Wentworth, with some inward wonder, pointing towards Lady Adela's corner. "I saw him there just now."

"Ah!" said Pateley, "all right," hardly knowing if he was relieved or not, but desperately threading his way in the direction indicated, still followed by Rachel.

Wentworth looked after them in surprise.

"What is that you are saying, Mr. Wentworth?" said a voice in his ear, and he turned quickly and found himself face to face with Mrs. Samuels. "A performing dog? Where? I am quite sure it must be performing better than Princess Hohenschreien."

Wentworth replied by eagerly offering a ticket.

"Let me offer you a ticket, Mrs. Samuels, and then you shall see for yourself."

"Well, I will take a ticket," she said, "on condition that you will tell me honestly what the performance is."

"Certainly," said Wentworth, with a bow, offering the ticket and receiving a gold piece in exchange. "It is Lady Chaloner's Aberdeen terrier. He sits up and begs with a piece of biscuit on his nose while somebody says 'Trust!' and 'Paid for!'"

"That is a most extraordinary and novel trick," said Mrs. Samuels gravely.

"It is unique," said Wentworth; "and sometimes he tosses the biscuit in the air when they say 'Trust,' sometimes when they say 'Paid for,' but generally he drops on all fours and eats it before they have begun."

"Thank you," said Mrs. Samuels. "I am afraid Princess Hohenschreien's performance will be best after all." Then Wentworth suddenly saw from her face that some other attraction was approaching from behind him, and turned quickly round as Mrs. Samuels, with her most beguiling air, advanced and offered her basket of cakes to Lord Stamfordham.

"Now, milord," she said. "I am sure you must be hungry."

"And what makes you think that?" said Stamfordham, whose air of willing response and admiration made it quite evident that Mrs. Samuels's blandishments were not usually exercised in vain. "Do I look pale, or haggard, or weary?"

"None of these," said Mrs. Samuels; "but I am sure it is a long time since I had the privilege of offering you a cup of tea at my stall. Quite half an hour, I should think."

"Quite possible," said Stamfordham. "All I can say is that it seems to me an eternity since I last had the pleasure of receiving anything at your hands. Pray give me a bag of those cakes. You baked them yourself, of course?"

"Of course," Mrs. Samuels said, with a little rippling laugh. And then in answer to Stamfordham's smile of incredulity, "All is fair in ... bazaars and war, you know."

In the meantime, Wentworth, enlisted, he himself did not understand how or why, in the anxious quest in which he saw Pateley and Rachel engaged, had hurried after Pateley, whose broad back he saw disappearing, to tell him of Lord Stamfordham's whereabouts. Pateley turned quickly round. Lord Stamfordham was coming towards them, with Mrs. Samuels, wreathed in smiles, at his side.

"I think," she was saying, "when you have eaten those cakes you can drink some more tea, don't you think so?"

"It is not improbable," Stamfordham replied. "But was our bargain that I was to eat them all myself?"

"Certainly," Mrs. Samuels replied.

"My dear lady," Stamfordham said, "I will engage to eat every one of them that you have baked, I can't say more. And in the meantime I am bound on a very foolish errand. I have sworn to go and have my fortune told," and as Mrs. Samuels's eye, with a careless and ingenuous air, rested upon Lady Adela's name above the tent, she smiled inwardly at the thought that what that astute lady might possibly prophesy would also perhaps come true if, as well as prophesying, she eventually brought her intelligence to bear upon its accomplishment.

"Wait one moment," Pateley said, almost nervously, to Rachel. "There is Stamfordham, he is coming this way," and as Stamfordham drew near the door of the tent Pateley accosted him.

Lady Adela, it may be presumed, had some occult means of discovering from inside who was drawing near her fateful quarters, or else she had the simpler methods more usually employed by mortals, of looking to see. At all events, as Stamfordham came towards her enclosure, she appeared on the threshold and winningly lifted the mysterious curtain, burlesquing a low curtsey in reply to Stamfordham's bow.

"Lord Stamfordham!" Pateley said hurriedly. Stamfordham, in some surprise, looked round. He had been seeing Pateley on and off during the day. Why did he accost him in this way? But the urgent note in his voice arrested his attention. Then, as he looked up, he saw an anxious pale-faced, girlish figure standing by Pateley, looking at him with large brown eyes filled with indescribable anxiety. It was a face that he knew, that he had seen somewhere. Who was it? For one puzzled moment he tried to remember. Pateley took the bull by the horns.

"Lord Stamfordham," he said, "Mrs. Rendel wants to speak to you."

Mrs. Rendel! Of course it was Mrs. Rendel. He had last seen her that day at Cosmo Place. Again a wave of indignation rushed over him. Rachel advanced desperately, looking as though she were going to speak. Stamfordham, involuntarily looking round him at the crowd of observers and listeners, said quickly in a low voice, "I am very sorry, it is no good. It is impossible." And then to Pateley, "It is no good, I can't do anything. You must tell her so," and he passed through the curtain which Lady Adela let drop behind him. Rachel looked at Pateley, then to his amazement and also to his involuntary admiration she lifted the curtain and passed in too.

The two people inside stood aghast at her appearance. She had followed so quickly upon Stamfordham's steps that he was still standing looking round him at his strange surroundings, Lady Adela facing him with a smile of welcome. The apparatus of the fortune-teller apparently consisted in certain cabalistic properties—wands, dials with signs upon them, and the like—arranged round a table. Stamfordham spoke first. He was absolutely convinced that Rachel had come to appeal to him for mercy, and was as absolutely clear that it was an appeal to which he could not listen.

"Mrs. Rendel," he said, "I am afraid I am obliged to tell you that I cannot listen to anything you may have to say. I can guess, of course, why you have come here, and I am sorry for *you*," he said, leaning on the pronoun. "But I can do nothing," and he spoke slowly and inexorably, "I can do nothing for either you or your husband." But Rachel had now lost all fear, all misgiving.

"I don't think," she said, unconsciously drawing herself up and looking straight at him, "you know what I have come to say, and I must ask you to listen for a moment."

"I think I do know," Stamfordham said sternly, and she saw he meant to go out.

"I have come to tell you," she said, quickly standing between him and the door, "that my husband was wrongfully accused of the thing that you believed he did." Stamfordham shook his head: this was what he expected to hear. "I know who did it, I have found out to-day," and she grew more and more assured as she went on. Stamfordham started, then looked incredulous again. "I have come to tell you who did it, that you may know my husband is innocent." Then she became aware of Lady Adela, who, having at first been much annoyed at her brusque intrusion, was now suddenly roused to interest, even to sympathy. Rachel turned to her. "I must say this," she said. "Don't you see, don't you understand, what it is to me?"

"Yes, yes, you must," the other woman said, with a sudden impulse of help and sympathy. "Go on," and she went outside. Stamfordham felt a slight accession of annoyance as Lady Adela passed out; he felt it was going to be very difficult for him to deal as cruelly as he was bound to do with the anxious, quivering wife before him. He stood silent and absolutely impenetrable. Rachel went on quickly in broken sentences.

"I didn't know about this at the time. I have been ill since. I could not remember. You brought some papers for my husband to copy, and he locked them up so that no one should see them, and while he went down to speak to you they were pulled out of his writing-table from outside, by somebody else who was there, and who showed them to Mr. Pateley. Mr. Pateley came in and went out again. Frank didn't know he had been there." Stamfordham stopped her.

"They were taken out by 'somebody,' you say; do you mean—in fact I must gather from your words—that it was—do you mean by yourself?"

"Oh no, no," Rachel cried, as it dawned upon her what interpretation might be put upon her words. "Oh no, not myself! I wish it had been, I wish it had!"

"You wish it had?" Stamfordham said, surprised. "Who was it, then? Who was it?" he said again, in the tone of one who must have an answer. "Who got the paper out and showed it to Pateley?"

Rachel forced herself to speak.

"It was—my father," she said, "Sir William Gore." And with an immense effort she prevented herself from bursting into tears.

"Sir William Gore!" said Stamfordham, "did *he* do it?"

"Yes," said Rachel; "I only knew it to-day, and I am telling you to prove to you that it wasn't my husband."

Stamfordham stood for a moment trying to recall Rendel's attitude at the time, and then, as he did so, he made up his mind that Rendel must have known.

"But," he said, after a moment, still somewhat perplexed, "you say you didn't know about this?"

"No," said Rachel, "I didn't. My father," and again her lips quivered and told Stamfordham what that father and his good name probably were to her, "was taken very ill, and I had an accident at the time and did not know anything that had happened. Frank told me nothing. Then my father died, and I was ill, and we came here and I did not know it at all till my husband came in and told me"—and her eyes blazed at the thought—"told me what had happened to-day..." She stopped. Stamfordham felt a stab as he thought of it.

"But," he said, "did he know? Did he tell you then? Did he know that it was Sir William Gore?"

"Oh no, no," Rachel said; "it was Mr. Pateley, and he brought me here to tell you that you might know." Then Stamfordham began to understand.

"Mrs. Rendel," he said, with a change of voice and manner that made her heart leap within her. "Where is your husband?"

"He is at our house, the little pavilion behind the Casino garden."

"Will you take me to him?" Stamfordham said.

Rachel looked at him, unable to speak, her face illuminated with hope—then she covered her face in her hands, saying through the tears she could no longer restrain, "Oh, thank you, thank you!"

"Come," said Stamfordham gently, but with decision. "You must dry your tears," he added with a smile, "or people will think I have been ill-treating you." And to the speechless amazement of Lady Adela, who was standing outside the curtain waiting until, as she expressed it to herself, she too should have her "innings," Stamfordham passed out before her eyes with Rachel, saying to Lady Adela as he passed, "Will you forgive me? I am going to take Mrs. Rendel back." Then looking round him at the jostling crowd he said to Rachel, offering her his arm, "Will you think me very old-fashioned if I ask you to take my arm to get through the crowd?" And, leaning on his arm, hardly daring to believe what had happened or might be going to happen, Rachel passed back along the room through which she had just come with Pateley, the crowd this time opening before them with some indescribable tacit understanding that something had happened concerned with the incident which, as Rendel had foreseen, nearly everybody at the bazaar had heard of. They did not speak again until they reached the pavilion.

Latchkeys were unknown at Schleppenheim, and the inhabitants of the little summer abodes walked in by the simple process of turning the handle of the front door. Rachel and Stamfordham went straight in out of the sunlight into the cool little room into which, in long low rays, the setting sun was sending its beams. Rendel had been trying to read: the book that lay beside him on the floor showed that the attempt had been in vain. He looked up, still with that strange, hunted expression that had come into his face since the morning—the expression of the man to whom every door opening, every figure that comes in may mean some fresh cause of apprehension. Rachel came into the room without speaking, something that he could not read in the least in her face, then his heart stood still within him as he saw Stamfordham behind her. What, again? What new ordeal awaited him? He made no sign of recognition, but stood up and looked Stamfordham straight in the face. Stamfordham came forward and spoke.

"I have come," he said, "to apologise to you for what took place to-day, to beg you to forgive me." Rendel was so utterly astounded that he simply looked from one to the other of the people standing before him without uttering a sound.

"I have just learnt," Stamfordham went on, "the name of the person who did the thing of which I wrongfully accused you." Rendel made a hurried movement forward as if to stop him.

"Wait, wait one moment!" he cried, "don't say it before my wife—she doesn't know." In that moment Rachel realised what he had done for her.

"Do you know?" asked Stamfordham.

"Yes," Rendel answered.

With the old friendliness, and something deeper, in his face and voice, Stamfordham said —

"Mrs. Rendel knows also. It was she told me."

"Rachel!" cried Rendel, turning to her. "Do you know?"

"Yes," said Rachel, trying to command her voice. "I know—now—that it was—my father," and the eyes of the two met.

Stamfordham advanced to Rendel.

"Will you forgive me," he said again, "and shake hands?" Rendel held out his hand and pressed Stamfordham's in a close and tremulous grasp, which the other returned. "I must see you," he said. "Will you come to my rooms some time? I shall be here for a week longer." He held out his hand to Rachel. "Thank you," he said, "for what you have done." And he went out.

Rendel turned towards Rachel, his arms outstretched, his face transformed by the knowledge of the great love she had shown him. His heart was too full for speech: in the closer union of silence that new precious compact was made. The veil that had hung between them so long was lifted for ever.